LAURI ROBINSON

'...obinson's talent for period detail shines.'
—*RT Book Reviews* on *Her Cheyenne Warrior*

LYNNA BANNING

'Lynna Banning has penned a delightful and
passionate western.'
—*RT Book Reviews* on *Her Sheriff Bodyguard*

CAROL ARENS

'Arens' newest romp is filled with characters we can't
help but root for.'
—*RT Book Reviews* on *Wed to the Montana Cowboy*

A lover of fairy tales and cowboy boots, **Lauri Robinson** can't imagine a better profession than penning happily-ever-after stories about men—and women—who pull on a pair of boots before riding off into the sunset…or kick them off for other reasons. Lauri and her husband raised three sons in their rural Minnesota home, and are now getting their just rewards by spoiling their grandchildren. Visit: laurirobinson.blogspot.com, Facebook.com/lauri. robinson1, or Twitter.com/LauriR.

Lynna Banning combines a lifelong love of history and literature into a satisfying career as a writer. Born in Oregon, she graduated from Scripps College and embarked on a career as an editor and technical writer and later as a high school English teacher. She enjoys hearing from her readers. You may write to her directly at PO Box 324, Felton, CA 95018, USA, email her at carowoolston@att.net or visit Lynna's website at lynnabanning.net.

Carol Arens delights in tossing fictional characters into hot water, watching them steam, and then giving them a happily-ever-after. When she is not writing she enjoys spending time with her family, beach camping or lounging about a mountain cabin. At home she enjoys playing with her grandchildren and gardening. During rare spare moments you will find her snuggled up with a good book. Carol enjoys hearing from readers at carolarens@yahoo.com or on Facebook.

WESTERN
CHRISTMAS BRIDES

Lauri Robinson,
Lynna Banning,
Carol Arens

MILLS &
BOON

Published in Great Britain 2017
by Mills & Boon, an imprint of HarperCollins*Publishers*
1 London Bridge Street, London, SE1 9GF

Western Christmas Brides

© 2017 Harlequin Books S.A.

ISBN: 978-0-263-92611-8

The publisher acknowledges the copyright holders of the
individual works as follows:

A BRIDE AND BABY FOR CHRISTMAS by Lauri Robinson © 2017
MISS CHRISTINA'S CHRISTMAS WISH by Lynna Banning © 2017
A KISS FROM THE COWBOY by Carol Arens © 2017

Our policy is to use papers that are natural, renewable and
recyclable products and made from wood grown in sustainable
forests. The logging and manufacturing processes conform to the
legal environmental regulations of the country of origin.

Printed and bound in Spain
by CPI, Barcelona

CONTENTS

A BRIDE AND BABY FOR CHRISTMAS

Lauri Robinson

Dedicated to my granddaughter Karlee Jo.

Love you forever and ever.

Dear Reader

I've had so much fun writing about the community members of Oak Grove, and was especially excited to spend the holidays with them. From the time she made an appearance in *Winning the Mail-Order Bride*, I knew Hannah would have her own story—and because she needed a bit of a miracle, a Christmas story was perfect for her. And Teddy… Well, he was absolutely perfect for her. He just didn't know it.

While I was writing this story Teddy's actions reminded me of my grandfather. When I was in grade school my family moved from Northern Minnesota to Kansas. I remember hearing my mother talking to my grandfather on the phone. She told him the store had trees for sale, but they were so dried-out she was afraid to put one in the house. A week or so after that conversation a UPS truck delivered a tree wrapped in burlap to our door. My grandfather had cut down a tree on his property and obtained a special permit to ship it out of state so we could have a 'real' Christmas tree.

That's what this season is about. Miracles. Whether they are trees, cradles or babies. Take a moment to remember *your* Christmas miracles. And smile.

Blessings to you and yours!

Lauri

Chapter One

Although moments ago she'd seen Teddy White out the window and watched him walking across the field that separated the house from town, the quick knock on the door startled Hannah Olsen so fully, the papers she'd been stacking scattered across the table and onto the chair. Hannah sucked in a deep breath and scooped the papers into a pile before calling, "Come in."

Teddy stepped in quickly and closed the door behind him. "Good day, Mrs. Olsen," he said while removing his narrow-brimmed hat. "Fiona asked if I could stop by and pick up your etchings."

Having grown used to people adding "Mrs." to her name Hannah no longer flinched at that. However, a flutter happened inside her—and it wasn't her unborn child. Teddy's voice did that to her, and she should have prepared herself for it. For months, her heart had taken to fluttering whenever he was near, and lately, it had gotten worse.

Forcing herself to speak around the frog in her throat, she said, "Yes, thank you, Mr. White." Shaken enough already, she kept her attention on the papers and wooden blocks. Looking at him would only make the flutters worse. "I'm sorry I didn't have them completed earlier, but I do now."

"I'm sorry Abigail insisted upon so many this week." He stepped closer to the table. "It's because of the holiday. She wants plenty of pictures in the Thanksgiving edition."

His sincerity surpassed her will not to look at him. Tiny specks of snow clung to his leather jacket, which was the same shade of brown as his eyes. Genuine regret sat in those eyes today. Hannah had seen that before. He often apologized for his sister.

"It wasn't too many," she assured, while stepping away from the table. "I just let time slip away when I shouldn't have."

"I'm sure you're busy with many other things," he said.

Hannah's hands went to her stomach. She had very little to do, except worry. Her father had said her baby would be ridiculed for not having a father, just like Herb Lundberg had been. A day hadn't gone by where Herb hadn't been blamed for something, even on the days he hadn't been in school. That wouldn't happen to her child. She'd make sure of it. That's why she'd left Wisconsin, and would never go back. Not about to admit all that to Teddy, she searched for something else to say. "The wind is bitter today."

"Yes, it is," Teddy said with a smile, and a glance toward the stove.

"Oh, would you like a cup of coffee?" She squeezed her hands together to quell their shaking. Teddy stopped by the house regularly to visit with

Brett, but this was the first time they'd been alone together.

"If it's no trouble."

"None at all," she said while forcing her feet to walk across the room to the cupboard. "Fiona keeps a pot on the stove for Brett. He always comes home a couple of times during the day." She had no idea why she said that. Other than because babbling might help. It didn't. Her heart thudded even faster now.

"I stopped and saw Brett on the way here," Teddy said.

Hannah nodded as she took down two cups. Teddy and Brett were close friends, which is why she'd been given the job of etching pictures into the blocks of wood for the newspaper. Her grandfather had taught her the skill years ago, mainly as a way to keep her busy. Having been born eight years after her next older sister, she'd spent most every winter in the care of her grandparents while the rest of her family had been out in the woods cutting lumber for their logging company. Perhaps that's why she enjoyed winter. She had many wonderful memories of staying with her grandparents during Thanksgiving and Christmas.

The time she spent living with Gram and Pappy had been fun and peaceful. There had been no fights, no blame, no hate.

"Hannah?"

Turning about, she pinched her lips as she looked at Teddy, hoping a bit of what he'd said had filtered through her musing.

"If you'd prefer I didn't attend, that's fine," he said.

Her musing had been too thick, leaving her with no idea what he referred to. "I'm sorry." She filled a cup and held it out. "I didn't hear what you said. I—uh—I was thinking of the holidays up home."

"Holidays can be tough to get through those first few years." He took the cup. "It does get easier."

His parents had died years before, some of the women in the quilting club had mentioned that, and how he and his sister, Abigail, had settled in other towns before ending up in Oak Grove. From what had been said, Abigail had stirred up trouble in those towns, which is why they'd packed up and left.

"Thank you," Hannah replied. "I'm sure it will."

Cupping his coffee cup with both hands, he glanced around before he said, "Earlier, I'd said that Brett has invited me to Thanksgiving dinner, but if you'd prefer I didn't attend, I'd understand."

"That would not be up to me, Mr. White," she said. "This is Brett and Fiona's home. I would never dream of implying one way or the other that someone was not welcome here."

"I know you wouldn't," he said. "That's why I mentioned it in private. No one but you and I will know. If it would make you uncomfortable, I won't come."

Lifting her chin, she forced a swallow around the solid lump that formed in her throat. He made her uncomfortable all right, because of all the eligible men in Oak Grove, he was the only one she could imagine marrying. Getting married just so her child would have a name, a father, may not be right, but late at night, in the quiet of the house, her father's voice declaring he wouldn't allow her to bring shame upon their family by having a child out of wedlock echoed inside her mind. She had to close her eyes to stop that thought from going any further. It took a moment, but once she felt stable enough, she said, "You do not make me uncomfortable."

He nodded, but there was doubt in his eyes.

There was doubt inside her, too. Her baby was due around the first of the year, which gave her little time to decide what she would do. A few of the women friends she'd made since arriving in Oak Grove knew her secret. Fiona, Martha Taylor, Mary Putnam and Maggie Miller were good friends and continuously assured her no harm would come from allowing others believe she and Eric had been married before he'd died. However, the closer the time came for her baby to be born, the more she understood that it didn't matter what others believed. What mattered was the truth. She'd never been married, and therefore her baby would be born out of wedlock. Born without a name, just as her father had claimed.

It would take a miracle for that to change. Setting her cup on the counter, she said, "I look forward to having you—" she had to brace herself in order to continue "—and Abigail join us for Thanksgiving dinner."

"Abigail won't be joining us."

The relief that washed over her was greater than

she'd expected. Even the baby seemed to rejoice by shifting. She placed both hands on her stomach as the precious rolling continued. The movement filled her with more warmth than the stove did the house.

"Is that your baby moving?"

Still focused on the contentment that filled her, she nodded.

"Your skirt is moving," he said.

"He or she must be trying to get comfortable." She loved the tiny being inside her so much, and couldn't wait to meet him or her. Flattening her skirt, she smiled at the visible movement of the material as the baby continued to move.

"Does it hurt?"

"No. It feels amazing." Used to sharing the wonderful movement with Fiona, Hannah said, "Give me your hand."

He did and she placed it on her stomach, palm down.

She knew the moment he felt the baby move. Not only had she felt it from inside her, but his eyes lit up with amazement.

He set his cup on the counter, and holding up that hand, too, he asked, "May I?"

She nodded, and rested her hand atop the other one he placed against her stomach. The sensation was so remarkable, so unexplainable, she closed her eyes to fully cherish the moment.

The baby moved again and Teddy chuckled. "That's incredible."

"Yes, it is." Completely at ease, she opened her

eyes to add, "Except for when a foot or knee gets caught beneath one of my ribs."

His expressions were easy to read. Sympathy was there now.

"It hurts then?"

"No," she answered, smiling. "It's just a bit uncomfortable."

They stood there for several minutes, softly laughing as the baby continued to move. She shouldn't be enjoying it as much as she was. It was surely scandalous, but exactly what she wanted. Someone to share these precious, wonderful moments with her.

"He or she must have fallen asleep," Teddy whispered after a time of no movement.

"Or just finally got comfortable," she said. The stillness also caused a wave of embarrassment to wash over her and she removed her hands from atop his.

He dropped his hands and took a step back. "I—uh—"

She shook her head, not wanting him to apologize. He hadn't done anything wrong. She had. If his sister learned of what had just happened, Abigail would have more reason to shed scorn. Since the first time they'd met, Abigail's contempt-filled glares had showered Hannah with more shame than her father's hateful shouts had back home.

"I have your money here somewhere," Teddy said, digging in his coat and pants pockets with both hands. "Ah, yes, I put it in this pocket so I'd find it easy." Handing her an envelope, he said, "There's also a note from Abigail as to what she'd like for next month. There are some special ads local merchants would like created, as well. She explains them in her note, but they won't be due for a couple of weeks."

A tinge of remorse washed over Hannah. In spite of all her instincts, she had to be thankful for Abigail White. If not for the opportunity to create the etchings, she'd be even more indebted to Brett and Fiona. The money she received from the *Gazette* allowed her to contribute to the household and to purchase the things she needed. Four months ago she'd arrived with little more than a satchel holding one extra dress and underthings.

"Thank you, Mr. White," she said. "I'll begin working on them right away."

"The thanks goes to you. Before you, the newspaper was rather dull. Though we tried, neither Abigail nor I have the drawing skills that you have. I'd wager no one in Kansas has the skills you have."

"I find that very doubtful," Hannah answered. "It's hardly a skill. Just something I like to do."

He gathered the stack of papers and etchings closer to his side of the table. "Do you need more supplies? Wood or paper?"

"No. I have plenty of paper and Brett has cut up a rather endless supply of wood blocks. He also sharpens the burins regularly, and Rhett and Wyatt enjoy sanding the blocks smooth for me," she added, referring to Fiona's two young sons.

"It's good you have so much help," Teddy said. "I'll bid you good day, then. If you hurry, you might still be able to join the quilting club. I'd be happy to walk you to Martha's dress shop."

She'd forgone the quilting club session today in order to complete the etchings, and had no desire to venture out in the cold. "Thank you, but no, I'll remain home today."

He nodded as he replaced his hat. "It's a good day to stay inside." After picking up the stacks, he added, "By tomorrow it could be warm enough to go without a coat. This is Kansas. The weather changes hourly."

"I've noticed how unpredictable the weather can be here. Other than the wind."

"Aw, yes, the wind. Now, that is something you can count on."

It was rather amazing how casually they conversed. She was thankful for how he'd made her forget that she'd been embarrassed a short time ago. Which she should have been. Allowing a man to touch her like that. Eric had been the only man to touch her and... Her thoughts paused momentarily as she looked at Teddy. That was the other unique thing about him. He made her forget how badly she missed Eric. How severely she'd mourned his death.

Their gazes locked and held in such a way her heart skipped several beats before he looked away.

"Good day, Mrs. Olsen," he said, moving to the door.

A sudden desire to stop him from leaving had her stepping forward. Unsure why she didn't want him to leave, she instantly concluded it had to do with not wanting Abigail to discover what had just happened. "Why isn't your sister joining us for Thanksgiving dinner?"

"She's joining the mayor and reverend at Rollie Austin's place that day."

"And you weren't invited?" That seemed terribly rude, even for Abigail.

"Yes, I was invited, but I eat at the hotel almost every day. Brett's invitation sounded more enjoyable."

His smile enticed her to offer one in return. "Then I hope you won't be disappointed."

"That would be impossible." He touched the brim of his hat. "Good day, Mrs. Olsen."

"Good day, Mr. White." Upon closing the door behind him, she drew a deep breath and leaned her forehead against the solid wood for a moment. Why? Why couldn't any of the other men on her list make her heart thud? Teddy was as opposite from Eric as a man could be. Eric had been loud and impulsive— two things Teddy certainly wasn't.

However, he did have one thing in common with Eric. His family hated her. She had lived with hatred her entire life, and was determined her child would never experience it.

Chapter Two

Teddy willed himself not to turn around for a final look. Hannah had already closed the door, so he wouldn't see her. Other than in his mind. A place where her image was etched as perfectly as the pictures she flawlessly carved into the blocks of wood. He'd been printing newspapers for as long as he could remember and producing multiple copies of pictures was not an easy task. Leastwise it never used to be. His and Abigail's engravings always collected ink and left globs that bled into the print. That hadn't happened once with Hannah's creations.

Her etchings were as flawless as her beauty. He'd been alongside Brett the day Hannah had stepped off the train, and had tried to keep his distance from that moment on. He'd fallen for a forlorn young woman once before and promised himself it would never happen again.

Keeping his distance had been easy at first. Brett's mother had sent Hannah to Oak Grove and Brett and Fiona had taken her into their home and protected her as strongly as a mother bear would a cub in spring. The entire town discovered why when Hannah's shape had begun to change.

Teddy let out a long sigh as his hands started to tingle. Touching her, feeling that baby move inside her, had been amazing. Miraculous even. And caused a large amount of compassion to well inside him. She was so young to be widowed and now was expecting a child all on her own.

Only she wasn't on her own. Brett and Fiona treated her like family and would continue to.

Still, in a town the size of Oak Grove, which was small compared to many but growing steadily, a single woman—widowed or not, expecting or not—was a highly sought after commodity. Last summer the town had formed a Betterment Committee in order to bring suitable women of marrying age to town. Several men had married the mail-order brides, but although he'd contributed to the committee, too, he hadn't sought out any of the brides. Hadn't even considered doing so. He'd only gone along with the cause for appearance's sake. Five years ago he'd gone down the road that led to marriage, but had hit a painful roadblock, which had taught him a valuable lesson.

That was part of the reason he'd kept his distance from Hannah and would continue to, even though her growing stomach made her all the more beautiful to him. He could imagine her having a baby girl with golden curls and blue eyes as lovely as her mother's.

A tremendous sense of satisfaction grew inside of him as he once again recalled touching her stomach. Feeling the baby move. He couldn't believe that had happened. Knew it shouldn't have happened, because every time he looked at her, he was reminded of another young girl carrying a baby. One he'd been ready to claim as his own.

A gust of wind caught him off guard. Teddy tightened his hold on the papers and blocks of wood in his hands, but relentless, the wind won and the bottom piece of paper caught the air. Teddy hurried after it, and stopped it with a stomp of one foot. While bending down to pick it up, he paused. Rather than a drawing, this one held writing. Neat and stylish penmanship he instantly recognized as Hannah's.

He grasped the paper and turned about, all set to return it to her, until he scanned the sheet a bit more closely.

A shiver that had nothing to do with the blustery wind, or the bits of ice it tossed about, raced across his shoulders. It was a list of men. Of men he knew full well were actively looking for a wife. And his name wasn't on it.

That should make him happy, yet his shoulders slumped as his gaze bounced between Brett's house and the list a couple times.

"What are you studying so hard?"

Teddy spun around at the sound of Brett's voice. Teddy had said he'd stop by on his way back and knew Brett would be watching for him. Stuffing the paper into his pocket, he replied, "Just a list."

"Of Hannah's drawings?"

He gestured to his arm load. "Got them all right here."

"I was just walking over to check on you. You were there quite a while."

"She offered me a cup of coffee and I accepted."

With black hair and shoulders as broad as the back end of a horse, Brett towered over most men in town. His size didn't intimidate Teddy, but he did respect Brett, and valued their friendship.

As Brett glanced toward his house again, Teddy said, "I've already spoken to Abigail. She won't request so many etchings all at one time again. I hadn't realized it was so many."

"Make sure she doesn't," Brett said. "Hannah's time is getting closer and she needs her rest."

"When did you become a doctor?"

Brett grinned. "I'm not, but I should be with half the women in town asking about Hannah and giving me advice about what she needs to do, including my own wife." Brett's face turned serious. "Hannah's become awfully quiet lately, like she was when she first arrived. I'm worried about her, Teddy. Real worried."

His heart skipped a beat. "Do you think she's ill?"

"Fiona says she's not. But she's back to barely eating enough to keep a bird alive."

Recalling something Hannah had said, Teddy suggested, "Maybe she's homesick. She mentioned thinking about the holidays back home."

"That could be it," Brett said, turning about.

Teddy fell into step beside his friend. Brett's blacksmith shop as well as the feed store he owned was on the edge of town and only a short distance from his house.

Most of the blacksmithing took place in the lean-to,

and as they skirted the far wall, Teddy let out a whistle. "That wind is brutal today." Thankful to be out of the biting wind he moved closer to the blazing fire in the open forge in the center of the open area.

"Yeah, it is," Brett replied. "Homesick, huh?"

Teddy nodded. "The first few holidays after our parents died were hard for me and Abigail."

"That's why Fiona suggested inviting you to Thanksgiving," Brett said as he rubbed his chin. "She thought the company would do Hannah good. I'll talk to her about inviting others."

Teddy's first instinct had been to say no when Brett had invited him to Thanksgiving, but out of respect, he'd said yes. Now his concern was for Hannah. "I don't know about that," he said. "Too many would just be more work for her and Fiona."

"That's true," Brett said.

"And don't forget the recital at the school that afternoon. There will be a lot of people there."

"It would be impossible to forget about that," Brett said, grinning. "Rhett and Wyatt have been practicing their lines so often I know Lincoln's proclamation by heart."

Teddy laughed. Brett had taken to Fiona's two boys as soon as they'd hit town, and treated them as if they were his own. Teddy turned to stare into the flames of the fire. He'd been willing to do that once. Love a child that wasn't his. It hadn't come to be, though. A week before the wedding, the real father had shown up. He'd stepped back, told Becky he understood and buried the pain of rejection.

To others Becky may only have been a barmaid who'd gotten herself into the family way, but she'd been more than that to him. He'd fallen in love with her, and when she'd first said she was going to have a baby, he'd thought he was the father. She'd insisted he wasn't. That it was a cowboy who had visited her regularly, but hadn't come back since she told him about the baby. Without any contemplation, he'd told her not to worry, that he'd marry her and claim the baby as his own, and had set plans in place to do just that.

Shaking aside ghosts of the past, Teddy moved away from the forge. "I better get these over to the office," he said.

"Thanks, Teddy," Brett said. "You've been a good friend, and helped Hannah out by letting her make those etchings."

"She's very good at it," he answered honestly.

Brett nodded. "She is, but..."

The hair on the back of his neck tingled. "But what?"

Brett seemed to shrink a bit as he shook his head slowly. "Hannah's been through some rough times."

"Well, she seems to have handled it well," Teddy replied. "Maybe she's stronger than she looks."

Brett shook his head with more purpose this time. "You haven't heard her crying herself to sleep at night."

Teddy had no answer for that, and the paper in his pocket suddenly felt as hot as the flames of Brett's forge.

Chapter Three

With so much that needed to be done, Hannah was up early. Quietly, so not to wake Brett and Fiona, whose bedroom was off the kitchen, she stoked up the fire and then gathered a knife and bowl to start cleaning out the three pumpkins sitting on the counter.

She loved all the cooking that went into preparing Thanksgiving dinner. A wave of sadness that she wouldn't be there to help Gram this year had her squeezing the knife a bit harder as she sliced the top off the first pumpkin. She missed Gram and it made her heart hurt to think of never seeing her and Pappy again. They were the only two people, besides Eric, who truly cared about her. But the warning from her father never to return to her family couldn't be ignored.

A sound on the porch had her spinning about, and the knock that sounded a moment later had her glancing toward the closed bedroom door before she started across the room.

It was awfully early for company. The sun was just starting to rise. Cautiously, Hannah pulled open the door just wide enough to see who stood there. Her heart thudded at the sight of Teddy.

"T— Mr. White, what are you doing here so

early?" she asked, taking a step back, away from the blast of cold air.

The bedroom door opened just then. "Come in, Teddy," Brett said, poking only his head around the door. "I'll be right out."

Teddy stepped into the kitchen and closed the door. "Brett and I are going turkey hunting this morning." His gaze dropped to her side, to her hand specifically. "Do you always answer the door with a butcher knife in hand?"

His question, or perhaps the twinkle in his eyes, allowed her to relax enough that the air she'd been holding whooshed out. "No, I was cleaning pumpkins," she answered, using the knife to gesture to the counter.

"Oh, I see," Teddy said.

She hadn't made any coffee yet, so couldn't offer him that, and was in the midst of wondering what to say next and how to maneuver around him when the bedroom door opened and Brett strolled out. She used that opportunity to scurry across the room, hoping the distance would calm her insides.

"Ready to shoot a bird?" Brett asked Teddy.

"I wouldn't be here if I wasn't," Teddy replied.

Brett sat down in the chair to pull on his boots. "Hannah, I told Fiona I'll do the chores when I get back," he said. "There's no need for either of you to go out in the cold this morning."

"We'll have breakfast ready when you get back," Fiona said, walking out of the bedroom.

Tall and slender with long brown hair and hazel

eyes, Fiona was a pretty woman, but it was her happiness that made her beautiful. It was as if she was part angel the way she floated around, smiling and glowing. Having seven sisters, all married, Hannah had been around a lot of couples, and Brett and Fiona had to love each other more than any two people she'd ever seen. The longer she lived with them, the more deeply she wanted to experience love like that. To have someone look at her the way those two looked at each other.

"There will be plenty for you, too, Teddy," Fiona said, "so come back hungry."

"Thank you."

The sound of his voice sent her heart into another unexpected bout of hammering and Hannah dropped the knife. She caught it before it fell all the way to the floor, but flinched as the blade nicked the end of her finger.

"Are you all right?" Teddy asked, instantly arriving at her side.

"Fine, just clumsy." Hannah set the knife down, but wrapped the tip of her finger with her other hand. It couldn't be very deep, so it shouldn't be bleeding too much. There was no reason for any of this. Not for her heart to pound so hard, or for him to have rushed to her side.

"Let me see," he insisted.

"It's nothing, really," Hannah replied, cautiously unfolding her fingers to take a peek. Relieved, she held the finger up. "See? It's not even bleeding."

He took ahold of her hand to give her finger a

thorough inspection, and she was glad she'd set the knife down, otherwise she'd have dropped it all over again. Her heart was racing faster than ever, and her hand, where he touched it, burned as if on fire.

"Here, let me see," Fiona said.

"It's fine," Hannah said, pulling her hand to her side as soon as Teddy's hold relaxed. "Really." She stepped back, and tried to slow her breathing.

"Well, you men best get going," Fiona said, while giving her a scrutinizing gaze.

Hannah turned about and moved the pumpkins around just for something to do.

As soon as the men left, Fiona asked, "Are you doing all right? You've seemed a bit preoccupied lately."

Hannah started scraping the inside of a pumpkin. "I'm fine. Just excited about the holidays. They've always been my favorite time of the year." That was true. Despite everything, the joy the holidays always instilled in her was still there. The idea of hope, of miracles happening, still lived within her.

"I'm more excited about them than I've ever been."

Something in Fiona's soft tone had Hannah turning to look at her. "You haven't always enjoyed them?"

Fiona shook her head. "Most years they were no different than any other day. There wasn't the money to have special meals. I always managed to come up with some small gifts for Rhett and Wyatt on Christmas Day, but…" She sighed and wiped her hands on her apron. "That's in the past. This year will be the best Christmas ever. And Thanksgiving, too. I can't remember the last time I ate turkey."

Hannah couldn't help but notice how Fiona was rubbing her stomach. As their eyes met again, Fiona's smile grew. Comprehension hit Hannah like a gust of wind. "You're expecting."

Fiona glanced over her shoulder, toward the parlor where stairs led to the second floor and the bedrooms Wyatt and Rhett slept in. "Yes, but we haven't told the boys yet. Haven't told anyone. Dr. Graham confirmed my suspicions last week. I saw him after attending the quilting club. Brett and I decided we'll tell the boys on Christmas Day."

Hannah wiped her hands clean in order to hug her friend. "They will be so happy."

"I believe they will. So many things have happened this past year, since their father died," Fiona said. "I'd almost lost hope. Then we moved out here and I married Brett. Some days I pinch myself, just to make sure I'm not dreaming. That my life really is this wonderful." Fiona pressed a hand to her stomach as they parted. "I love my sons with all my heart, but I can't say I was ever this excited about being pregnant. With each of them, I worried about feeding them, providing for them. I no longer have those worries, all because of Brett."

"He loves you very much," Hannah said. How Brett and Fiona behaved toward one another had influenced her thoughts when it came to considering her options for a possible husband. They were kind to each other, which seemed obvious, but it hadn't been that way in her family.

Fiona's smile grew soft. "Brett is so easy to love. At first that seemed so strange to me. He's the exact opposite of Sam."

"He is?" Hannah asked. Fiona had made mention of her first husband, but never said much about him.

"Oh, yes," Fiona said. "But it's more than that. My love for Brett is different than what I felt for Sam. Love is like that. We can love different people, in different ways. Sam was Rhett and Wyatt's father, and I will always honor his memory, but I will also embrace my new life for what it is now." She giggled. "You could say I now look at things with a whole new perspective." Fiona closed her eyes as she laid both hands on her stomach. "This baby is more than a blessing. It's a true gift from God."

Hannah couldn't help but place a hand on her own stomach and wonder if she would ever look at things with a new perspective. She and Eric had loved each other very much, and planned on leaving Wisconsin, leaving all the hatred between their families behind. The very hatred that had ultimately killed him.

"Oh, listen to me, going on," Fiona said. "I'm sorry."

"Why would you be sorry?" As soon as she asked, Hannah read the sadness in Fiona's eyes.

"Your baby is a blessing, too," Fiona said. "Just think about it. Our babies will grow up together. They'll be as close as siblings."

Hannah forced the smile to remain on her lips.

"Yes, yes they will." It was a wonderful thought, but her baby needed a father before siblings. However, she refused to dampen Fiona's joy.

A thud sounded overhead and Fiona squeezed her hand. "The boys are awake. I need to start their breakfast."

Hannah squeezed Fiona's hand in return. "And I have pumpkins to get in the oven."

While Fiona made breakfast and sent her boys off to school, Hannah cleaned and baked the pumpkins. The slices were on the counter, cooling so she'd be able to peel and mush the fruit to use for pies, when the door opened. She was glad to not be holding the pan. If hearing Teddy's voice had made her drop the knife, the sight of him now would have had her dumping the entire pan of pumpkin on the floor.

His eyes were shining like usual, but so were his cheeks. They were red from the cold wind, but it was the smile on his face that made him look even more charming than ever. More handsome.

Teddy thought he knew what to expect, as they'd only been gone a couple of hours, but the sight of Hannah caught him off guard. The smear of flour across her cheek, along with the apron that made her stomach more prominent, made her look beyond pretty. Beyond beautiful. She looked like a wife. A wife a man would want to come home to. And that had his blood pounding harder than when he'd shot the turkey. He didn't want a wife, dang it. So why did she make him think along those lines all the time?

His hearing seemed to kick in from nowhere and he turned toward Fiona.

"Yes," he replied to her question about whether they'd had any luck. "We got a big one. Must be close to thirty pounds."

"Oh, that's wonderful," Fiona replied as she glanced at Hannah. "Isn't it?"

"Yes," Hannah said before turning her back on him.

"Where's Brett?" Fiona asked.

"Getting a tub," Teddy answered. "He asked me to have you put water on to boil." His gaze kept bouncing back to Hannah. She was as attractive from the back as she was the front. Her blond hair was tied at the nape of her neck and the long curls hung down her back almost to her apron ties.

"Of course, but he doesn't plan on cleaning it, does he?" Fiona asked while she added a log to the firebox of the cookstove.

"We figured you two were busy enough," Teddy answered. "Thought we'd go ahead and clean it."

"Nonsense." Fiona crossed the room and grabbed a shawl hanging by the door. "He's the one who has to work today. I'll be right back."

Hannah turned around as the door closed. When their eyes met, he said, "I think we'll leave them alone for a moment."

"I think that's a good idea," she replied.

The smile on her face made his heart thud. Drawn forward, he paused when she took a step sideways—away from him. Flustered because he shouldn't be drawn to her, he searched for an excuse as to why he'd moved. Eyeing a kettle on the counter, he said, "I'll fill this with water and put it on the stove." He then quickly asked, "How's your hand?"

She shook her head slightly. "Fine. I'll get another kettle. If the bird is as large as you say, we'll need plenty of hot water."

"It's as big as I say," he assured. "One of the biggest turkeys I've ever seen." Setting the pot on the stove, he asked, "Do you like turkey?"

"Of course. Who doesn't like turkey?"

"I certainly do." He crossed the room to collect one of the buckets filled with water. "But then there's not a whole lot I don't like. How about you?"

"Nothing that I can think of." She set the second kettle on the stove. "However, I have made some things that weren't very tasty."

He laughed while filling both pots with water. "I have, too."

She frowned. "You cook?"

"Every day." He set the empty bucket on the table. "Except for the meals I eat at the hotel."

"What about Abigail? Doesn't she cook?"

"As little as possible, luckily." He turned about and smiled. "Her cooking is worse than mine."

"It is?"

"Abigail's usually so busy writing, she burns everything." Noting her frown, he changed the subject while nodding toward the counter. "Are you making pumpkin pies?"

"Yes." Her smile was as soft as her voice. "Do you like pumpkin pie?"

"It just happens to be my favorite."

"I'm using my grandmother's recipe."

"I can hardly wait."

Silence encircled around them as they stood there, Hannah near the stove, him next to the table, their gazes locked. He wanted to say something, but the heart in his chest hammered against his rib cage, stealing his ability to form a single rational thought. Other than ones about how blue her eyes were, and how they kept moving slightly, as if she wanted to look away but couldn't.

The lines of her face were soft and graceful, and the lashes around her eyes long and dark. Her lips were pale pink and glistening. This time he counteracted the pull inside him that had him wanting to step closer to her by resting a hand on the back of a chair.

Like every other time he laid eyes on her, a deep sense of wisdom or logic, or some other sensation he couldn't quite explain, overcame him. Perhaps it wasn't her he was drawn to as much as it was her condition. It reminded him of Becky and the baby he'd already looked forward to before she'd told him the wedding was off. That she was marrying the baby's father. He'd been hurt and disappointed, but never let it show. Abigail had. She'd been furious, and when she had taken out her anger in her newspaper articles, he'd sought out a new town looking for a newspaper. Within a month, he and Abigail had moved. Two years later, they'd moved again, to Oak Grove. When they'd arrived, he'd promised himself, and warned Abigail, this was their last move. He wasn't hauling that press another mile ever again.

Frustrated that he was remembering all that, and that Hannah was the reason, he glanced away. The best thing that could happen would be for her to marry one of the men on that list she'd written out.

The list was in his pocket, and at the moment seemed to be singeing his thigh. He'd carried it with him every day and thought nonstop about giving it back to her, but— "Who else will be here tomorrow?" he asked.

"No one that I know of," she answered. "Angus stopped by yesterday, to let us know that he'll be taking his meal with Maggie and Jackson."

Angus O'Leary was an eccentric old Irish bachelor who had more money than he had brains. That wasn't true. Angus was smarter than men half his age, which had to be pushing three-quarters of a century, and he knew how to charm the ladies. Perhaps it was his tall top hat, or his three-piece suits, but women adored the old codger.

Including Hannah.

Every Sunday, and whenever there was a community event, Angus was the one to escort Hannah. Old or not, Angus took his role of keeping others at bay when it came to Hannah seriously, and did a fine job of it.

Up until this moment, Teddy hadn't considered

that. How well Angus kept others at bay, including those on her list.

"Why?" she asked.

"Just making sure there will be plenty of pie for me." That wasn't the reason, but he wasn't exactly sure what his reasons were. Or why it mattered to him at all.

A shy smile formed as she shook her head slightly. "You certainly must like pumpkin pie, Mr. White."

"I do," he admitted, "and do you think you could call me Teddy? I assure you it wouldn't be improper. Most everyone in town does, even Rhett and Wyatt, and you do call Angus by his first name."

"Yes, I do," she said. "Because he insists upon it."

Suddenly it meant a lot to him to have her call him by his first name, too. "Will it help if I insist, too? Because I will."

She shook her head, but the smile that grew on her lips gave him hope.

A clatter on the back steps and the opening of the door stopped her from answering. Teddy had to swallow a growl of frustration at the interruption as Brett and Fiona walked in. He should be happy about the interruption. Actually, he should just leave.

"My wife and I have come to a compromise," Brett said, grinning down at Fiona. "She and Hannah will finish making us breakfast while we clean the turkey you shot. How's that sound, Ted?"

"Sounds like a fair deal to me," Teddy answered

while he gaze once again settled on Hannah. "How does that sound to you, Hannah?"

Her cheeks took on a pink tinge as she nodded. "I believe that is a very fair deal, Teddy."

Chapter Four

Teddy shut the door of the cupboard he'd thoroughly searched and crossed the room to yell up the stairway. "Abigail, where's that jar of pickles I bought from Rollie?" Their print shop took up the front two rooms of the building, but the back three rooms as well as the three bedrooms upstairs were their living quarters.

"Why?" Abigail asked as she appeared at the top of the stairs.

"Because I need to take them to Brett's," Teddy replied.

Tying the bow of her flowered hat beneath her chin, she started down the stairs. "I ate them."

"You ate them?"

"Yes. I was up late writing last night and got hungry."

Normally he didn't anger easy, but her statement unleashed the coil of frustration that sat inside him lately. "Now what am I supposed to take to Brett's?"

She shrugged. "I'm sure they'll have plenty to eat."

"That's not the point," he growled. Overlooking her attitude was not in him today. Hadn't been the past few days. Never overly pleasant, she'd been even pricklier lately. "It's good manners to take a gift to the host," he pointed out.

She rolled her eyes, but said, "You could join the mayor and I at Rollie's."

Her attitude irked him. She was his sister, therefore he loved her, but on occasion didn't like her much. "Is that why you've been so testy lately? Because I'm not joining you?"

"You should be joining me," she said.

There were also times when arguing with her wasn't worth the effort, and this was one of them. He crossed the room and grabbed his hat off the coatrack.

"Before history repeats itself," she said.

Although he'd kept his thoughts of late hidden, he should've known she'd say something about Hannah sooner or later. "There is no history to repeat."

"Do you think I'm blind? Or have you forgotten how devastated you were the last time you took up with a pregnant woman?"

"Give the Austins my best," he growled as he opened the door and strode out.

She shouted his name, but he kept walking, ignoring her. He hadn't forgotten anything about Becky, including how Abigail had reacted. She'd been against him marrying Becky and then furious when it hadn't happened.

Giving his head a clearing shake, he looked up at the bright blue sky and told himself he was attending dinner at Brett's place for no other reason than Brett was his best friend and had invited him. There was no history to repeat itself because he would never fall in love again. As much as he didn't want to admit it, Abigail was right. He had been devastated when Becky had cast him aside. He was older now, and smarter, and would never go down that road again.

Several hours later, Teddy wondered if he should have gone with Abigail. Brett and Fiona were gracious hosts and the meal had quite easily been the best he'd ever eaten. However, the joy that kept weaving its way around inside him came from Hannah. She was happier than he'd ever seen her. Talkative and carefree as she teased Rhett and Wyatt about eating so much they'd forget their parts in the upcoming recital.

It could just be the jubilation filling the house that was affecting him. Children had a way of doing that, and Rhett and Wyatt, who were five and seven, kept everyone at the table laughing.

Both boys had speaking parts in the program the new teacher had prepared for the entire community. The children were to recite the Thanksgiving proclamation President Abraham Lincoln had delivered back in 1863, making the day a national holiday. The boys insisted the more they ate, the better they'd perform and shortly after their plates were empty, they were itching to leave.

"Rhett and Wyatt sure are excited," Teddy said to Hannah as he closed the door behind them.

The boys had been the first out the door, followed by Brett and Fiona, who'd given a quick apology, stating they needed to hurry or the boys would have their suits dirty before they got to school. Teddy had no choice but to assure them that was fine, that he'd escort Hannah to the school.

"I'm sorry," Hannah said sheepishly. "I just can't move as fast as I used to."

"No reason to be sorry," he said. "We aren't in a hurry."

"The boys are," she said. "They've been practicing their lines all week."

He chuckled. "I think I heard the entire proclamation while we were eating."

She giggled. "I've heard it for the past week. I think I know it by heart."

"The new teacher must be doing a good job," he said. "I don't ever remember being that excited about anything happening at school."

The smile on Hannah's face as she glanced his way made his heart kick like an old mule. "I imagine you were an excellent student."

"I wouldn't go so far as to say that," he answered.

She giggled again, but then said, "Fiona certainly thinks Miss Burnett is a wonderful teacher, and I read the article in the newspaper that Abigail wrote about her. Miss Burnett seems to be very qualified."

"Josiah had purchased ads in newspapers far and wide hoping to find someone suitable. It appears he has, but I don't believe she'll last any longer than the past few have." Teddy bit the end of his tongue, not sure why he'd said that.

"What do you mean?"

"I've heard that Don Carlson is at the school every

day, dropping off and picking up his children." It was the truth, he'd seen it himself, but pointed it out mainly because Don Carlson was on the list of Hannah's potential husbands currently in his pocket. The list he still hadn't returned. It wouldn't hurt for her to know a few of the men on that list may not be a good choice for her. "Last year, Tess Creswell only lasted a few months as the teacher before Art married her. They just had a baby a few months ago."

She nodded. "I've met Mrs. Creswell."

"Don doesn't have a wife and it appears he believes Miss Burnett is what he's been looking for."

"I wasn't aware of that," she said.

"Jules Carmichael has also been seen at the school," he said, mentioning another name on her list. "Jules lives in a small cabin on Russ and Henrietta Gibson's dairy farm, which might not be as appealing to Miss Burnett, coming from the city as she did. The same goes for Jess Radar. He's shown interest in the new teacher, too, but he lives in Steve Putnam's bunkhouse. A woman such as Miss Burnett might be more comfortable in their own home, don't you think?"

Hannah's smile wobbled slightly as she nodded. "I suspect you're right."

Guilt assaulted his stomach. What was he doing? He'd told Abigail more than once that making others look bad did not make her look better. Nor would it make him look better. Which shouldn't matter because he didn't want to look better to Hannah. He didn't want to be one of her choices.

"Have all the eligible men in town shown an interest in Miss Burnett?" Hannah asked.

He shrugged.

"Or just the ones on my list?"

Teddy stumbled slightly.

Hannah had searched for her list. For a while, she'd feared the list had been amongst the drawings she'd given Teddy last week, but since he'd never mentioned finding it, she'd assumed it must have accidently gotten burned. Until a moment ago, when out of nowhere a sinking feeling told her he had it, and knew exactly what it was. The remorse in his eyes said she was right.

They'd stopped walking, and not sure what else to do, she merely held her hand out. He dug into his hip pocket and pulled out a piece of paper. She didn't unfold it. Just slipped it into the pocket of the button-up jacket Fiona had insisted she wear.

"I planned on giving it back to you," he said. "Would have before now, but never had the opportunity."

She couldn't look him in the eye. Selecting a spot over one of his shoulders, she kept her head up, her gaze averted.

"I'm sorry, Hannah," he said. "I should have given it back last week, but—"

"But what?" She still didn't look at him. "You wanted to make sure you had something bad to say about each one of them first?"

"No, I—"

"You what?" She was more upset than she was angry, which was foolish. Making that list had been foolish.

"I just wondered why I wasn't on your list."

The baby moved so suddenly, it startled her as much as his statement had. She placed a hand on her stomach, and he gently touched her arm.

"Is something wrong? Is it the baby?"

She took a deep breath and shook her head. "The baby is fine, and so am I. We should get to the school now." She still hadn't looked at him, didn't have the courage to do that, but noticing his sister amongst the crowd walking toward the school gave her the wherewith to put one foot in front of the other. Abigail's flowered hat was impossible to miss. Even the sight of the back of it caused a sinking sensation inside Hannah.

"We can go back to the house if the walk is too much for you," he said.

"The walk is not too much for me." She drew another deep breath. But all the deep breaths in the world wouldn't give her the fortitude to tell him his sister was the reason he wasn't on her list. The past few nights had been full of sleepless hours, and for most of those hours she'd contemplated what she wanted. Brett and Fiona were wonderful and would let her live with them forever, but she didn't want that. She wanted the baby to have a family. A mother and a father, and eventually siblings. Her thoughts always led her to think about Teddy, and ultimately Abigail. And how much his sister disliked her. The people who would say that didn't matter had never experienced living with hatred. She had. And she knew the consequences.

"Are you sure?" he asked.

She tried to hide a heavy sigh while saying, "I'm sure."

Chapter Five

The children's program didn't last long, but what followed seemed to take forever. Teddy had secured her a chair, of which Hannah was thankful. The school was large enough for the children on a daily basis, but with the entire community in attendance, there wasn't nearly enough room. People stood outside, watching the program through the windows and doorway. She was proud of Rhett and Wyatt, how they performed their speaking parts without a single mishap. The other children, too. She couldn't help but think of the future and how her child would someday be old enough to participate in such performances.

That thought also left her unsettled. What Teddy said had been the truth. About Don Carlson, Jules Carmichael and Jess Radar. She'd already known what he'd said about each of them, and had determined none of them was a suitable choice for her. He had only confirmed her list was much shorter than she'd wanted to believe. And then hearing Rhett whispering to his mother had her thinking about other things.

After the children had taken their final bow, Reverend Flaherty, using words from Lincoln's Proclamation, had led a prayer of inestimable peace, harmony and prosperity for all of Oak Grove. Then Mayor Melbourne had walked to the front of the room. He'd been talking for ages already, and under his breath, she'd heard Rhett tell Fiona that he sure was glad she hadn't married the mayor.

That tiny whispered voice echoed inside Hannah's head for the rest of the mayor's speech. Marrying someone just so her baby would have a last name wouldn't be what was best for her child. Or her. Finding the right man, one she could love and who would love her and her baby, was what she truly wanted. Love like Brett and Fiona had. Like her grandparents had. That's why she'd loved being with them so much, because they'd loved her in return. Outside of their house, all she'd known was hate. Her father had been so full of it, it had spread far and wide. There had been no escaping it.

"Come," Teddy said, taking ahold of her arm. "We'll slip out the side door and avoid most of the crowd so you won't have to be on your feet so long."

"I'm fine," she said in protest, but gladly rose now that the mayor had finally concluded his speech.

Hannah then shivered from head to toe when a squeaky voice sent an icy tremor up her spine.

"Teddy!" Abigail repeated.

He appeared to ignore his sister while walking toward the door, but once outside, he paused long enough for Abigail to catch up with them. Hannah forced a smile to form and prepared herself as she turned to face the other woman.

The glare was there. As icy as the tremor had

been. Having lived with such glares her entire life, Hannah's heart sank. She just couldn't endure that again. Wouldn't.

"I want an etching of the children's performance for the paper next week," Abigail said, never once glancing toward her brother.

"I'm sorry, Miss White," Hannah said. "I didn't bring any paper with me."

"Abigail—"

"You can't draw one from memory?" Abigail interrupted Teddy. "To hear my brother talk, you can draw anything. Everything."

"You've commented on what an expert artist Mrs. Olsen is, too, Abigail," Teddy said. "As has the mayor and practically every person who has seen one of her drawings in the *Gazette*."

"That I have," Mayor Josiah Melbourne said. "Every week when I read the newspaper." Patting Abigail's arm, the man continued, "You certainly can't expect Mrs. Olsen to draw all those children from memory."

Hannah figured she could draw a few, but not all of them, and sincerely hoped Abigail would agree with the mayor. Josiah and Brett had butted heads when it came to Fiona—mainly due to the fact the mayor had brought her to town to marry him— and Hannah certainly didn't want to be the cause of Brett standing against the man again. Or Teddy. That would be even worse. Especially in Abigail's eyes, which were narrowing and making her face all the more hawkish.

"I expected you to realize an event this large would need a picture to go along with my article," Abigail said, holding up her pad of paper. Of course her pencil was stuck behind one ear as always.

"I didn't," Teddy interjected, "and I own the paper." Taking ahold of Hannah's arm once more, he nodded. "Now, if you two will excuse us, we have pumpkin pie waiting for us."

"So do we, Abigail," the mayor said.

Abigail didn't speak as she spun about. Didn't need to. Her eyes had said all Hannah needed to hear.

"I don't believe the mayor has missed too many desserts in his life," Teddy said with a smile as they started walking.

The mayor was portly, and short, and Hannah had a hard time believing Fiona had ever considered marrying the man every time she saw him. That wasn't what she thought of now. Although Teddy was obviously trying to make her think of other things, she couldn't. Nor could she stop the heavy sigh that escaped her as they crossed the street.

"Don't let Abigail bother you." Teddy's hold on her arm tightened while they stepped onto the wooden walkway that ran the entire length of the street, including past the *Gazette* office.

Hannah shook her head. "I don't know what I've done to make her dislike me so much."

"You haven't done anything," Teddy said. "Abigail has never learned how to make friends. I've tried to make her understand things, but…" He shrugged. "I thought she'd grown out of it."

"No," Hannah insisted. "I know hatred when I see it." If she had the wherewithal, she would kick up her heels and run back to Brett's house, but in her condition, that wasn't an option. At most, her gait would be a fast waddle.

"It's not you," Teddy said. "It's me. She's upset because you're, well, similar to a woman I was engaged to marry once."

Hannah footsteps faltered briefly. "I am? Engaged to? What happened?"

He shrugged. "She married someone else."

There was no shine in his eyes, no smile on his face, and Hannah got the impression he regretted saying as much as he had. After several quiet moments, she said, "Eric's family hated me. Still do. They hate my entire family. Always have. And my family hated him. His entire family. The feud has been going on for years. Long ago, two brothers were in the fur trade together, but when one stole the other one's wife, the two became enemies. They moved to opposite sides of the lake, and one changed the spelling of their name."

"Their name?"

"Olsen. One of them changed it from an *O-l-s-e-n* to *O-l-s-o-n*, according to my father. According to Eric's father it was the opposite way. From *o* to *e*, not *e* to *o*." She wasn't sure why she'd told him all that. Maybe because in a somewhat different way, she knew how he felt. Not being loved by someone you wanted to love you. "The feud was reignited when I was a baby. By then both families owned logging companies. Eric's grandfather and my grandfather both tried to claim an island in the middle of the lake, wanting to harvest the lumber off it."

"Who won?" Teddy asked as they turned the corner and started walking toward Brett's blacksmith shop and seed company.

"Neither. A fire burned all the trees to the ground. Both sides claimed the other one started the fire."

"What does your grandfather say?"

"He died in the fire. So did Eric's grandfather. They were the only two on the island."

After a few steps, he asked, "I thought your grandfather taught you how to draw and etch wood."

"He did. But Pappy is my mother's father. John and Glenda Gunderson." Saying her grandparents' names added to her melancholy. She missed them terribly. "I stayed winters with them from the time I was a baby. I'm the youngest. My sisters and mother went to the logging camp to cook for the men. When I got old enough to go to the camp, too, Gram asked if I could stay with her and Pappy instead because they were getting older and could use my help. I have plenty of sisters—seven, actually— so my mother agreed I could stay behind, and my father... Well, he was glad to not have me around. I angered him. Because I was supposed to be a boy." The baby inside her shifted and she placed her hand upon her stomach as a familiar and special feeling eased some of her sorrow.

"Surely that didn't really matter to him."

"Yes, it did. The other Olsons had sons to carry on

the family name." Tired of the hurt that encompassed her when thinking about her father, she changed the subject. "Pappy didn't mind that I was a girl and he was proud of my etchings. He's a carpenter. Makes furniture as fine as Jackson Miller here in town. But Pappy's pieces are all uniquely carved. Pinecones and oak leaves, birds, fish and many other personal designs. They are truly wonderful." The memory of one particular piece made her sigh. "When I was a baby, he made a cradle for me to sleep in while I was at their house, and always said that my children would sleep in it, too. It's beautiful."

"I'm sure it is." They walked in silence for a few more steps before he said, "Did things get better between your families once you and Eric—"

"No," she answered before he could finish. She didn't want to lie to him, but wasn't ready to reveal she and Eric had never been married. "One of his brothers saw Eric talking to me at the lumberyard one day. Both of our families sold logs to Brett's family's sawmill. His father made sure my father heard about it, and we were forbidden to see each other."

"But you didn't stop."

"No," she replied, "we didn't." Her throat was suddenly on fire, and swallowing only made it worse, but she continued, "Eric died because he loved me. He may have drowned while floating logs across the lake, but he wouldn't have been given that job if his father hadn't been mad at him because of me."

* * *

Teddy wanted to tell her that couldn't be true, that she couldn't blame herself for Eric's death like that, but tears weren't the only thing in her eyes. There was so much grief, so much sorrow, it stole his breath. They'd crossed the field and now stood near Brett's house. Still holding one of her elbows, he grasped her other arm, to pull her close to offer comfort, but she shook her head.

"His father told me so. Told me I was the reason his son died. Eric was a faller. He loved cutting down trees." She blinked back several tears while pinching her lips together. "But he hated the water. Was afraid of it. Everyone knew that. Especially his father, but he'd made Eric float the logs across the river as a punishment for loving me."

The desire to pull her close grew at every tear that fell from her eyes. "Hannah—"

"I don't want my baby to ever know that kind of hatred. That's why I left Wisconsin." She twisted against his hold until he released both arms. "And that's why you aren't on my list." Covering her mouth with one hand, she hurried toward the steps.

Teddy watched her enter the house as new and unusual emotions flooded him. It was a moment before everything connected in his head. He wasn't on her list because of the way Abigail treated her. For the first time in his life, he didn't feel the tiniest desire to defend his sister. Instead, he wanted to protect Hannah. Protect her from all the people who had ever hurt her, and from any of those who might ever do so in the future.

He now fully understood why Brett's mother had sent her to Oak Grove when she had. Under the ruse of becoming Brett's wife. And he understood why Brett had been so protective over her since the day she'd arrived. Hannah had been hurt badly. Compared to flesh wounds, inner ones took longer to heal. Some never healed. His grandfather had explained that to him in a way he'd never forget.

Around the age of ten or so, after a fight with Abigail, who was five years younger than him, where he'd said some mean things to her, his grandfather had taken him into the print shop and pulled a sheet of paper off the same press Teddy still used to print the *Gazette*.

A person's heart is like this paper, Grandpa had said. *It's as fragile as it is strong. When someone's heart gets hurt, for whatever reason, it crimples a bit, and though we can smooth the crinkles out, the paper will never be the same. If it's run through the press, ink will gather in the fine creases, remnants of the crinkles, and the print will be smudged. A man should take care to never say or do something that will crimple someone's heart.*

He'd never forgotten that lesson. It had gotten him through the ordeal with Becky. Although his heart had been crimpled, he hadn't wanted hers to be, so he had generously wished her well in her marriage to Rex Arnold.

His mind had momentarily gone to Becky, but

his gaze was still on the house. Hannah's heart had been crimpled for as long as she could remember.

The sound of his name had him turning about.

"Did you like the performance, Teddy?" Rhett asked as the two boys slid to a stop beside him.

"Yes, I did," he answered, ruffling the boy's mop of brown hair, which earlier had been combed smooth, but was no longer. "It was the finest recital I've ever seen."

"That's what Brett said, too," Wyatt answered, beaming. "And now we get to eat some of Hannah's pie!"

Teddy had been looking forward to that pie as much as the boys—they'd talked about the dessert even while eating the turkey and fixings. He no longer felt like eating pie. Might never feel like eating again.

"Aren't you joining us for dessert?" Fiona asked as she and Brett arrived, holding hands.

"No," Teddy replied. "I have to go to the hotel, but thank you, Fiona. That was the best Thanksgiving dinner I've ever had."

Brett laid a hand on his shoulder as he said to Fiona, "I'll be in shortly."

Fiona eyed them both curiously, but hurried inside.

"What happened?" Brett asked. "Where's Hannah?"

"Inside," Teddy answered. "She told me about her and Eric's family. About the feud. How they hated each other."

Brett huffed out a sigh. "Her father and Eric's are cruel men. From what my mother said in her letters, it's gotten worse over the years, and it would be best if Hannah never saw either of them ever again."

"How can grown men…" Teddy shook his head, knowing Brett would have the same sentiments, and no answers. Some people were just mean. Too mean. Couldn't see past their own noses when it came to recognizing how their behaviors hurt others.

"You care about Hannah, don't you?" Brett asked.

Glancing toward the house, Teddy admitted, "More than I should."

Chapter Six

❧❧❧❧❧

The slamming of cupboard doors said Abigail was as angry this morning as she'd been when she went to bed last night. Teddy continued setting type. She had plenty to be mad about—in her mind. He'd forced her to leave the hotel and confronted her on how she'd spoken to Hannah. Her response had been to inform him they would be doing their own etchings again.

He'd disagreed, and would stand his ground on that, as well as on a few other things.

"Did you not make any coffee this morning?"

"If you want some, make some," he answered.

"You didn't even build a fire."

"If you want one, build one."

"I don't have time. I have articles to write today, and—"

"And several to rewrite," he interrupted, pointing to the two articles he'd already edited this morning.

She flew across the room and grabbed the sheets of paper off the desk. "There is nothing wrong with these."

He walked up behind her and pointed to one particular section he'd circled.

Oak Grove Community members will be excited to learn that every store in town will be hosting special sales for the upcoming Christmas Season. Except for Blackwell's Blacksmithing and Feed and Seed. Evidently, Mr. Blackwell doesn't believe in the Christmas Spirit.

"What's wrong with that? I'm being honest," she said, jutting out her chin. "That's the first thing a reporter must be. Honest. Brett hasn't purchased an advertisement about any Christmas specials, so he must not be having any."

"That's not being honest, that's being rude." He took the papers from her. "Articles like this are the reason we've moved so many times. I was serious when I said no more, Abigail. And I still am."

"That's not why we left Missouri," she snapped. "And that's what won't happen again." She spun about and marched over to her desk in the corner. "I won't let it." She opened a drawer and pulled out a newspaper he didn't recognize. "Hannah Olsen will give birth to a bastard. She. Was. Never. Married."

The chill that raced over him was colder than water pulled from the well in January. "What have you done?"

Hannah held her breath against an onslaught of sensations that made her shake. She couldn't help but glance across the street, toward the front office of the *Gazette*. Someone was on the other side of the glass and she quickly glanced away. Even on the other side of the street she could feel the glower that Abigail was sending her way.

"Rhett, slow down," Wyatt said. "Hannah can't walk that fast."

Pulling her attention back to the two boys walking with her, she said, "I will one day soon," she said. "I think I'll challenge you both to a footrace after this baby is born."

Rhett, who had listened to his older brother and slowed down, laughed. "Mothers don't have footraces."

"They don't?"

"No."

"We'll have to see about that." Winking at Wyatt, she added, "Right after I beat you in one."

While Rhett laughed again, Wyatt changed the subject. "Are you really going to draw a picture of all of us?" he asked.

"If it's all right with Miss Burnett," she answered. The idea had come to her last night. If Abigail wanted an etching of all the children, that's what she would receive. Despite how the other woman might feel toward her, Hannah was not going to promote hatred in any way. She'd left Wisconsin to get away from it. Forever.

She'd thought about that late into the night, and while unable to sleep had remembered something Brett's mother had said to her. *Whenever hatred is allowed to thrive, bad things follow. But where there is love, there's goodness and grace.*

At the time, she'd taken that as a simple statement of truth, but last night, she'd begun to look upon it as a piece of advice, as well as Fiona's idea of looking at things from a different perspective. It might prove hard, but her first thought had been that Abigail was Teddy's sister, and Teddy was very easy to like. He was also at the core of her thinking. She couldn't help but wonder how or why the woman he'd been engaged to had married someone else.

"Hannah came to school with us!"

Rhett's shout pulled her attention back to the task at hand.

"Hello, Mrs. Olsen," Miss Burnett said as they arrived at the school building. "I hope you enjoyed the recital yesterday."

"Oh, I did. Very much," Hannah answered. "So much I have a favor to ask of you."

"What is that?"

"I'm hoping to spend some time in the classroom today. I didn't think to bring a piece of paper with me yesterday, and I'd like to draw a picture of the children during their performance."

"Whatever for?"

"The newspaper," Hannah answered. "I promise it won't take long. But I will need everyone to stand at the front of the room like they were yesterday. Just long enough for me to get an outline, then I'll sit in the back, drawing some of their features." For the etching, she only needed a prominent feature for each child, so they'd be somewhat recognizable, mainly to their families.

"The newspaper? The children would love that," Miss Burnett said. "Of course, come in."

"Is this everything?" Teddy asked, holding the newspapers in one hand and Abigail's arm in the other. The newspapers had come from Wisconsin and Minnesota. He hadn't read them, but believed Abigail's claim that they held articles of Eric's accident.

"Yes," she growled.

She was furious. So was he, and he wouldn't allow Hannah to be hurt, not in the harmful, hateful way Abigail had been plotting. He ripped the newspapers in half, then again.

"She's going to destroy you, just like Becky did." Abigail stomped a foot. "I don't care what Brett says, that woman came here to find a husband. To find a father for her baby."

"What's wrong with that?" he asked.

"She'll never love you, no more than Becky did."

"I'm not marrying Hannah." As he said the words, his heart lurched and he glanced toward the window Hannah had walked past a short time ago.

"Does she know that?"

"Yes," he said. "She wouldn't marry me if I asked, and do you want to know why? Because of you."

"Me!"

Releasing her arm, he tossed the torn papers into the box beneath the desk. "When I do decide to get married, you will have no say in it because I don't care what you think. But, in the meantime, if you do anything to Hannah, you will answer to me, and I won't be as kind as I have been in the past."

"She's lying. I haven't done—"

"You wield that pencil behind your ear like a sword, and though it makes me sick to admit it, I've let the fact our parents died when you were young be your shield." Grabbing his jacket, he shook his head. "I'm done doing that."

"You'll be sorry," she shouted.

Opening the door, he said, "No more than I already am."

The street was empty, and assuming Hannah had walked Rhett and Wyatt to school, he started in that direction. He had no idea what he might say to her, but if he could prevent her from having her heart crimpled again, he had to do it.

Upon approaching the school, his ears picked up the teacher telling the students to listen to Hannah. It was warm, even for November, and the door was open, so he quietly snuck just over the threshold, to where he could peek around the corner of the storage closet. All the children stood at the front of the room, along with their teacher, while Hannah sat in a chair near the front row of desks.

"Thank you, Miss Burnett," Hannah said. "Children, I asked you all to stand this way for so long because, as Miss Burnett said, I'm drawing a picture. What she didn't tell you is that the picture is for Miss White."

"What for?" one of the children asked.

"Because she's writing an article for the newspaper about what a wonderful performance you gave yesterday and she wants a picture to print along with the article."

"So we'll be in the newspaper?" someone asked.

"Yes," Hannah said, "but, I think we should all keep that a secret. Think how surprised your parents will be when they see the paper next week with you in it, and read about what a wonderful job you all did in reciting Lincoln's Proclamation."

Teddy grinned at the squeals of delight and mumbles of agreement.

"Can you do that?" Hannah asked. "Keep it a secret?"

Shouts of yes echoed off the walls.

"Wonderful," Hannah said. "I'm going to be here for a while longer drawing, and if I ask you to smile at me, it's because I'm drawing your face and want to get it right."

Teddy eased out of the door. There was no one else like her on this earth. No one. As he started down the steps, he paused at a sinking sensation. Now he was going to have to make sure Abigail published the etching.

His life may have just gone from bad to worse.

Chapter Seven

Hannah's hands hurt, and her eyes ached, but as she gently brushed the etching clean, satisfaction spread throughout her. Smiling, she carefully touched several of the tiny faces. This may very well be her best work. Maybe it was just her, but she could recognize each child.

"Can I see it now?" Fiona asked as she poured hot water into the teapot on the counter.

Sitting at the table, Hannah covered the block of wood with a piece of paper. "I wish you could, but that wouldn't be fair to Rhett and Wyatt."

"I know what it is," Fiona said.

"I'm sure you do," Hannah answered. "But you'll act as surprised as every other parent in town when the paper arrives."

"I'll have Brett take it to the *Gazette* in the morning," Fiona said.

"No, I don't want him to see it, either. I'll walk it over there myself. I just hope they haven't printed the paper yet."

"Teddy doesn't print it until Saturday."

"But he lays it all out on Friday." Which is why she'd worked on the etching nonstop all day.

"I'm sure he won't mind redoing a page or two in order to include that," Fiona said. "Now, it's late, everyone else has been asleep for hours. I have tea and biscuits ready to take upstairs. You barely stopped working long enough to eat supper."

"Thank you, and I'm sorry for not being any help to you today."

"Nonsense. I enjoyed seeing you so engrossed in something. You really enjoyed doing that."

"I did. I've never etched people before."

"I can't wait to see it." With a nod toward the paper-covered etching, Fiona said, "Gather your things. I'll follow you up the stairs."

The following morning, as soon as the breakfast dishes were washed and put away, Hannah set half of a pumpkin pie in the bottom of a basket, covered it with a plate, and then put in the etching and corresponding drawing, as well as a smaller etching and drawing. On top, she stacked the drawings the children had made. After covering the basket with a cloth, she retrieved her coat and left the house.

Everyone from Brett down to Rhett had offered to accompany her to the *Gazette* office, but she'd declined, stating she'd be back shortly. Although her baby was calm and quiet as she walked toward town, nerves had her stomach churning. Offering this olive branch, which is how she chose to think of her actions, was scary, but she wanted better things for her child than what she'd known, and she had to do something to make that happen. It wasn't easy, but few things worth doing were easy.

The space between the house and the *Gazette* office had to have shrunk because before she was fully prepared, she'd arrived.

Abigail was on the other side of the glass window, staring at her, and so was Teddy. Hannah willed her courage to remain, and even managed to produce a smile as Teddy pulled open the door.

"H— Mrs. Olsen, what are you doing here? Is everything all right at Brett's place?"

The genuine concern in his eyes made her heart swell. "Everything is fine," she said. "Brett and Fiona say hello." Holding up the basket, she said, "I have something for Ab— Miss White."

"What?" Abigail asked.

Ignoring Abigail's tone and glare, Hannah held her smile in place. "May I?" she asked, gesturing toward the counter.

"Of course," Teddy said. "Allow me." He took the basket and set it on the counter.

While removing the cloth, Hannah said, "I made an etching of the children's recital for you to include with your article."

"Teddy has already completed the typeset for this week's edition," Abigail said, stepping up behind the counter. "We won't be able to use it."

Refusing to allow her disappointment to show, and seeing how Teddy was preparing to protest, Hannah said, "I understand. I told the children I may not have it completed in time." Taking the children's drawings out of the basket, she handed them to Abigail. "They asked me to give you these either way."

She'd purposefully put Wyatt's letter on the top of

the pile. Frowning, Abigail started flipping through the pieces of paper.

"Some of the children are too young to write, so they drew pictures," Hannah explained.

Teddy leaned across the counter and picked up Wyatt's letter. "'Dear Miss White. I haven't read the article yet, but thank you for writing about our recital. It was fun and my ma and pa are going to like seeing my picture in the paper. Sincerely, your friend, Wyatt Blackwell.'"

Hannah smiled at how well Teddy had deciphered some of the misspelled words.

He picked up another one that said Abigail was a very good reporter, and another one that said having their picture in the paper was very exciting. That usually only outlaws got their pictures in newspapers.

Laughing at that one, Teddy picked up the one that Rhett had drawn. It was of several small stick people and one large one with "thank you" written at the bottom. "These are adorable." Transferring his smiling eyes toward his sister, he said, "Aren't they, Abigail?"

Abigail didn't respond, but did seem to be concentrating on a longer letter written by one of the older children. Hannah knew the letter. It was from Patty Owens and claimed she'd like to become a reporter someday.

"May I see the etching?" Teddy asked.

"Of course," Hannah replied, taking it and the corresponding drawing out of the basket. "I listed all of the children on the drawing," she said. "In case you were able to print it and wanted to include their names."

"Wow," he said, examining the block of wood. "I recognize each one of the children. We have to print it." Handing it to his sister, he said, "Don't we?"

Abigail didn't reply, but took the etching.

"I'm afraid it's larger than any others I've done, but I had to make it that big to fit everyone in."

"It's perfect," Teddy said. "Perfect."

Hannah's stomach was still churning and she couldn't quite seem to catch her breath—that was due to standing so close to Teddy. She had thought long and hard about the list he'd given back to her, and how she couldn't marry any of those men. She'd told herself she'd created the etchings because of Abigail, but in truth, she'd made them because of Teddy. He was so kind and generous and deserved that in return.

Pulling her trailing thoughts back to the task at hand, she reached into the basket. "I made another etching, Abigail." The other woman's name hadn't rolled off her tongue easily and she hoped no one had noticed that. Handing Abigail the small etching, Hannah said, "I made this one of you, in case you'd like to use it."

Abigail took the block of wood, and Hannah's stomach completely flip-flopped. Drawing Abigail from memory had been easy. The hard part had been softening her features to make her look as attractive as possible. While drawing, she'd focused on the feature Teddy and Abigail shared—their eyes. So rather than squinting, she'd drawn Abigail's eyes as round and prominent as Teddy's were. She'd also changed Abigail's hair a smidgen. Rather than having it pulled back so tightly, she'd loosened it and drawn a few stray curls near her temples, but had made sure the pencil behind one ear was still visible.

Nervous beyond compare, Hannah said, "My thought had been that you might like to use it if you wanted to print one of the thank-you notes from the children. If there was room in the newspaper, of course."

Abigail glanced up from the etching, and for the first time ever, there wasn't loathing in her eyes.

Swallowing a hiccup, Hannah handed Abigail the final piece of paper out of the basket. "Here's the corresponding drawing." It was much larger than the etching.

Abigail placed a hand over her mouth as she took the paper with her other hand and stared at it.

Not sure what to do next, Hannah lifted the pie out of the basket. "I brought this, too," she said to Teddy. "You left before having any dessert on Thanksgiving."

Teddy had never seen such a genuine act of kindness in his life, and may never witness one that would compare to this if he lived to be a hundred and one. He wanted to force Abigail to respond, to say something positive, but had accepted Abigail was her own person and needed to accept her own responsibilities.

So did he. "Thank you," he said. "I was sorry to have missed tasting your pumpkin pie. I believe I'll have a piece even before I start pulling type."

"No."

Teddy balled his hands into fists at Abigail's voice, and at Hannah's dejected look. To her credit, she never faltered in putting the cloth back into the basket.

"I'll pull type, Teddy," Abigail said. "While you escort Hannah home before Brett and Fiona start to worry about her."

"That's not necessary," Hannah said.

As Abigail stacked the letters from the children into a pile, she said, "It's the least we can do."

Teddy was surprised, but agreed. "It is the least we can do."

"These," Abigail said, while picking up both etchings, "are amazing, and we will print them in this edition. Thank you for making them. And thank you for bringing them over this morning."

Relief washed over Teddy, especially as Hannah's face took on a glow as she placed a hand on her stomach.

"You're very welcome," Hannah said. "The children were so excited about the prospect."

"We'll print extra copies," Teddy said, "so they each get their very own copy."

"They'll like that," Hannah answered.

"Teddy," Abigail said, "shouldn't you get your coat so you can walk Hannah home?"

"Really, that's not—"

"Yes, it is," Teddy said, almost afraid to leave the two women alone. "Wait here. I'll be right back."

He hurried around the counter and then through a doorway into the back of the building to grab his coat. Rushing back toward the office, he heard Abigail speak again.

"This was very thoughtful of you," she said. "Very thoughtful."

He entered the room as Hannah lifted the basket off the counter.

"I—I sincerely appreciate you providing me with the opportunity to make etchings for the newspaper," she said. "It's helped me and my situation considerably. More than you know."

"It has helped us considerably," Teddy said. He wasn't totally sure if Abigail was being sincere, or just acting. It was hard to tell at times, but either way, he was glad she'd behaved. Shrugging into his coat, he rounded the counter and told her, "I won't be gone long."

"Take your time," Abigail said. "I'll just be pulling type."

"I can do that when I get back."

"No," she replied, looking at the picture of herself. "I can do it. I want to make some changes to the story, too."

The likeness was very good. It reminded him of her when she was younger.

"I'm sorry to have caused more work for both of you," Hannah said as he took the basket from her.

"It's no problem," he said. "We're used to last-minute changes. It's part of the publishing businesses. Isn't it, Abigail?"

"Yes." Abigail held up one of the children's drawings. "And the *Gazette* is the best newspaper in all of Kansas."

That was exactly what the piece of paper she held said, with a couple of misspelled words and backward letters. Teddy had to take a second look at his sister. He hadn't seen her smile so big in a long time. The giggle beside him had him shifting his gaze.

The shine in Hannah's eyes was the brightest he'd ever seen, and was enough to make his heart hammer harder than his printing press when cranking out newspapers.

"That was one of my favorites," she said.

"I look forward to reading them all," he said, opening the door and gesturing for her to cross the threshold first.

"You'll enjoy them," she said.

"I'm sure I will. Thank you for delivering them. And thank you for the etchings. They are remarkable, Hannah."

"Thank you, Teddy."

It sounded as if she'd said his name as a test, or an afterthought, which was how he'd said her name. A sort of test to see if she'd protest.

"I enjoyed making them, and the children were

thrilled with the idea of being in the newspaper. The thank-you notes were Miss Burnett's idea."

The wind tugged at her bonnet as they walked and he took her elbow to direct her closer to the buildings for a bit of protection. "I'm sorry for the way I left the other day."

"That's why I brought you some pie. I knew you'd been looking forward to it."

"Thank you for that as well, and I will eat it as soon as I get home, but I meant for how I left you. You were upset. I should have—"

"No, you shouldn't have, Teddy. I needed to be alone."

"Well, I shouldn't have said what I did about Jules Carmichael and Jess Radar. They are good men and once married, I'm sure they would secure different living quarters."

"Probably, and I'm sure they are good men. Don Carlson, too." She glanced up at him.

"Yes," he admitted, with a hint of chagrin. "Don, too. The others on your list are as well, and—"

"I burned it."

Taken aback by her interruption, he asked, "Burned what?"

"The list. Right after you gave it back to me." She wasn't looking at him, but straight ahead, toward the corner they would soon turn down and head east toward Brett's house.

"Hannah, I—"

"It wasn't because of anything you said or did.

It was me." She glanced his way. "Can I ask you a question?"

"Sure."

"Were you in love with the woman who didn't marry you?"

He paused before answering. "I thought I was at the time." He wasn't so sure now. Becky had been young and alone, not so different from Hannah, except that Hannah had Brett and Fiona. Becky hadn't had anyone and that had worried him.

"You thought?"

Becky had been in his thoughts lately, as well as what his life might have been like if she had married him, and he questioned the absence of any ache, of any sense of loss. "I was worried about her and wanted to help her."

"Why? Was something wrong?"

He couldn't stop his eyes from darting to her waist. Lifting his gaze, he shook his head. "Not necessarily wrong." Becky had left him for a man she loved. Hannah still loved Eric, and he had to wonder if that would be worse. She might always love Eric, and where would that leave him? Needing to change the subject, and curious, he asked, "How are you feeling?"

"Fine." Her smile increased. "I loved etching all of the children. I'd never drawn people before, and wasn't sure if I could."

"Well, those etchings are amazing. Your grandfather must have been an excellent teacher."

"Oh, he was. He and Gram are the best."

"You miss them."

She nodded and put one hand on her stomach. "I do. Very much." Her sigh caught on the breeze as they turned the corner to walk toward the blacksmith shop. "I was never scared or worried while at their house."

"But you were at your own home?"

She nodded.

"I've already told you my father wanted a boy instead of me. It was worse that Eric's family continued to have children. Boys to carry on the family name, and our side of the family didn't."

Anger rolled inside Teddy. He couldn't imagine a father—any man—blaming a child for something that was so out of their control. It was ludicrous. "Being born a girl was not your fault, Hannah. You had nothing to do with it."

She shook her head solemnly. "It went beyond that. I couldn't do anything right in his eyes. Including my etchings."

"Well, I believe your etchings are remarkable. And I'm not the only one. Every time someone inquires about an advertisement, they ask if you'd be able to create a picture to accompany it."

"They do?"

The shine in her eyes made his heart skip a beat. "Yes, they do. You've been very good for our business." He added a wink, hoping that she understood it was the truth, but he was also teasing her a bit.

She giggled. "I'm glad. It feels good to know I'm helping someone and I do enjoy it very much."

"Good, because we'd lose customers if you stopped."

She playfully slapped his arm. "You would not. You're just teasing."

He patted the hand she still had on his arm as his mind came full circle back to the list she'd created. If she did marry one of those men, she might become too busy to etch any more pictures. "I'm not teasing," he admitted. "I'm proud of you, Hannah. Proud of your etchings."

Her expression grew serious, yet content. "Thank you, Teddy. Thank you very much."

Rhett and Wyatt shot from around the blacksmith shop and ran toward them. "Are you going to print the picture, Teddy? Are you?" Rhett asked.

Hannah laughed and leaned a bit closer to say, "I warned them you might not be able to, but if you did, they were to keep it a secret."

He knelt down as the boys arrived and put on a serious expression as he whispered, "I can't tell you if you're going to run around shouting about it."

"We won't," Wyatt assured, casting a glare toward his younger brother.

"I was only shouting 'cause it was you," Rhett said. "I won't tell anyone else. I promise."

"Cross-your-heart promise?" Teddy asked.

Both boys nodded and used a fingertip to draw an X over their chests.

"Then, yes, I'm going to print it, and I'll make sure you each get your very own copy."

The giggle from Hannah, and the way she

squeezed his arm as he stood up, filled him with more happiness than he might ever have known before.

Fiona and Brett walked around the building just then.

An unusual wave of disappointment washed over him as Hannah let go of his arm.

"Thank you for walking me home," she said. "I hope you enjoy the pie."

"I will," Teddy answered, having totally forgotten about the pie. He graced Fiona with a smile before nodding at Brett.

When the women were several steps away Brett said, "I don't know what she was etching, but she worked all day on it yesterday."

Still watching her walk away, and knowing the boys were within hearing distance, Teddy replied, "It's a secret. That's all I can tell you."

The boys giggled before they ran off, and a thought shot across Teddy's mind. He wondered what Brett would say if he said he wanted to marry Hannah. It wasn't the first time he'd had that thought, but he was still unsure if that was what his heart truly wanted, or if he was just worried about her like he had been about Becky.

"I wasn't happy about letting Hannah do all this work for your paper in the beginning, but Fiona insisted it would be good for her," Brett said. "I guess she was right."

"She enjoys it," Teddy replied. "And she is also very good at it."

"Yes, she is," Brett replied. "She'll make some man a wonderful wife."

Teddy buckled a bit inside. He'd thought he'd kept his thoughts buried too deep for anyone to see. Before he could say anything, Brett slapped his shoulder.

"I got a wagon wheel calling my name," Brett said. "See you later."

Teddy nodded, yet his eyes were once again on Hannah as she and Fiona disappeared into the house across the field. "See you later," he said, after swallowing the lump that had formed in his throat at the idea of Hannah making someone a wonderful wife. And that someone not being him.

Chapter Eight

Hannah wasn't exactly sure what had happened. She couldn't give all the credit to how much Abigail had liked the etchings, or to the fact that Teddy was proud of her. The only person who'd ever said that they were proud of her was Pappy. A true sense of peace filled her as she and Fiona hung their bonnets and coats on the hooks in the kitchen.

"I'm assuming that went well," Fiona said.

"Very well." Smiling, Hannah said, "Looking at things in a different perspective isn't as hard as I'd imagined. Thank you."

Fiona frowned. "Why are you thanking me? What do you mean?"

Her contentment was so profound, Hannah sighed at how wonderful she felt. "The day before Thanksgiving you said were looking at life with a new perspective." She grinned. "I decided I should do that, too."

"So that's why you made that etching for the newspaper."

"Yes," Hannah said. "And it was the right decision." For the first time in months, her stomach growled. "Are there any biscuits left over? I'm hungry." The craving for food increased. "And honey. I'd love some honey."

"You haven't been hungry since I met you," Fiona said. "We've had to force you to eat."

"I know." Hannah rubbed her stomach. "Maybe I'm ready to make up for all those missed meals." She was ready for other things, too. Rather than mulling over lists, she was going to focus on what she wanted, which was for Abigail to like her, because once that happened, maybe someday she'd feel comfortable enough to ask Teddy how he'd feel about becoming a father. She wouldn't get her hopes up that it would happen by Christmas, nor would she dwell on it. Although a father for her baby would be the most wonderful Christmas miracle ever.

Actually, Teddy would be the most wonderful Christmas miracle. Not just because she wanted her baby to have a father, but because she wanted Teddy to be her husband. It seemed strange to admit that, but it was true. He was so caring and kind. Very unlike the men she'd known all her life. She couldn't imagine him treating anyone in rude or hurtful ways. He was too full of goodness and grace, and that was what she wanted. A life like Gram and Pappy had. A life like Fiona and Brett had.

"Would you like tea with your biscuits and honey?" Fiona asked.

"Actually, I think I'll have a glass of milk," Hannah said. "A big one."

Her appetite remained with her all day, as did the contentment. It seemed to have taken root inside her and that night she slept better than she had in a very long time. She was dressed and ready for church along with everyone else, but remained behind. Angus O'Leary, who was a dear old soul, had made it a habit to walk her to church on Sundays from the time she'd arrived in Oak Grove.

When the knock sounded on the back door, she slipped on her coat while walking across the room. Her heart skipped a beat at the same time the baby moved, which was also the same moment she opened the door and saw Teddy standing there.

Although happy to see him, she was also concerned. "Where's Angus?"

"Nothing to worry about," Teddy said. "Angus asked me to come escort you to church because his knee is acting up a bit."

She let out a sigh of relief. "I hope it's not too bad."

"He's escorting Abigail, so you'll still see him." He gestured toward the steps. "Are you ready?"

"Yes, yes I am, and thank you for escorting me, but I could have walked with Brett and Fiona and the boys."

"You could have," he said, pulling the door closed behind them. "But I'm extremely glad you didn't."

She was, too, but stopped herself from saying that. "You seem very happy today."

"I am," he said. "It's a beautiful day, and I'm escorting a beautiful woman to church, and that gives me much to be happy about." Leaning closer he said, "And all three hundred copies of the *Gazette* are printed and folded."

"Three hundred copies?"

"Yes. Abigail thought people might like to buy extras to mail to family members."

"Oh, they might, for sure."

"Want to know a secret?" he asked.

The teasing glimmer in his eyes had her biting her lip to keep her smile from growing too large. "What?"

"The children will receive their copies at church this morning."

She clapped her hands at the excitement that instilled. "Oh, they will love that! Rhett and Wyatt have been counting the hours until Monday."

"I can't take the credit," he said. "Abigail decided we should distribute them a day early and was up half the night folding the papers. I've never seen her so excited about something."

"I'm so happy she liked the etching and that you were able to use it. I can't wait to see the paper myself."

"I thought so." With an extra-large grin, he pulled a copy of the *Gazette* out of the inside of his coat.

"Oh, thank you!" They'd crossed the open field and were near the blacksmith shop. As she took the paper, she increased her speed and hurried around the side wall so the wind wouldn't rip the paper as she folded it open. The picture, with all the children's names printed below it, took up most of the top half of the first page. She'd seen several of her etchings in the paper, but had never experienced the amount of delight that filled her right now.

"As I said before, it's amazing," Teddy said quietly.

Tears of happiness stung her eyes as she looked up at him.

"And I'm so proud of you," he whispered.

Then he did something that made her heart and the baby do a somersault. He leaned down and placed a soft, warm kiss on her cheek.

Teddy held his breath. The kiss had been an impulse, one he hadn't even had time to consider. Until now. He was proud of her, and he was fond of her. Growing fonder every day.

The air was still locked in his lungs when Hannah opened her eyes. The smile that settled on her lips was gentle and so serene the air seeped out of his lungs. Her eyes were so blue, her features so perfect, he could spend hours just looking at her.

"We better go," she said. "We don't want to be late."

Thankful she didn't question his impulsive kiss, he gestured toward the paper. "Would you like me to carry that for you? I have a large pocket inside my coat."

"Please."

After tucking the paper in his pocket, he held out his arm. She folded her hand around the crook of his elbow as they started to walk around the blacksmith shop. They conversed about the weather and a few other things, including how he'd eaten the pie she'd delivered. He had thought of her with every bite he'd taken of that pie, and about being married and having a family. The idea was growing on him.

This time it definitely wasn't because he felt sorry for someone. This went much deeper and was much stronger. Far deeper than pride. He was proud of her, but it was more than that. He truly admired her. Unlike Becky, who had cried on his shoulder because of her situation, Hannah not only thought of others, she forged ahead.

Arriving at the church, he led her up the aisle to where Brett, Fiona and the boys sat on one side. Abigail usually sat in the front, but today she was sitting with Angus across the aisle from Brett's family.

Abigail patted the bench space beside her. "We saved places for you."

Teddy remained silent, letting Hannah choose where she wanted to sit.

Her smile never faltered as she stepped between the pews. "Thank you," she said to Abigail before glancing around her to ask Angus, "How is your knee?"

"Fine. 'Tis fine. It was just being testy this morning, lass. I hope you don't mind that I asked the lad Teddy to escort you on this fine morning."

"Not at all," she said, "but I do expect you to have Dr. Graham examine your leg if it's not completely better by tomorrow."

Teddy took the seat beside her and nodded toward Angus as Abigail leaned closer to Hannah.

"Did you see it?" Abigail asked.

"Yes," Hannah replied in a whisper. "Thank you. The children will be so happy."

"Thank you," Abigail replied. "I believe it's the best edition we've ever printed."

A mixture of satisfaction and pride filled Teddy. It might be too much to ask for these two women to become friends—Abigail didn't acquire those very easily—but that was another thing about Hannah. She had the ability to look beyond the surface and touch the core of people. It would be good for his future wife and his sister to be close.

His future wife. What was he thinking? He hadn't decided that, had he? Hannah may not want that. She'd said she'd burned her list. Did that mean she didn't want to get married at all now? What would that mean for her baby? Surely she didn't plan on raising him or her all by herself? She made some money etching, but not enough to live on, and she couldn't plan on living with Brett and Fiona her entire life.

Teddy shifted slightly in his seat, just to take a quick sideways glance at Hannah. He hadn't thought much about the mail-order bride idea when Josiah had first mentioned it. Wouldn't have donated to the Betterment Committee if Abigail hadn't insisted upon it. She'd said it was expected of him. As time went on and he found himself amongst men who'd truly wanted a wife—especially Brett—the idea of getting married still hadn't appealed to him, although he'd pretended it did. He wasn't lonely like the other men, not with Abigail living with him. And he had her to consider. She'd been so young when their parents had died, he knew he would continue to provide for her as long as necessary. Actually, having another woman around, one who could teach her the things he'd never been able to, might be a good idea. Hannah could teach her a lot. Especially when it came to being nice to others.

He'd never considered that before. Truth be known, his thoughts were more selfish. The desires Hannah evoked in him were like no others, and not just physically.

Daydreams had formed lately and had continued to grow every day involving her. He dreamed about her at night, too, dreams that left him aching in the morning. He'd tried not to admit that he was thinking of her along those lines, but he was, and those desires grew each and every time he saw her.

A gentle tap on his arm had him glancing toward her. Smiling, she gestured for him to stand along with her, and join in the singing of the hymn.

He did so, and then settled in to listen to Reverend Flaherty, hoping a solid lesson on righteousness would do him good. The reverend's sermon was about love and kindness and forgiveness, all of which had him reaching over and taking hold of Hannah's hand.

Hannah couldn't remember if she'd ever enjoyed a sermon so much. The reverend's message was full of hope as they embarked upon the Christmas season. In some ways, the holiday season had always seemed miraculous because when her family had descended upon her grandparents' home for the holidays there had been nothing but kindness and love shared. Pappy had insisted it be that way. That the holidays were a time to rejoice in all the blessings that had been bestowed upon her family, and even her father had obeyed that rule. Thanksgiving and Christmas were the only two days she'd felt as if he'd loved her.

She may not be with them this year, but she could still honor her grandparents' traditions. They would like that. Closing her eyes, she said a silent prayer of thanks, and rejoiced in how Teddy squeezed her hand. She'd been cherishing the warmth of his hand since he'd taken hold of hers earlier.

When people started gathering their coats and jackets, Reverend Flaherty said, "I'm going to ask you all to remain seated for a few minutes longer."

As a curious stillness filled the church, Abigail whispered, "Will you help me distribute the news-papers?"

"I'd love to," Hannah answered, truly honored.

Teddy stood and stepped aside, making room for her and Abigail to exit the row of pews. Hannah waited and then followed Abigail toward the front of the church where a table had been set up.

"At this time we'd like for the children to come forward," Reverend Flaherty said. "Miss White has something to give them."

The hushed squeals of delight made Hannah's heart sing. As her gaze met Teddy's smiling eyes, she whispered, "Teddy should be helping you, not me."

"No, he and I agreed it should be you," Abigail

said. "There are enough papers for each child to get one. Even those with siblings."

The children arrived at the table with excitement in their eyes and as the first few returned to their families, the jubilance that filled the church was so great, Hannah knew the heavens were smiling down upon them.

A short time later, Hannah had to hold her smile back a bit more.

Mayor Melbourne had made his way to the table and turned about to offer his thoughts to everyone on the newspaper, but Abigail quickly grabbed his arm. "Not today, Josiah," she said. "Nothing more needs to be said."

The mayor was shoved aside as the entire congregation made their way to the front of the church. Besides thanking Abigail and Teddy, and in many cases, her too, several mentioned they'd need an extra copy to mail to family members.

"The *Gazette* office will be open first thing in the morning," Teddy said. "With all the copies you'll need."

He'd placed an arm around her shoulders, and the pride that filled Hannah was like nothing she'd ever known. She shouldn't put too much into the action, for he had placed the other one around Abigail, but that didn't diminish how wonderful, truly wonderful, she felt.

As the crowd dispersed, Fiona insisted Teddy and Abigail come to the house for Sunday dinner, as well as Angus, who was singing the praises of the picture to all who would listen. Hannah noticed the old man's knee didn't seem to bother him at all, and the grin Teddy bestowed upon her said he'd read her mind and thought the same thing.

The exchange increased the joy dancing about inside her and the merriment that continued at the house reminded her so much of holiday gatherings at her grandparents' house she grew teary-eyed.

"Hannah, are you all right?" Abigail asked.

They were drying dishes as Fiona washed. "I'm fine," Hannah assured her. "Just laughing at that." She referred to the shouts coming from the front parlor, where the men and boys were holding a boisterous checker-playing championship.

Abigail, who had changed her hairstyle for the day, making it look similar to how Hannah had drawn it, giggled. "I do believe the Rhett and Wyatt are winning."

It wasn't just her hairstyle that made Abigail look much prettier today. The shine in her eyes as she laughed washed away the sharpness of her features profoundly.

"I'm sure it's because they have Angus on their team," Fiona said.

They all three laughed because Angus was taking a comfortable after-dinner nap in the chair next to the fireplace.

Chapter Nine

That day set a pattern for the days and weeks that followed. It became customary for Teddy and Abigail to join them for Sunday dinner, which was always enjoyable. However, it was the weekdays that Hannah enjoyed the most. Teddy made it a habit to stop by on a daily basis, and often joined them for the evening meal.

Even though she knew she'd see him the following day, saying goodbye to him grew harder each evening. Watching him walk away reminded her of leaving her grandparents each spring, when the logging camps broke up and she had to move back to her parents' house. She'd known she'd see them again, but being separated from them had made her heart ache in the worst way.

Each evening, she sent home a platter of treats for him and Abigail, and tonight was no different.

"We'll take those, if you don't mind wrapping up a second plate," Fiona said, pointing toward the plate Hannah had just tied a dish towel around.

Having not paid attention to the activity behind her, Hannah frowned at seeing Fiona, Brett and the boys all wearing their coats.

"We are going over to visit Maggie and Jackson

this evening," Fiona said. "I'm sure they'll enjoy the cookies."

There were more than enough for her to wrap up a second plate for Teddy. Since her appetite had returned, Hannah had been baking Christmas treats continuously. "Of course," she answered, handing Fiona the plate. "I wasn't aware—"

"Teddy will keep you company so you aren't home alone," Fiona said.

Hannah's heart skipped a beat, both at the prospect of Teddy remaining longer than usual and at the knowing glint in Fiona's eyes.

"I can walk you there if you prefer to go to the Millers'," Teddy said from where he stood beneath the archway leading to the front parlor.

"No." Heat stung her cheeks at how quickly she'd replied. "I—I'd rather stay home, if you don't mind."

Brett mumbled something, but Fiona shoved him out the door before Hannah heard what he'd said, or maybe she hadn't heard because her heart was thudding so hard her pulse echoed in her ears.

As Teddy took a step into the kitchen, her heart leaped. So did the baby.

"Did the baby just kick you?"

He seemed so intuitive about that. "Yes." Rubbing her stomach as the movement continued, she said, "Or maybe he or she is jumping rope."

Smiling, he asked, "May I?"

Nodding, she took the hand he held out and placed it on her stomach. He couldn't possibly know how much she appreciated and enjoyed his interest in her baby.

They both laughed as the baby moved nonstop for several moments. "See?" she said. "Jumping rope."

"Come," he said, placing his other hand on her back. "I think it's time you sat down. Give yourself and the baby a moment to relax."

He assisted her onto the sofa that was near the blazing fireplace in the parlor. Then he collected the footstool and, upon placing it in front of her, lifted her feet onto it one by one.

"How's that?" he asked.

"Very nice, thank you."

He then sat down beside her. "This is lovely, isn't it?"

Filled with contentment, she said, "Yes. This is what evenings were like with my grandparents. Gran would sit in the rocking chair knitting and Pappy would sit in his chair whittling. They have a collection of birds he's carved out of wood on their mantel."

"And what would you do?"

Memories made her smile. "Draw or etch. It was evenings like this when Pappy taught me. Probably just to give me something to do while they relaxed."

"Did you draw and etch while at your parents' house, too?"

"No, my father considered that idleness, something he didn't approve of." She'd thought about what Teddy had said, that being born a girl was not her fault. It wasn't. She didn't care if her baby was a boy or a girl, she'd love them the same either way. That's how it should be. That's how it would be in her life. It was so satisfying to have come to understand certain things lately. Still smiling, she asked, "What about you? What did your family do in the evenings?"

His eyes sparkled. "We sat in the parlor together every evening. Some nights we'd play checkers or guessing games, but usually my father read to us."

"What would he read?"

"Funny, wild stories about all sorts of things. He was a newspaperman because it was the family business, but he really wanted to write stories. And he did. He printed a few and sold them at the newspaper office. I wish I'd kept a couple of them, but didn't think of them when I was packing for Abigail and me to leave."

"Leave?"

He nodded. "Cholera wiped out complete blocks of the city we lived in back in Pennsylvania. I was the only one in our family who didn't get it. Abigail was still sick when we left town, but my mother insisted I take her and leave. My father had already died and Mother passed away before I found someone to help me load up the printing press."

"Oh, Teddy, I'm so sorry." She rested a hand on his knee. "How old were you?"

"Sixteen. That was ten years ago."

"That must have been scary," she said sincerely.

"I tried to make it not be for Abigail."

She could believe that. "Your father sounds like he was very nice."

"He was." Looking thoughtful for a moment, he added, "He was very loveable."

"Mine wasn't." She quickly covered her mouth, and said through her fingers, "I shouldn't have said that."

"Why not? There's nothing wrong with telling the truth."

"I know there's not, but I shouldn't have said it because I'll never see him again, and I only want to remember the good things."

"You don't know for sure that you won't see him again."

She had to pinch her lips together at the pain that was wriggling its way inside her heart. "I know for sure. He said I'd never be welcome in his home again, and he meant it."

Sorrow wasn't only in his eyes—it was on his face. "He shouldn't have said that. I'm sure he didn't mean it."

"Yes, he did." Although she'd known it for a long time, it still hurt to admit. "His hatred for the Olsons is far stronger than his love for his own family."

The arm he put around her was more comforting than a warm cloak and the way he pulled her head onto his shoulder was as consoling as it was reassuring.

"I'm sorry, Hannah. I'm sorry for the hurt you've experienced."

"You have nothing to be sorry about," she said,

closing her eyes. "It's made me see exactly what I don't want in my life. What I don't want in my baby's life."

"You're an awfully strong person," he whispered. "And a wise one. You'll be a wonderful mother."

The baby moved again, and Hannah had to close her eyes at the formation of tears. She would be a wonderful mother because she'd love her baby with all her heart. Yet, at the same time, she wanted that for herself. Someone to love her with all their heart.

Teddy's hand joined hers on her stomach, and they both sat quietly as the baby rolled. She lifted her head enough to smile at him. He was the wonderful one. Had been his entire life.

His other hand cupped her cheek and her breath caught as he slowly leaned forward until his lips gently met hers. The kiss was nothing like the few hidden ones she'd shared with Eric. This was unhurried and purposeful. Teddy's lips caressed hers with such divine tenderness she leaned forward, wanting more of the same.

He continued to kiss her, until her entire being was warm and content, as if everything was completely right in the entire world. Then he leaned back and guided her head to once again rest on his shoulder.

Neither of them said a word. None were needed as they sat there, simply enjoying just being together. Fiona was right. There were different kinds of love. She had loved Eric, but it had been different. Very different from what she felt for Teddy. Both she and Eric had been tired of the discord surrounding their families. His father hadn't been any nicer to him than hers had been to her. With that in common, they'd bonded, and planned on running away together. His father had told her he'd found Eric's packed bag. He'd told her father, too. The same day he'd come to the house and blamed her for Eric's death.

"Eric never knew about the baby," she whispered. "He died before I could tell him."

Teddy's arm tightened slightly and it felt as if he softly kissed the top of her head.

"I'm sure he would have been happy about it."

"I believe he would have been," she said. "And he'd be happy that I left Wisconsin. Got away from our families." Hannah bit her bottom lip. She wanted to tell him the truth, that she and Eric had never been married, yet the things her father had called her, a wanton, immoral and more, just wouldn't let her.

"Are you happy?" Teddy asked. "Because that's what matters now. You and your baby. If you're happy, your baby will be, too."

She let his question settle and as a peaceful harmony filled her, she said, "Yes, I am."

"Good. Then that's all that matters."

"Are you happy here?" she asked.

"Yes, Oak Grove is a good town. Full of good people."

"It is," she agreed.

They sat there, with her resting her head upon his shoulder until there was nothing but coals in the fireplace.

Teddy shifted. "I need to add a log to the fire before it gets too cold in here."

She sat up so he could move. "Would you like a cup of coffee and a cookie?"

He grinned. "Would you?"

She shrugged and nodded. "I seem to be hungry all the time now."

He held out both hands for her to take. "Dr. Graham says that means the baby is growing."

Taking his hands, for the assistance in rising was helpful, she asked, "How do you know that?"

He continued to hold her hands even after she was standing. "You told me he'd said that after your visit the other day."

She laughed. "I did, didn't I?"

"Yes." He then kissed her forehead. "Go get your cookie while I add wood to the fire."

"Do you want one?"

"Sure."

"And coffee?" she asked on her way to the kitchen.

"Sure."

She stacked several cookies on a plate and poured him coffee from the pot on the back burner. Putting everything on a tray, she added a glass of milk for herself.

"I'll carry that," he said, arriving at her side as she was about to lift the tray.

Knowing he'd protest if she refused, she let him carry the tray. Earlier, when she'd said she was happy, she'd almost told him why. It was because of him. He made her happy.

He frowned slightly. "What are you thinking so hard about?"

She shook her head and came up with the only excuse she could think of. "Do you remember some of your father's stories?"

"Parts of them," he answered.

"Will you tell me one? Your favorite one?"

"Why?"

"Because I want to hear it." She hooked her hand around his elbow. "If it's your favorite, I'm sure I'll like it."

"You're sure?"

"Yes, I'm sure."

Once in the parlor, he set the tray on the table and then helped her sit back down on the couch. Handing her the glass of milk and a cookie, he said, "My favorite was about a boy and his dog."

"I like it already."

He chuckled. "It might not be as good as I remember, or maybe I should say, I might not remember enough to make it interesting."

She patted the couch seat beside her. "It's already interesting to me."

They ate the entire plate of cookies while he told her about the escapades of a boy named Jack and a dog named Buck who got into trouble at every turn. When Brett, Fiona and the boys returned, Hannah was laughing so hard she hadn't heard the door open.

It was their home, but their arrival saddened her because it meant Teddy would leave soon. Which was what happened, but long afterward, while lying in bed, she relived the evening over and over, concluding that it had been the best night of her life. Her life was the best it had ever been. There was only one thing that could make it better.

Lying in his bed, staring at the ceiling overhead, a plethora of things raced across Teddy's mind. Hannah was front and center, and the reason other things came to mind. He hadn't mentioned his father's stories to anyone. Not even he and Abigail discussed them. Those stories had been his memories, his alone, and had kept him connected to his family all these years. Yet it felt good to share them with Hannah. His father had been a good man, a fair and honest man, and that had sent Teddy's thoughts to Hannah's father, and the things she'd said about him. He also thought about Eric, and wondered if he'd ever confronted Hannah's father.

Whether the man was the size of Brett or as short and pudgy as the mayor, nothing would have stopped Teddy from telling Hannah's father just what he thought of how she'd been treated. How could a man tell his daughter—his own flesh and blood— that she wasn't welcome in his house?

His mind twisted and turned and made its way back to something he'd done a couple of weeks ago. The letter he'd written. He hoped it had arrived, and that he'd soon get a response, because he wanted to make Hannah's Christmas very special.

Chapter Ten

A week later, Teddy discovered his letter had been received and his request had been fulfilled when Wayne Stevens stopped by. Tomorrow was Christmas Eve and he'd started to worry.

"Hey, Ted," Wayne said, walking into the *Gazette* office. "Thought you'd like to know a crate arrived for you on the train today."

Teddy set aside the bottle of ink he'd been about to pour into a tray. "That's great news," he said, removing the apron he wore to protect his clothes.

His plan had been to give it to Hannah on Christmas Day but, anxious to see the surprise and pleasure on her face when she opened it, he said to Abigail, "I'll be gone for a while."

"I'll finish filling the ink trays," she said. "So they'll be ready whenever you return."

Nodding her way, he collected his coat and asked Wayne, "Can you help me deliver it?"

"Sure. We'll need to get a wagon if we have to go too far," Wayne answered. "It's big."

Even though Brett's house wasn't far from the depot, he nodded. "I'll go rent a wagon and meet you at the depot."

The anticipation of seeing Hannah always thrilled him, but the excitement building inside him went beyond anything he'd felt before. She was going to love his gift. Love it almost as much as he loved her. He wasn't exactly sure when he'd finally admitted that to himself, but he was now absolutely certain he loved Hannah with all his heart. And wanted to marry her. He was going to ask her, too. Not right away, because she might not be ready yet. But she was bound to like her present.

They'd spent a lot of time together recently— however not nearly enough time *alone together*. Other than a few evenings, when Fiona and Brett went visiting, someone was always around. But even then, he and Hannah talked a lot. She spoke of her grandparents mostly, often mentioning how much she missed them. Each time he'd think of the letter he'd written, and hoped they'd respond with his request prior to Christmas. His hope was that Hannah would see that despite the feuding, there were people in her family who loved her. Had always loved her and always would. Surely that would heal her heart enough to consider loving again?

His wish had been granted, the gift had arrived in time, which proved this truly was the season of wishes and miracles.

Optimistic that he was making the right choice, he entered the livery in the best mood possible.

Hannah opened the door to the *Gazette* office and tried to contain her disappointment when Teddy was nowhere to be seen. "Hello," she said to Abigail. "I decided a walk was in order today, so thought I'd drop these etchings off."

"Hello and thank you." Abigail nodded toward the far side of the office. "You can set them on the desk. I was filling the ink trays and spilled one. I can't believe the mess I made."

Setting down the etchings, Hannah asked, "Is there anything I can do to help?"

"Actually, would you mind bringing me some newspapers from the box under the desk?" She held up two ink-covered hands. "Teddy keeps the misprinted copies just to clean up ink spills. This has to be the worst one ever."

Hannah had to grin, mainly because Abigail was. "Oh, goodness."

"This is worse than 'oh, goodness,'" Abigail said, still smiling despite the ink mess.

Hannah pulled out the chair and used the edge of the desk to help her kneel down. Such simple tasks were getting harder each day, and the ache that had settled in her back made it worse. Which was why she'd decided a walk was in order. Of course it was also a chance to see Teddy. She'd thought of little else lately. Seeing him was what she woke up looking forward to each morning, and she fell asleep each night thinking about how wonderful a time they'd had each day.

"I can't believe I've made such a mess," Abigail said. "I was being so careful."

"That's why they're called accidents," Hannah said. "Things happen, no matter how careful we are."

She flipped a handful of papers onto the desk, and then pulled herself upright again.

"I suspect so," Abigail said.

Hannah shuffled the papers into a stack and then carried them to the counter. As she set them down, the ache in her back formed a sharp pang. Startled, she inadvertently scattered the stack of papers.

"Are you all right?" Abigail asked.

The pain disappeared as quickly as it had hit, but the ache remained. "I must have twisted wrong when I got up," Hannah answered, gathering up the papers. One caught her attention. It wasn't a copy of the *Gazette*, but another paper she'd seen before. Her heart began to race as she slipped it away from the others. The newspaper had been ripped in half—a couple of times—but she knew it was one that contained the article about Eric's death. A sheet of writing paper that had also been ripped in half fell out as she lifted up the newspaper. Her stomach knotted as she read one handwritten line.

Eric Olson was not married at the time of his death.

Abigail snatched the paper out of her hand, and without a word used it to wipe ink from her fingers.

Hannah had read all she'd needed to. Her entire being shook, yet she held her stance, and the stare she'd settled on Abigail was steady.

Grabbing for another sheet of paper, Abigail said, "There is ink everywhere—"

"How long have you known?" Hannah asked.

Abigail didn't look up.

It might have been fear or perhaps anger that flared inside her. "How long?" Hannah asked.

Slapping a sheet of paper atop the ink, Abigail let out a groan. "Last fall, but Teddy—"

"So he knows, too."

Abigail nodded, then shook her head. "It was me, all me. He almost married a pregnant woman once before and I thought it was happening all over—"

Hannah's hands went to her stomach as a buzzing sound filled her ears. She spun around, knowing she had to leave.

"Hannah, wait! That's not what I meant!"

She didn't wait. She walked faster than she had in months. Out the door and down the street. Tears burned her cheeks as severely as the cold wind stung them as she crossed the field to Brett's house.

She should have known someone would investigate her story. That they'd want to know more. Abigail was a reporter, so it was reasonable that she'd be the one to do it. But knowing all of that didn't make the hurt any less severe. Neither did the fact that Teddy knew the truth, too, yet had never said anything. Not about Eric nor about...

She opened the door to the house, and seeing him sitting at the table sickened her.

He jumped to his feet and rushed forward. "Hannah? What's wrong? What's happened?"

"That other woman you were going to marry was pregnant?"

He stopped and glanced around as if looking for an escape.

"Is that why you didn't marry her? Because she was pregnant and you didn't want to raise another man's child?"

"No, hell, no." He shook his head. "How? How do you know about that?"

Getting her emotions under control, at least partially, she pointed to the door. "Goodbye, Teddy."

"Hannah—"

"Just leave, Teddy." Tears fell faster than she could swipe them aside. "Please, just leave." The pain filling her insides had nothing to do with the baby, yet she grabbed her stomach and dropped into the closest chair.

"No, not until—" Fear shot through Teddy. He'd never seen such anguish in someone's eyes. Such pain on their face. He wrenched open the door and shouted across the field. "Fiona!" As soon as he saw the other woman run out of Brett's blacksmith shop, he turned to Hannah. "I'm going to get Doc Graham."

He ran out the door. "It's Hannah," he told Fiona as they crossed paths, both running. "I'll be right back with Doc."

All sorts of terrible thoughts crossed his mind as he collected the doctor, raced back to the house and then paced the floor, while Hannah, Dr. Graham and Fiona were upstairs.

Hearing footsteps, he ran to the bottom of the

stairs. "What's wrong? Is she in labor? How's she doing? Can I see her?"

"She's not in labor," Fiona said. "But she doesn't want to see you. Not right now."

"But she's all right? Both her and the baby?" he asked.

"Yes. They're fine. Dr. Graham is giving her a thorough examination. He'll be a while."

That news relieved him, yet anger still roiled inside him. "Tell her I'll be back," he said, grabbing his coat.

Hours later, after talking with Abigail, he was back at Brett's house, standing on the back porch. "I have to talk to her. It won't take long."

Brett shook his head. "It won't matter what I tell her, Teddy. She doesn't want to see you. You're better off, and so is she, if you just stay away for a while. She needs to rest right now."

The pain inside him was real, and miserable, yet he couldn't deny she needed rest. "Will you make sure she opens the crate? It might help her feel better."

"I'll mention it," Brett said.

Teddy left, and after a sleepless night, during which he did nothing but think of Hannah, of his life with and without her, he was back at Brett's door the following morning.

"She still doesn't want to see you," Brett said sympathetically.

"Did she open the crate?" Teddy asked.

Brett shook his head. "Go home, Teddy. Maybe in time—"

"No," Teddy interrupted. "I won't go home." A compilation of anger and worry roiled inside him. All he needed was a chance. An opportunity to let Hannah know how much he cared about her. How much he loved her. "What if that was Fiona, Brett? Would you simply walk away? Go home and wait?"

Brett opened his mouth, but then closed it and shook his head. "Wait here."

Teddy paced the stoop, planning how he'd convince Hannah he was in love with her. When the door opened and Brett along with Fiona and the boys exited the house, Teddy shot forward, barely nodding when Brett said they'd be at the blacksmith shop.

His prepared speech vanished as he entered the parlor and saw Hannah sitting on the couch. The way she continued to stare into the fire, not acknowledging that he'd entered the room, said she wasn't prepared to hear anything he had to say.

Teddy pulled the hammer out of his coat pocket and walked directly to the crate sitting in the corner. Without a word, he pushed it across the room, until it was in front of her.

Apologies weren't what she needed. "I'll leave, Hannah, and never bother you again, once you open this crate."

"I don't want anything from you, Teddy."

Using the hammer claw, he loosened the nails on

one edge of the top. "It's not from me." He walked around the crate, released the other edge and lifted the top aside. "I only asked someone to send it to you."

Chapter Eleven

Hannah had been doing her best to not let anything show. Not how the sight of Teddy increased her heart rate and saddened her at the same time. How could she have been so wrong about him? No, it was herself she was wrong about. She'd been so focused on finding her Christmas miracle, she'd overlooked how he might feel about it. Had never asked him how he'd feel about— The uncomfortable tightening of her stomach that had started a few hours ago hit again, stealing her attention.

It didn't last long, and as she opened her eyes, they landed on the opened crate. Her fingers shook as she reached out to touch the top of one finely carved board. "It's my cradle."

"I wrote a letter to your grandparents." Teddy knelt down beside the crate. "It looks like they sent more than just the cradle."

The familiar feel of the wood beneath her fingertips filled her with memories. Good ones. As well as the knowledge that only Teddy would be this thoughtful. Loving him was so easy. That's why she'd forgotten to ask him how he felt about raising another man's child.

"I know how much this cradle means to you, how much you wanted your baby to sleep in it."

He would know that. They'd spoken of it, and of how much his family's printing press meant to him. It had kept him close to his family, even after all these years. He'd told her that just the other night.

"Go on," he encouraged. "Look what else they sent."

She unpacked quilts, clothes, nappies and various other baby items, as well as some carved wooden toys before reaching the bottom of the cradle, where two envelopes lay. One with her name, one with Teddy's.

She handed him his, and opened the other one. Her grandmother's handwriting made her eyes sting.

Dearest Hannah,
The letter from your young man was the miracle Grandpa and I had been praying for. We are so thankful that you are not letting the past rule your future and that you've found a man who loves you as much as we do…

The letter went on, but Hannah stopped reading to look at Teddy. "What did you tell them?"

He shrugged. "That you were here, safe, and how much you'd like to have the cradle before the baby arrived."

"It had to have been more than that."

Holding up his envelope, he said, "I also sent them the money to ship the cradle here, but they returned it."

"They are too honest to…" Honest. Her grandparents were, but she hadn't been. "I wanted to tell you that Eric and I had never been married, but I—"

"I," he interrupted, "don't care if you'd been married or not."

Her nose started to run, causing her to sniffle. "But you do care about raising another man's baby."

"Who told you that?"

"No one. I figured it out. That's why you didn't marry the woman you were engaged to and that's why you didn't want me to marry any of those men on my list. My father said that's what would happen. That no one would ever want to marry me, but—"

He pressed a finger to her lips. "Stop. Your father was wrong about many things. Any man would be proud to marry you." He put his finger under her chin, forcing her to continue looking at him. "I didn't marry Becky because the father of her baby returned to town wanting to marry her and raise his family, and I tried to convince you not to marry any of the men on your list because I was jealous of each and every one of them."

Her heart skipped a beat. "Jealous?"

"Yes, jealous because I was already falling in love with you."

Her heart swelled inside her chest. As tears formed, she glanced at the cradle and then back to him. "You were?"

"Yes, I was."

"Why didn't you—"

"Tell you?" he asked. "Because I didn't think

you were ready for that. You'd burned your list so I thought you didn't want to marry anyone just yet."

She shook her head and blinked back tears as he continued.

"I love you, Hannah. And I already love your baby." He laid his other hand on her stomach. "But most of all, I want you to be happy. If that can't happen here in Oak Grove, then I'm prepared to pack up and move. Anywhere you want to go, anywhere you will be happy."

Blinking back the tears, she said, "You can't move. What about Abigail? The *Gazette*?"

"Nothing matters as much as you do, Hannah." He sat down next to her. "Abigail wishes she had never written that letter, or ever received those newspapers. She swears she won't tell anyone, but if you are afraid of gossip, we'll leave. We'll leave today if you want to."

Hannah glanced again at the letter in her hand, at the line about the past ruling her future. She'd already decided that wasn't going to happen, yet at the first impediment, she'd given in to the heartache rather than stand up to it. "We can't run from the past. Not forever."

"It's not likely, but I'll do my damnedest to try if you want."

The love inside her spread out so fast, so thoroughly, she laughed. Shaking her head at his frown, she said, "That's one of the things I love about you— your honesty."

"I'm afraid I haven't been very honest with you,"

he said, bowing his head. "I should have told you about Becky, and about falling in love with you. I knew how you'd been treated and should have realized you'd think the worst of me."

"But I shouldn't have thought the worst of you. You gave me no reason to. It was me. All me. I was so focused on what had happened to me before, and how I didn't want it to happen again, that I made it happen." She shook her head. "That sounds as confusing as it is."

"No, it doesn't," he said. "Because that's what was happening to me, too."

"It was?"

"Yes." He kissed her hand. "I was afraid to love you because I thought maybe I was just feeling sorry for you like I did with Becky. It wasn't until you asked me if I'd loved her that I realized the difference. I should have told you the entire story then, but I didn't want to scare you off. Wasn't sure you were ready for that."

She wrapped both of her hands around his. "I burned that list because you weren't on it."

"You did?" he asked hopefully.

Leaning forward, she brought her lips close to his to whisper, "Yes, I did. I knew you were the only man I'd consider marrying. I love you, Teddy. I love you very much."

As their lips met, he wrapped his arms around her and pulled her close. The overwhelming peace and joy that filled her said she'd let the past fill an entire night with worry when there hadn't been anything to worry about. This was Teddy, and he wasn't anything like anyone from her past.

As their lips parted, he grinned widely. "So…"

She copied his grin. "So…?"

"Will you marry me?"

She bit her bottom lip, only because the vast amount of happiness welling inside her made her want to shout. Gaining control, she nodded and whispered, "Yes."

"Yes!" he shouted triumphantly and then kissed her so hard for so long they were both breathless when they parted. They both laughed after filling their lungs with air, and then kissed again.

"When?" Teddy asked when they both needed air again. "When do you want to get married?"

The tightening of her stomach occurred again, but this time it was strong enough to make her gasp and send a groan into her throat as it clutched her entire stomach and back with a long agonizing pain.

"What's wrong?" Teddy laid a hand on her stomach. "Hannah?"

"I think this baby is about ready to be born." As the pain subsided, a slight wave of sadness washed over her. "It was so close."

He glanced around. "What was so close? The baby?"

She had to giggle as she shook her head. "No. My Christmas miracle. A last name for my baby."

He grinned. "How does baby White sound to you?" Teddy planted a fast kiss upon her lips. "I believe in Christmas miracles, too."

He was out of the room before she had a chance to ask where he was going. A moment later, a single gunshot echoed outside of the house. Within minutes, the house was full of people.

It was chaotic at first, until Teddy took charge. The first thing he ordered was an examination from Dr. Graham, who said she was in labor, but that there wouldn't be a baby for several hours.

Hannah was already deeply in love with Teddy, but the way he organized everything, all the while making sure the arrangements were fine with her, made her love him all the more. By noon, all of her things, including the new cradle, and her were moved into his house, where Reverend Flaherty performed their wedding.

Before the ceremony, Abigail, with tears in her eyes, apologized—several times—and promised to be the best aunt on earth. Hannah believed she would be, and told her so.

Her wedding was all she'd dreamed it would be—minus a labor pain or two—because the man marrying her would love her until his dying day. He not only vowed it, he'd already proven it. She vowed to love him just as long, and would.

The afternoon hours were spent with women and the doctor checking on her as she lay in Teddy's bed. Throughout the day, Teddy sat beside her, held her hand, hugged her, kissed her and told her she was doing great. He made the pain bearable.

Shortly after midnight, the doctor ordered everyone but Fiona out of the room.

"I'll be right outside the door," Teddy said as he kissed her cheek.

Her heart tumbled at the concern on his face. It was her turn to be strong, to assure him all would turn out just as he'd promised. "I'll be fine," she said, squeezing his hand. "I love you."

"I love you, too," he whispered before kissing her again.

Teddy once again found himself pacing, except this time it was the hallway of the upper floor. Abigail was there too, and so was Brett. A handful of others were downstairs, filling coffee cups and sending them upstairs. He'd carried around several cups, but had never taken so much as a sip. His mind was in the bedroom. With his wife.

A pain-filled scream almost brought him to his knees, but the next instant, the sound of a baby crying had him standing tall and accepting congratulations from those around him.

It seemed like hours before he was admitted into the bedroom, where he was told he had daughter. While looking down at the adorable red and wrinkled face he'd love until his dying day, devotion like he'd never known filled him.

Turning to Hannah, he asked, "How are you?"

"Happy," she said, looking more beautiful than ever. "So, so very happy."

"Me, too," he said.

Later, when the house was completely quiet, he

carefully crawled onto the bed and stretched out beside Hannah.

She opened her eyes and smiled. "I love you, Teddy White."

"I love you, Hannah White."

"That sounds amazing, doesn't it? Hannah White."

"Yes, it does." Reaching across her, he touched the tip of the tiny nose on the baby lying in the crook of her arm. "What will her name be?"

"I'm thinking Theodora Abigail White. After her father and favorite aunt."

His heart swelled so fast and hard, it made his eyes sting. "Theodora?"

"We'll call her Dorie," Hannah said. "Dorie White. Doesn't that sound wonderful?"

"Yes," he admitted. "Absolutely wonderful." He leaned across her to kiss the top of the baby's head. "Merry Christmas, Dorie."

Then he kissed Hannah and wrapped an arm around her as he lay down beside her again.

She snuggled her head upon his shoulder. "This has really been a Christmas full of miracles, hasn't it? My favorite time of the year."

"Yes, and it will forever be my favorite time of the year, too." Pulling Hannah closer, he rested his hand upon baby Dorie's head. He'd forever believe in miracles, too. "Merry Christmas, Hannah," he whispered.

"Merry Christmas, Teddy," she said. "Merry Christmas, one and all."

* * * * *

MISS CHRISTINA'S CHRISTMAS WISH

Lynna Banning

To the millions of immigrants
who have come to America.

You enrich our culture
and help make our country the land of the free.

Dear Reader

To me, Christmas is a time of reflection about what
is important in life. It's a time to connect with those
we love, and a time to give to others the gift of our
attention, our understanding and our acceptance.

Lynna

Chapter One

The train engine chuffed into the station and rolled slowly forward until the cars lined up with the platform. With a final billowy puff of white steam, the passenger compartment slid to a halt, the uniformed conductor leaped down and unfolded an iron step, then stepped back inside.

"Smoke River," he bawled at the top of his voice. "Now ya see it, now ya don't."

Christina frowned. She leaned toward the harried mother sitting beside her. "Whatever does he mean?"

"He means—" the woman corralled a wriggling child and plopped it onto her lap "—that this town's so small if you blinked, you'd miss it."

"Oh."

Small was exactly what she needed. If she failed here, she didn't want a big audience. She edged past the woman and her child, grasped the handle of her travel valise and headed for the exit, where the conductor stood waiting.

He lifted the satchel out of her hand and set it on the platform below, then helped her down the iron step. "Got all yer things, miss?"

"Yes, thank you." She had all her "things," yes. What she didn't have, Aunt Lettie would have said, was a lick of good sense and a big helping of self-confidence.

Well, it was too late now, she thought, peering at the sprinkle of people waiting to board the train. She had never retreated from a challenge before, and she most certainly wasn't going to start now. Besides, for better or worse, she was here in Smoke River.

The woman and her child stepped down onto the platform behind her, and Christina turned to intercept her. "Excuse me, which way is the main street?"

"Main street? Yer lookin' at it, dearie. Just past the station house over yonder." She tipped her head toward the low white-painted building behind her. "Got a freight service of sorts if you've a mind," the woman volunteered. She shifted the squirming child to her other hip and puffed the drooping feather on her hat out of her face.

"No, thank you, I can manage." Her valise wasn't heavy. She'd packed only an extra shirtwaist, three camisoles, some underdrawers and her notebooks. She would walk into town to save a few cents. She picked up her suitcase and headed off down the wooden platform onto a wide board sidewalk.

It led past a mercantile with bushel baskets of shiny red apples out in front, Poletti's barbershop, the Smoke River Hotel, an adjacent restaurant and Stockett's feed store. Across the street was the Golden Partridge saloon, the sheriff's office and a bakery. She would ask at the mercantile if there was a boardinghouse nearby.

Suddenly a hand-lettered sign in the front window of the bakery caught her eye.

ROOM FOR RENT
CHEAP

She pushed open the door and stepped inside. Then she drew in a deep breath and closed her eyes. Oh, what a heavenly smell! Something lemony made her mouth water. And chocolate! Or was it molasses? Both, she decided.

"You like cookie?" The diminutive Chinese man behind the glass display case smiled and offered a frosted square.

"Oh, no, thank you. I came about your sign in the window, about the room for rent?"

"Can eat and look, too!" He proffered the cookie again.

"Thank you, Mr...?"

"Name Ming. But everyone call me Uncle Charlie."

"I am Christina Marnell. The new schoolteacher," she added.

The man's black eyebrows waggled. "Ah. Much work to do in school place."

Christina laughed. "Oh, I do hope so. I haven't traveled all the way from St. Louis to *not* work."

"You come, see room upstairs." He led the way up the narrow staircase at the rear of the bakery and at the top opened the door to reveal a spotless, sunny apartment with cream walls and blue curtains fluttering at the two large open windows.

Uncle Charlie beamed. "Is mine. You like?"

"Yes, it's lovely. But why are you renting it?"

"Get married soon. Wife come from China, so

need more room. Buy house in back from newspaper man."

Christina gazed around her and set down her valise. "This will be perfect, Mr—Uncle Charlie."

"Ah, good. I leave curtains?"

She smiled at him. "Yes, please. I have almost nothing except for what is packed in my valise. My trunk could be delivered tomorrow."

"Need stove? Table? Maybe bed? I buy all new for wife, so you can have these."

She blinked. "Really? Oh, Uncle Charlie, you are an angel."

He reached out and patted her hand. "Buddha maybe, missy. Not angel. Now, you come. I show you best cookies."

An hour later, replete with chocolate-molasses wafers and two restorative cups of hot tea, Christina made her way back to the railway station to arrange delivery of her trunk. On purpose she walked very carefully along the tree-lined street in order to hide her uneven gait.

Ivan Panovsky watched the young woman step out of Uncle Charlie's bakery and head down the main street, moving slowly enough to attract a good deal of interest. Long dark blue skirt, somewhat swirly around her ankles but not fancy, and some kind of shirtwaist with ruffles at the wrists. The straw hat she wore had a brim so wide it shaded all but her chin, and the ends of the wide blue ribbon around the crown streamed down her back. Like a picture he saw once in a book. He wished he could see her face.

He knew he had never seen her in Smoke River before. He started to turn away from his second-floor window across the street from Uncle Charlie's when he noticed something else about her. She was limping.

He watched until she reached Ness's Mercantile across the street. Then he clapped his wool cap on his head, moved to the doorway of his small room over Stockett's Feed & Seed and tramped down the back stairs to head for the sawmill.

"Hey, Panovsky! You goin' to the square dance tonight?"

Ivan continued to slice his ax through the bark on the huge pine log he was straddling. Ike Bruhn, his boss at the sawmill, had asked him that same question every single Saturday since he'd been hired four years ago. And he always gave Ike the same answer.

"No. Have letter to write."

Smitty, working the log beside his, snorted. "You say that every week, Ivan. You got a girlfriend back in New York or what?"

No, he didn't have a girlfriend back in New York, or anywhere else for that matter. He had no time for a girl. He was working two jobs and saving every penny he could. Girls cost money.

As usual, Smitty didn't give up. "You sayin' you're too good for a barn dance?"

"I have nothing to say," Ivan said evenly.

"Mebbe you got something against dancin', huh?"

"Knock it off, Smitty," his boss yelled. "None of your business."

"Hell, Ike, I was just bein' friendly."

Ivan went back to skinning the log. He didn't mind Smitty's joshing. But it was nobody's business why he did not go to dances or join the other mill workers at the Golden Partridge, or visit Sadie's bawdy house and it had nothing to do with not being friendly. He had other things on his mind. More important things.

He huffed out a long breath and reminded himself what his mama had told him: "If you pray for potatoes, you must pick up a hoe."

Chapter Two

Christina had almost finished unpacking the lace-edged muslin sheets and towels she had spent all summer finishing when three imperious raps sounded on her door. She swung it open to find a tall, unsmiling woman facing her.

"I am Verena Forester," the woman announced. "Your neighbor next door. Charlie told me you'd taken the room. I only hope you will be as quiet as he was."

Christina worked up a smile. "How do you do, Miss Forester. I am Christina Marnell, from—"

"St. Louis," Verena finished for her. "I asked around at the railway office."

"Um…won't you come in? I was just unpacking my trunk, but I could make some tea if you—"

"Don't drink tea. Just coffee."

"Oh, I'm sorry, but I don't have—"

"Makes no never mind," the woman snapped. "I hear you're the new schoolteacher."

My, word traveled fast in a small town out West! "Well, yes, I am. I've just graduated from—"

"I'm the dressmaker," Verena announced. Her flinty gray eyes assessed Christina's skirt and creased shirtwaist. "Looks like you'll be needin' some duds when school starts."

Christina blinked. Her trunk was crammed with

"duds," skirts and dresses that were conservative enough for a classroom. "Oh, no, I don't think—"

"Things from back East are too fancy for out here in Oregon. Come on over to my shop in the morning and I'll see what I can do."

"Miss Forester, I am grateful, really I am. But—" Christina swallowed "—but you see I have no way to pay you until I fulfill my year's teaching contract."

The woman's narrow face scrunched into a frown. "Makes no never mind, my girl. Most everybody in town owes me for what's on their back. Sooner or later I always get paid."

Christina recognized the remark as a kindness meant to be welcoming, but the woman also intended it to drum up some dressmaking business. Very well, she would play the game. "That is most generous of you, Miss Forester. I will pay you a visit tomor—"

"Make it today if you don't mind. Tomorrow's Sunday, and I always attend church on Sunday. You a churchgoer?"

Christina gulped. She hadn't attended church since she was nine years old. However, she was not about to confess that to Verena Forester. Some things were private.

"I'm afraid I must spend today preparing my lessons. School starts Monday morning."

The dressmaker shot her a sympathetic glance. "Well, good luck to you. Won't be easy, I'm thinkin'."

When the woman left, Christina indulged in a calming cup of tea and nibbled thoughtfully on the six oatmeal cookies Uncle Charlie had left on her doorstep early that morning. *Why won't it be easy?*

she wondered. Were the children badly behaved? She knew that the previous teacher, Eleanor Starks, had left abruptly when the term was over last June; apparently she had eloped with the head of the schoolboard, and in Oregon a married woman was not allowed to teach school.

Was there more to it than that? Had the students been too unruly to handle? Perhaps they hadn't liked Miss Starks and…

Her breath caught. Oh, Lord, would they like *her*? *Will they laugh at me?*

She had wanted to teach school ever since she could remember. She loved learning, and after Mama died and she had gone to live with Aunt Lettie, she had spent the last of the meager inheritance from her father to attend the St. Louis Teachers Academy. She had excelled at her studies, especially music.

But she had to admit she had not excelled at conquering her fear of standing up in front of people and—she shuddered—talking to them. And never once in her teacher training had she faced a room full of schoolchildren who would stare at her.

Face it, Christina. It is learning *you love, not people.* Especially not a whole classroom full of wriggly, boisterous students.

She poured another cup of tea and tried to control her shaking hands.

Ivan looked up from the counter as the bell over the door clanged and Thad MacAllister stepped into the feed store. "Need ten pounds of seed corn, Ivan."

"Is not too late in the season to plant corn, Thad?"

"Maybe. But you know me, I like experimenting with crops."

Ivan nodded. Rancher Thad MacAllister's venture into growing winter wheat was the reason every farmer in Oregon now sowed a winter-wheat crop, and why Ivan's boss, Abraham Stockett, was getting rich selling them seed.

"Say, Ivan, you fancy comin' out to the ranch for supper tonight? Leah's making cabbage rolls, and I know you Russkies love cabbage."

Ivan hefted the bag of seed corn onto the wooden counter. "That most kind of you, Thad, but I cannot. That will be two dollars."

Thad slapped some coins onto the counter. "Don't do much socializing, do you?"

"No, I do not."

"Oughtta think about it. Might be you'd want to get married someday."

"Not marry yet," Ivan said quickly. "Something there is I must to do first." He knew Thad MacAllister was too well-mannered to ask what that something was. Maybe he would tell the friendly rancher some day. MacAllister could keep a secret. "Yes, perhaps I will marry someday."

Thad gave him a quizzical look. "You keep sayin' that, Ivan, and 'someday' will never come." The rancher lugged his purchase out to the wagon waiting in the street, and Ivan locked the door behind him. Then with a tired sigh he climbed the back stairs to the bachelor quarters over the store Stockett had let him have. Inside the small room, he brewed a pot of strong coffee, buttered three slices of day-old bread from Uncle Charlie's bakery and settled down at the battered oak desk under his front window.

Ah, what was this? Directly across the street, in the apartment where Charlie had lived all the years Ivan had been in Smoke River, a lamp flared to life and he saw a dark head bending over a desk. It was the girl he'd seen leaving the bakery that morning! He forgot all about his bread and coffee and began to watch her.

Half an hour went by, and the girl didn't stir. She was writing something, dipping a pen into what must be an ink bottle and leaning over a paper or something on her desk, but never once did she raise her head. He wanted her to look up so he could see her face.

But she worked on and on while his coffee grew cold and his curiosity warmed up. She couldn't be Uncle Charlie's new wife from China, could she? No, she didn't look Chinese. Besides, a Chinese woman wouldn't wear a pretty wide-brimmed straw hat with a blue ribbon hanging down the back.

All at once he understood. Charlie had rented his quarters over the bakery to the new girl in town. And from the looks of it, he guessed she was writing a long, long letter to someone. He watched as long as he could stay awake, then gobbled his three thick slices of bread and took himself off to bed.

In the morning he gulped the dregs of his cold coffee, toasted his last slice of bread and tramped down the stairs to open the feed store. He glanced out the front window to the apartment across the way, hoping to catch another glimpse of the girl, but now the blue curtains were closed.

For the rest of the morning he straightened shelves and reorganized the heavy burlap bags of feed behind displays of new plows and hoes and garden rakes. Townspeople drifted past on their way to church, and an hour later they drifted back again, some stopping in to purchase chicken feed or tomato seeds. Edith Ness stepped in from her father's mercantile store across the street to buy more red nasturtium seeds, and Billy Rowell, the sheriff's nephew, rode past on his red pony, delivering his newspapers.

He watched the churchgoing stragglers, hoping to catch another glimpse of the blue-ribbon lady, but the long, lazy Sunday afternoon gradually drew to a close without a single glimpse of her. It was a good thing Uncle Charlie's bakery stayed open on Sunday; around closing time, Ivan strode across the street to get another loaf of day-old bread.

Chapter Three

Christina twitched the folds of her gored brown poplin skirt one last time and picked up her satchel. She was ready.

Oh, no, she wasn't the least bit ready. She would never be ready to face a room full of strangers—even half-grown strangers. Large—or even small—gatherings of people had always made her nervous. From the assembled well-wishers listening to her college graduation speech to crowds of townspeople singing carols at Christmas, she had always felt ill at ease among strangers. She was shy, Aunt Lettie said. But inside she knew she was more than shy; groups of people frightened her. Books didn't frighten her, but *people* did.

However, sooner or later she would have to walk into the lion's den, so she might as well get it over with. She sucked in a fortifying gulp of air, smoothed her skirt one last time and started off.

The schoolhouse was half a mile from town. She had glimpsed it from the train window when she'd arrived, a pretty little red building with lots of windows, nestled in a grove of pine and maple trees. The leaves were starting to turn gold and orange.

It took her a good twenty-five minutes to walk the distance at her halting pace, and on the way she concentrated on calming her nerves and trying to remember her opening speech. To add to her anxiety, beyond "good morning, students," she couldn't recall a single word. She prayed it would all come back to her when the time came.

The gardens along the way were beautiful—roses and asters and bushes covered with tiny white daisy-like flowers; she admired the gardens as she passed by. The air was soft and warm and smelled of grass and baking bread. Her stomach rumbled. She'd been too nervous to eat anything before she left her apartment.

At the schoolhouse she unlocked the door and stepped inside. Three rows of wooden seats faced a large oak desk at the front of the room. Light from the bank of windows splashed across the floor and over the blackboard on the wall, illuminating the pull-down map roll and the wall clock. A small black potbellied stove stood in one corner, flanked by an empty wood box and a wooden water bucket with an iron dipper. Nails for coats and mittens were studded along the wall nearest the door. A battered box of McGuffey's Readers and a single volume of Tennyson sat in one corner of the room; all the books looked well-worn at the corners.

At one minute until nine she opened the school-room door, stepped into the doorway and clapped her hands sharply. "School is starting, children! Come inside."

She retreated to her desk and waited as a tumult of bodies spilled into the room and banged into their seats. Shoes thumped on the polished wood floor. The double-seat desks filled up rapidly, and squabbles broke out over who would share a seat with whom.

The cacophony of voices rose until Christina could scarcely hear herself think. *Merciful heaven, this is bedlam.* She stood up, pondering what to do, and then she sucked in her breath, purposefully edged out from behind her desk and stood facing the students. They merely stared blankly at her. She would stare them down, she decided. She waited, arms folded across her midriff, until she caught the eye of every single one of them.

It worked. As her gaze connected with that of first one, then another of the worst troublemakers, the noise level gradually began to recede. Some of the girls began shushing their companions, and then the loudest of the boys fell silent as her gaze—steely eyed, she hoped—moved from one student to another.

Finally, *finally*, it was quiet. "Well," she said in her most carefully controlled voice, "is this how you behave at home?"

"Sometimes," a tall, rugged-looking boy with a shock of blond hair answered. "When I can get away with it."

That brought snickers from the other boys and a few giggles from the older girls.

"Really," she said as calmly as she could manage. "And what does your father do about it?"

"Ain't got no pa!" the speaker retorted.

One of the girls laughed, then clapped her hand over her mouth. Christina swallowed and clenched one fist in the folds of her skirt. "My name is Christina Marnell. You may call me Miss Marnell."

Dead silence. "Where you from?" a wiry boy with red hair and a torn collar blurted out. "You talk funny."

"I am from St. Louis, Missouri. I guess I 'talk funny' as you put it, because I went to school in the East."

He nodded, pursing his lips.

"You talk funny, too," she said.

He shot her a startled look. "Oh, yeah?"

"It's 'Oh, yeah, *Miss Marnell*,'" she enunciated clearly. She waited four heartbeats, then went on. "Now, students, I am not here to teach you good manners. I am here to teach you other things."

"Yeah?" the red-haired lad said. "What things?"

Christina studied him. "Things you don't know."

"Like what?" the blond boy snorted.

At least she had their attention. Now she had to figure out how to keep it! "Like exactly how far your proboscis is from that of the girl across the aisle from you."

"Whatza 'proboscis'?" a boy called.

Christina drew in a long breath. She had them. Almost. Anyway, it was a beginning.

"Well, now, I would guess that you are all very intelligent boys and girls, so why don't you tell *me* what you think a proboscis could be?"

"A thing that tells time!" someone shouted.

"A nose," a resonant voice from the back of the room said.

Christina narrowed her eyes. "Who said that?"

A slim, dark-skinned boy with a shock of black hair over his forehead half raised one hand. "I did."

A murmur ran around the room.

She met the boy's hostile black eyes. "And your name is?"

"Sammy Greywolf."

"I am pleased to make your acquaintance, Mr. Greywolf. You are correct."

The dark eyes flicked down and then up again. This time they were shining. Suddenly she realized she didn't have to make an opening speech. She simply had to pique their curiosity and go from there. She pivoted and walked back toward her desk to retrieve her notebook and pencil and heard a collective indrawn breath.

"Golly Moses," someone exclaimed. "Miss Marnell is crippled!"

Chapter Four

No sooner had she turned her back and started for her desk than the whispers turned to murmurs and then to a loud buzzing. She ignored it, opened her notebook and pointed at the girl at the head of the first row. "Your name, please?"

"I'm Roxanna Jensen, Miss Marnell. I'm nine years old and I live on a ranch out of town. I have my own horse."

Christina quickly wrote the information down. "Next?"

Then came Billy Rowell, twelve years old, whose uncle, Hawk Rivera, was the sheriff. Last was Sammy Greywolf. He was Indian, Christina noted. Age eleven and very smart.

"And now I will tell you about myself," Christina announced.

The class suddenly sat up straighter.

"I am from St. Louis, where I attended college. I am twenty-three years old. And I am going to teach you many things. Are there any questions before recess?"

A hand stabbed into the air. "Miss Marnell, how come you're crippled?

From that moment on, Christina's first day of teaching went downhill. The fact that she walked with a limp somehow undid the control she thought she had managed to establish, and during the lunch hour she watched surreptitiously through the window as the older boys clopped gleefully around and around the school yard in exaggerated parodies of her gait.

She had endured such taunting for years; in fact, she had grown so good at ignoring the barbs and cruel comments they scarcely registered any longer. But seeing her halting gait imitated in the exaggerated, mean-spirited actions of her students cut her to the quick. She tried her best to eat her lunch of cheese and a ripe apple, but her throat was so dry she found it hard to swallow.

After an hour all the students clattered back into the classroom. Christina took a deep breath and pasted a smile onto her stiff face. While she assessed her students' reading and arithmetic skills, the rest of the class buzzed and fidgeted. The girls whispered and giggled, and occasionally she heard the purposeful, uneven clumping of heavy boys' boots on the plank floor. She knew it was done to annoy her.

At the end of her grueling first day of teaching she stood up and looked over her students. "Class is dismissed," she said with a sigh. She was exhausted. Her temples pounded as if little men inside her head were shoving wagon wheel spokes into her brain.

The schoolhouse quickly emptied, and in blessed silence she sank onto the chair behind her desk. Never, *never* had she expected teaching school to be so difficult. Or so tiring. She felt as if she were staring at a mountain of ignorance and disinterest in front of her, and she was heartsick. She had wanted to teach so desperately, but after today it looked…impossible.

The thought of an entire school year made up of days like today made her physically ill.

She locked the schoolhouse door and managed to limp slowly across the grassy yard until she reached the main street. With her last ounce of strength she stopped in at Ness's Mercantile. The short, narrow-faced man behind the counter pinned watery blue eyes on her.

"Kin I help you find somethin', ma'am?"

"Oh, I do hope so. I need an umbrella, and—"

"You sure? Ain't rainin' yet."

"Yes, I am quite sure. Eventually it *will* rain, and I wish to be prepared. I also need some sort of bell for the schoolhouse."

"Might try a cowbell. If that don't get the kids to school on time, they must be hard of hearin'." Not even a hint of a smile crossed his thin lips.

"Then I will need two, no, make that three boxes of blackboard chalk, a large bottle of ink, a stout ruler and…" Her mind went completely blank.

"And?" Mr. Ness prompted.

She added four ripe apples, a block of yellow cheese and a tin of tomatoes and one of beans.

"That'll be, let's see, a dollar and forty-seven cents all together. You wanna open an account?"

Christina nodded, and Mr. Ness wrapped her purchases in brown grocery paper and bid her an unsmiling farewell. She gathered up her parcels and on trembly legs slowly headed for her apartment over the bakery.

Maybe I will never, ever be able to teach anything

to anyone's children, ever. All the chalk and ink in
the universe can't bring about miracles.

Ivan reached over the glass bakery case to shake
the owner's pudgy, flour-dusted hand. "Thank you,
Charlie. When you want window added to your new
house?"

"Bride come this week," the Chinese man said
with a grin. "Put window over sink in kitchen. I pay
you many loaves of bread."

"Good." He gathered up the two loaves of stale
bread Charlie had set aside for him today and turned
toward the door. Just as he reached for the knob, the
door burst open and a young woman with shiny dark
hair caught in a loose bun at her neck and a blue-
ribboned straw hat clutched in one hand barreled
straight into his chest. Her armload of packages skit-
tered onto the floor, along with his precious loaves of
bread. She gasped and looked up at him with desper-
ate, dark blue eyes that were brimming with tears.

A sharp-toothed saw bit into his heart. God in
heaven, she was beautiful! He stared into her startled
face until she blinked, and he remembered to close his
mouth. Her eyes were magnificent! And he could not
pry his gaze from the sprinkle of tiny freckles over
her nose. Little-girl freckles. But she was not a little
girl. She was a woman all grown up. The enchanting
contrast sent a bolt of hot steel into his belly.

"Oh! I am terribly sorry!" She turned her face
away, but he saw the shimmer of tears on her pale
cheeks. He swallowed hard.

A dark stain seeped through the brown wrapping

paper around one parcel and something oozed across the floor. Ink! He scooped up the paper and dumped it into the metal wastebasket Charlie held out. Then four red apples rolled into the muck.

Ivan grinned at her. "You need another bottle of ink and new apples."

"I— Yes, thank you. Oh, Charlie, I am sorry about your floor. I will scrub it for you tomorrow after school."

"No need, missy. All time spill things."

"But not ink!" She clasped and unclasped her hands. Ivan watched her bite her lips until they looked like ripe raspberries, then forced his gaze away. He could not let himself think about ripe raspberries. He could not think about a pretty woman with tears spilling onto her lashes, raspberries or no raspberries.

All at once he wanted to gather her into his arms and protect her from whatever was causing those tears. He stuffed his hands into the back pockets of his jeans, then remembered his ink-stained fingers. Charlie was down on his hands and knees scooping up the spilled parcels and her loose apples and his two loaves of bread.

He felt completely helpless. He knew what to do when he was straddling a thick spruce log with a double-edged ax in his hands, or feeding it into a muley saw, but the sight of her quivering lips turned him into an idiot with his head in a cloud.

What was wrong with him?

Charlie shoved the bread loaves against Ivan's chest and gave him a wide, knowing grin. "Confucius say, easy to lose brain when belly empty. Heart, too," the twinkly-eyed man added under his breath.

"What?"

"Heart," Charlie murmured. "You understand?"

It did not help. No matter how short of breath this pretty blue-eyed girl made him, there was nothing he could do about it. But every inch of his body wanted to follow that enticing backside that was now gently swaying up the stairs into her apartment.

He shook his thoughts back into coherence. "Charlie, who is lady?"

"New schoolteacher from East. You like?"

"I do not know her." But he *did* like her. And that was a problem. The *last* thing he wanted to do was like her.

He tramped across the street and up the back stairway to his sparsely furnished room over the feed store. His brain was so fuzzy he poured ground oats into the coffee grinder.

The last thing he needed right now was a pretty schoolteacher with tears like diamonds on her eyelashes who made his groin swell. He had withstood his fellow sawmill workers' jokes about why he never joined them at the saloon or attended barn dances because there was something else he had to do, something he had worked hard for the last five years to accomplish. He could not let anything get in his way.

But now he wanted… God in heaven, what did he want? Suddenly he did not know.

He gritted his teeth, ground up a handful of coffee beans and remembered the advice his Russian grandfather had once given him: when in doubt, do nothing.

Chapter Five

By the time Christina started off for the schoolhouse the following morning, she had managed to somewhat shore up her flagging confidence and instill some calming thoughts into her skittery brain. Was teaching always like this, two steps forward and one step back? If that were true, how did students ever get educated?

She rounded the corner and started toward the grassy school yard. Her satchel, stuffed with the cowbell, notebooks and boxes of chalk, grew heavier with each step. By the time she reached the schoolhouse door, she was short of breath and perspiring in the crisp fall air. Inside she quickly unloaded her lunch and the supplies she had purchased into the empty desk drawers. Then she paced back and forth in front of the open door, trying to calm her nerves.

Students began collecting in the yard in groups of three or four, except for little Manette Nicolet and the Indian boy, Sammy Greywolf, who stood by themselves off to one side. The other boys congregated in a tight knot near the honeysuckle-swathed outhouse, apparently cooking up some devilment.

At nine sharp she stepped into the open doorway and rattled the cowbell.

Twelve startled faces swiveled toward her, but no

one moved except for little Manette. Dressed in a starched pink pinafore, the girl practically danced past Christina and took a seat in the first row of desks. The other students began tumbling through the door, laughing and scuffling for seats. The noise level rose.

Her second day of teaching was worse than the first. Every single time she turned her back to write an arithmetic problem on the blackboard, pandemonium erupted. First Kurt Jorgensen tumbled out of his seat onto the floor to the uproarious guffaws of the other boys and the giggles of the girls.

"Kurt was passing a love note to Noralee Ness," someone yelled.

Christina stared at them. In the time it had taken to write "18 X 4" on the blackboard, discipline in her classroom had evaporated. Once more she faced the blackboard and heard scuffling and muffled laughter at her back. The instant she turned around, quiet fell. Except for Noralee, who was snuffling into her lacy handkerchief. Christina's temples began to throb.

Not one student did the arithmetic problem correctly until Sammy Greywolf's quiet voice pronounced, "Seventy-two."

Christina smiled at the boy. "Your answer is correct, Sammy."

That prompted a chorus of jeers from the boys. "Smarty-pants, smarty-pants, your jeans are all baggy and full of ants!" She ignored the noise, and the morning dragged on. By noon she was exhausted and disheartened, and when the hands on the clock finally—finally!—crept forward until they were both straight up, she cut short Kurt Jorgensen's labored reading of McGuffey's first primer and dismissed the students for lunch.

The room emptied, and she sank onto her desk chair and unwrapped her sandwich, but before she could take a bite she heard angry shouts from the school yard. She raced to the window to see what the noise was about.

All the boys and many of the girls were gathered around someone, shouting taunts. Kurt and Adam occasionally darted through the crowd to land blows on whoever was trapped in the center. She ran to the door and headed clumsily for the crowd as fast as she could force her crippled ankle to move.

The girls spied her first and scattered, but Kurt and Adam were so intent on inflicting damage on the hapless person they did not see her. The other boys melted away, leaving the two older boys in the center with their unfortunate victim, Sammy Greywolf. Kurt had his arm locked around the boy's neck, and Adam was stomping on Sammy's soft-toed moccasins.

"Stop it!" she shouted. "Stop! Just what do you think you're doing, ganging up on one boy?"

"He ain't a boy," Kurt yelled. "He's an Injun."

"Shame on you, both of you!"

Both boys stood before her, their heads drooping. They dug the toes of their boots into the dirt while Sammy Greywolf stood quietly where he had obviously been cornered, his dark eyes defiant.

She rounded on Kurt and Adam. "I will say this only once," she said, working to control her voice. "If I ever catch either of you ganging up on anyone or attacking anyone else, *anyone* else, you will be expelled. Do you understand?"

"Yes, ma'am," both boys mumbled in unison.

Shaking, she moved back into the schoolhouse and shut the door, then threw the rest of her lunch into the wastebasket, put her head down on her desk and burst into tears. What made people attack other people just because they were different? Was it something in human nature? Something handed down from the time of cavemen?

She sat up and mopped at her wet cheeks. These undisciplined children needed much, much more than arithmetic and spelling lessons.

At midnight Ivan laid his pen aside and closed his eyes. It had been five years since he had laid eyes on Annamarie. Would she even remember what he looked like?

He knew the years had changed him; shoving logs into the hungry jaws of a muley saw had added muscles to his once-slim frame, but working day and night was wearing him down. He ate too much stale bread and not enough meat, and at night he dulled his loneliness by reading the books he had brought with him from his father's library. He hungered to talk to someone, to have a real conversation beyond "That'll be two dollars for the seed, mister" and "Ready for another log here, Panovsky."

He sighed and read over his letter.

Dearest Anna,
I miss you very, very much. I am working hard

at the sawmill during the day and at the feed store at night to save money for our future. The day draws closer when the house I am building for us will be finished, and soon I can send you the train ticket that will bring you to Oregon so we can be together.

I know that many years have passed, but please do not be discouraged. We will be together again, I promise.

Ivan

He jerked out of the chair and had his hand on the doorknob when he remembered that a cup of coffee at the Smoke River restaurant across the street cost five cents. But if he wanted to see Annamarie before she was another year older, he could not afford to waste a penny. He clenched his jaw and decided he would do without.

Chapter Six

After a restorative evening spent making new lesson plans and reminding herself why she had decided that teaching school was something she would be good at, she gave up and stumbled into bed for a fitful night's sleep. The next morning Christina started off for school with a renewed sense of dedication and six molasses cookies in her lunch bag for fortification. As she drew near the school yard she lifted her head at a sharp sound.

What on earth? It was only eight o'clock in the morning, far too early for any of her students to arrive. The sound came once again, followed by a thunderous crash. She quickened her pace to see what was going on.

At first all she could see was dust. Then it slowly settled to reveal a man straddling a felled tree. His back was facing her, his frame almost obscured by thick evergreen branches. He raised an ax and began lopping off limbs, working his way methodically from the thick trunk to the tip, hacking his way through the frothy greenery and tossing it into a pile. Finally he began slicing his ax into the tree itself, cutting the wood up into short lengths. Suddenly he made a half turn toward her and she gasped. It was the man she'd barreled into in the bakery!

Without looking up, he propped a short length of wood on a flat stump, raised the ax, and with a sharp crack split it neatly in half. Then he began splitting that into woodstove-sized lengths. He stopped to roll the sleeves of his red plaid shirt above his elbows, revealing tanned, muscular arms. That night at the bakery she hadn't noticed how well built he was; she guessed she'd been too distracted when she'd spilled ink all over Uncle Charlie's polished wooden floor to notice much of anything. But she remembered him— he was the man with the loaves of bread.

He hadn't heard her approach but kept steadily working away, keeping his back to her and his head bent. She noticed his overlong dark hair tended to curl at his neck.

The *ka-chunk* sounds continued as she edged past and didn't cease until she heard the laughter and chatter of her students as they began to arrive. "Oh, man," Billy Rowell sighed. "Who chopped all that wood? My ma makes my Uncle Hawk do that every Saturday."

She couldn't answer. She realized she had no idea what the man's name was.

For the rest of the morning she struggled to focus her thoughts on arithmetic sums and three-syllable spelling words, but the image of the slim dark-haired figure chopping wood in the school yard kept popping into her brain.

After an extremely disheartening day, she dismissed the class and headed for the sanctity of her room over the bakery and a fortifying cup of tea. On the stairs up to her apartment she paused to find

Uncle Charlie gazing up at her, his round face shining. "You help, missy? Must go to train, meet new wife."

"Your wife? Really?"

"From China," he said proudly. "Brand-new. You sell cookies to customers while I get married?"

"What, me? I've never sold a thing in my life."

"Easy to learn," Charlie assured her. "Count cookies, take money."

She hesitated.

"Give you nice lemon cake," he entreated.

That did it. She hungered for something sweet, something indulgent to fortify her for another long evening of making lesson plans. "How long will you be gone?"

"Not long. Meet train, go to church, get marry. Then come back. Take only one hour."

Christina laughed out loud. "Surely you will want to spend more time with your new wife?"

Incredibly, the smiley round face was suffused with pink. "Plenty time tonight, after bakery close. I cook special supper."

He looked so eager she simply couldn't refuse. "All right, Charlie. I will mind the bakery for an hour. But don't blame me if your customers are disappointed."

"Ah. Maybe *two* cakes. You choose."

The minute he disappeared out the door, Christina positioned herself behind the big glass case of baked goods and prayed that no customers would show up. Through the front window she watched Uncle Charlie hurry down the street past the Golden Partridge saloon toward the train station.

The entire bakery smelled enticing! She studied the orderly rows of oatmeal, molasses and chocolate cookies. Did she dare filch one? She chose one with a crinkly top and had just bitten off a big mouthful when the bell over the door tinkled. Oh, mercy, a customer!

Hurriedly she tried to swallow the cookie, but her dry throat refused to cooperate. Stricken, she looked up to see the firewood man in front of her.

Ivan closed the door and stopped dead at the sight of the young woman. Then he remembered she was the new teacher. "Where is Charlie?"

She looked stricken. Her eyes grew even larger and her mouth looked like she was trying to say something, but nothing came out. Instead, she shook her head.

"No Charlie?"

Another shake.

"He come back?"

She nodded.

"When?"

She pointed urgently at her cheek, and after a long pause she swallowed and gasped for air. "Charlie will be back in an hour. He has gone to the train station to meet his new wife."

Ivan blinked. "New wife? She's arrived already?"

"So he says," Christina managed. "He left me in charge."

"Ah. He leave bread for me, Ivan Panovsky? I live across the street, in room over feed store."

She smiled. "My name is Christina Marnell. I'm the new—"

"Schoolteacher," he finished. "I know. I stack wood at schoolhouse this morning."

"Oh, that was you? I heard the chopping." She ran her eyes over the bakery case, then the counter where the cash register stood. "What kind of bread was it?"

"Stale," he answered flatly.

"I beg your pardon? Did you say—"

"Yes, is stale. Charlie give me two loaves every night after work."

"Must it be *stale* bread?"

Ivan exhaled a long breath. "Yes, is stale bread. Charlie give for free."

Her dark eyebrows went up. "Oh," she said after a long moment. "I see." She studied his face with penetrating blue eyes. "Well, let me look…"

All at once he wanted to explain. "I save up for train ticket," he blurted out. "For my—for someone in New York."

He thought a shadow of something—disappointment?—fell across her face.

"You need not explain, Mr. Panovsky. If you will wait just a minute I will wrap up your bread." She turned away, snatched up two loaves of bread, which Ivan knew Charlie had baked fresh that morning, and began to bundle them up in brown grocer's paper.

He couldn't utter a word. She must know that wasn't stale bread, so why had she…?

"Here you are, Mr—"

"Ivan."

She smiled up at him, her lovely eyes warm and understanding. "I hope you enjoy it."

"Thank you. Is very good bread."

At that moment Uncle Charlie swept in through the back entrance, looking for all the world like a cat with a surfeit of cream. Christina stifled a grin.

"New wife very beautiful!" he announced. "I take home extra-big cake."

"Congratulations, Charlie," Christina said quietly.

The Chinese man peered at the parcel under Ivan's arm. "You have bread?"

"Yes," Ivan acknowledged. "Thank you, Charlie. Also, congratulations. Not every day a man is married."

Christina ran up the back stairs, set the kettle on the stove for tea and thought about Charlie's new bride. Imagine coming halfway around the world to marry someone you'd never laid eyes on before! Charlie was positively beaming with happiness; she wondered if his bride felt the same way.

But why on earth would she be happy, finding herself all alone in a new country? She sipped her tea and thought about it. Marriage, even to someone you knew well, was a terrible gamble. Both her parents had been dissatisfied, so unhappy that one day Papa had just walked away, and a year later both he and Mama had died.

Christina had never even considered marrying. Long before she was allowed to wear long skirts she had decided marriage was risky and her life's work would be teaching, bringing the world of ideas to young minds.

* * *

Ivan kept a sharp eye on the window of the second-floor apartment across the street, wishing that the schoolteacher, Christina Marnell, would pull back the curtains so he could see her. Every night she worked at her desk, twisting a strand of her dark hair in concentration or staring absently out the window.

Tonight was no different. He pulled off two hunks of bread and sliced off some cheese with his pocket-knife and stared across the street. He wished he could talk to her. Deep inside he admitted he was lonely. The men at the sawmill and the customers at Stockett's Feed & Seed didn't come close to making him feel less alone.

But there is Anna. And she will be here soon.

Of course, they had exchanged letters, but he hadn't laid eyes on her for so many years she might not even know him! He gulped a swallow of black coffee and set the mug on his desk. Worse, *he* might not know *her*.

By the time he had devoured half the loaf of bread and a hunk of the goat cheese Carl Ness at the mercantile had saved for him, his gnawing physical hunger had subsided. Now he sat sipping his coffee and studying the figure framed in the window across from him.

What would it be like to talk to her? Maybe go on a picnic, or walk back to the bakery from the schoolhouse with her some afternoon? He suspected girls thought he was dull because he did not speak good English. And if a girl did speak to him, he felt tongue-tied. People thought he was unfriendly. Perhaps he *was* unfriendly. Or maybe he hadn't met a girl he really wanted to talk to until now. Maybe he could invite Miss Marnell to tea at the restaurant beside the hotel… Ah, no, he could not. Tea would cost money, and he must save every penny for Annamarie.

He dropped his head into his hands. He loved Annamarie. He hoped what he was doing was the right thing.

Chapter Seven

It rained steadily for three straight days, a soft fall rain that left the air smelling of hay and pine trees, but kept Christina's students inside at recess and—worse—during the lunch hour. Today she racked her brain to think up something—anything—to keep them entertained while they were all cooped up together.

A spelling bee? No, they had held one on Monday.

A geography contest? Unfortunately, that had been Tuesday's challenge.

An arithmetic race? That had been held on Wednesday.

Now here it was Thursday, and she decided the afternoon would be spent in teams of two, studying geography and long division. As usual, Sammy Greywolf picked up any new material long before the other students, which earned him smirks and surreptitious pokes when she wasn't looking.

By three o'clock she was tired out. If it rained again tomorrow, she would…what? She could read aloud, perhaps a chapter of *The Last of the Mohicans* or a tale from *One Thousand and One Nights*. Or they could play History Charades, where the students acted out historical events. Kurt Jorgensen would love that—he craved being the center of attention.

At three o'clock, the children shrugged into their coats and knitted wool caps and rain boots and bolted outside into the wet. Christina slowly gathered up her lesson notebook and an advanced-reading workbook and made her way to the schoolroom door, unfurled her umbrella and started for home. Ahead of her she noticed that Adam Lynford was carrying Edith Ness's books. That made her smile.

When she reached the bakery, she stopped short at the window and stared. A unfamiliar woman was standing behind the glass display case, a short, very tiny, woman with a bun of jet-black hair, wearing an odd-looking long-sleeved tunic of dark blue silky-looking material and matching trousers.

Charlie's new wife.

The instant Christina moved through the doorway, the woman's black eyes met hers. Christina extended her hand. "I am Christina Marnell," she said to introduce herself. "I live upstairs." She gestured at the ceiling.

The woman's face lit up. "I am Iris Ming, though I expect some will call me Missus Charlie."

"You speak English very well!" Christina exclaimed.

The woman smiled. "I attended a missionary school in my village in China. The nuns taught me to speak English."

"Welcome to Smoke River, Mrs. Ming."

"Oh, thank you! It is quite strange here, so different from China. But I like it. I like especially the roses."

"Roses?"

"Along the fences in front of the houses, yellow and red and pink, even though it is almost winter. Soon I will have a garden—vegetables and flowers. Tomorrow I will dig up the earth in front of my house with my new shovel."

"You have a new shovel?"

The Chinese woman nodded. "A wedding gift from Charlie."

"Charlie is no fool," Christina blurted out. Both women laughed.

She bought half a dozen molasses cookies, and with a friendly wave at Iris Ming she climbed the stairs to her apartment. While she ate her supper of scrambled eggs and toast she idly thought about Adam Lynford walking the Ness girl home, and a little pain darted into her chest. Nobody had ever walked *her* home. She wondered what it would have been like.

Christina tightened her grip on the satchel and stuffed her free hand into her skirt pocket. This morning was downright cold! As she drew near the schoolhouse she noted the stack of wood against the front wall had been replenished. As the days grew colder, she needed to keep the schoolroom toasty.

Even so, after a morning of reading recitations and multiplication problems, at lunchtime all her students bolted out the door into the chilly school yard. The boys engaged in rough games of kickball or Run Sheep Run; the girls stood in tight circles of two or three, chattering away like magpies.

She watched covert glances slide from one group

to another, after which the whispering girls bent their heads together conspiratorially. Young girls certainly liked to gossip! Why could they not get along with each other? She remembered how painful it had been for her, being laughed at and excluded because of her limp and her interest in books and learning. It hurt so much some mornings her stomach ached at the thought of one more day of school. Young girls tolerated no one who was different; they wanted other girls to be just like them!

She kept a sharp eye peeled for anyone being excluded or picked on. Among the boys, only Sammy Greywolf was not accepted. Surprisingly it was only partly because of his Indian heritage; mostly Sammy's treatment was jealousy over his obviously quick mind and ready answers. It put all the other boys to shame.

Nine-year-old Teddy MacAllister was an exception. Teddy often went out of his way to strike up a game of marbles with Sammy, and today one of the younger girls, Roxanna Jensen, asked to join them. That was met with hoots of derision from both sides of the yard. Roxanna, however, excelled at marbles. She just grinned at the boys gathering around and knocked the biggest marble out of the ring.

At what age did boys and girls start to get along with each other? she wondered. Teddy MacAllister seemed partial to little Manette Nicolet, and so did Billy Rowell. But sunny-spirited Manette was friendly with everyone, even Kurt Jorgensen. Kurt, however, was more interested in lording it over the other boys than paying attention to anyone who wore a pinafore and a dress.

Christina took a bite of her sandwich and went on staring out the window. One morning last week Ivan Panovsky had turned up early with his ax and chopped wood for an hour before school started. And then—wonder of wonders!—Kurt Jorgensen had shown up early, as well. He helped stack all the wood Ivan split, and when the tall, lean man acknowledged the boy's presence, Kurt began to talk. And talk.

Ivan gave short, straight answers to Kurt's questions, and Christina finally understood it was not disinterest on Ivan's part but his rather taciturn way. Kurt's eagerness to be recognized and accepted made her heart ache. If she remembered correctly, Kurt had no father.

She took another bite of her sandwich and thought about Ivan Panovsky. She had to admit he interested her. The long-limbed sawmill worker was still subsisting on stale bread and moldy cheese; she knew this because she had asked Iris Ming about it, and Carl Ness at the mercantile had volunteered more information. "What that Russkie does with all my unsold cheese is anybody's guess," Carl had said. "Foreigners are funny!"

Foreigners? Ivan was no more a foreigner than anyone else in Smoke River; almost everyone in the county came from some other country. She'd mentioned Carl's remark to the dressmaker, Verena Forester, and got an earful about the night Teddy's stepmother, Leah MacAllister, who was half-Chinese, challenged the entire town about who among them was "a foreigner" and who was not.

Had Ivan come from Russia as a young man? Perhaps that explained his quietness. Perhaps he was unsure of his English? But it was said that he read books at night, so...

She gave herself a shake. Her mind was wandering, and lunch hour was almost over. It was time to rein in her rambling thoughts and write eight new spelling words on the blackboard.

Chapter Eight

Ivan waited anxiously in the railway station ticket line while the matronly woman ahead of him finally finished her business, then stepped forward to spread his hard-earned cash—fifty-seven whole dollars—on the counter.

"I would like one ticket from New York City to Smoke River."

"Don'cha mean from Smoke River *to* New York?"

"No. I mail ticket to New York and lady will use to come to Smoke River. How long will letter take?"

The man's bushy rust-colored eyebrows waggled. "More'n a week, I'd say. Best send a wire to let the party know the ticket's comin,' so's they'll be watching for it." He waited expectantly, his finger poised over the telegraph key. "Who's this telegram going to?"

"Miss Annamarie Panovsky."

"Address?"

"Greenfield Hall for Young Women in New York City."

"That a college or somethin'? Wanna add a room number?"

"No. It is not a college. Is a— Is not a college."

The telegraph key clicked away and Ivan folded the long, four-section paper ticket, slipped it into his pre-addressed envelope and sealed it.

"Gonna take three stamps, mister. Fourteen cents, please."

He slid two nickels and four pennies across the counter and watched the man affix three small blue stamps to his letter, grinned and turned away. He'd done it! He'd scrimped and saved every penny to finish the house he was building so Annamarie could join him; she had waited almost five years and now she would be here in two weeks!

Every night he had prayed his sister hadn't given up on him, and every morning he dragged himself out of his cot and stumbled off to the sawmill for another grueling day of feeding logs onto the carriage chain to be sawed into lumber. After his mill shift he went to his other job, manning the cash register at the feed store. He earned two dollars every two weeks, and to increase his meager earnings, he felled pine trees out by the schoolhouse and cut them up into firewood for the teacher's potbellied stove. For every cord he split and stacked, the Smoke River school board paid him fifty cents.

Ever since Christina Marnell had come to town, he looked forward to cutting the firewood, and it wasn't because of the precious money he was paid. He liked being anywhere in her vicinity. If stacking wood outside her schoolroom was as close as he could get, he would settle for that. Often he stopped trimming branches or splitting kindling long enough to watch her slow, uneven progress along the path from town. How would a crippled woman manage when it started to snow in the winter and she would have to break trail to reach the schoolhouse? She should have a horse, like the Jensen girl and Teddy MacAllister, who rode to school from ranches outside of town.

He strode from the train station onto the main street. Today was Sunday, and he spent the next eight hours at Stockett's feed store selling prime alfalfa and wheat seed to the ranchers in the county. Afterward, he headed for the mercantile to lay in beans and potatoes and canned tomatoes for when Annamarie would arrive.

Halfway across the street he halted. Annamarie had lived all her life in New York City. What if she hated living in a little town out in Oregon? What if she didn't like canned tomatoes? What if…

All at once he was scared right down to his boot tops. *Holy Mother of God, what if I have made a mistake?*

After an early-morning snowfall, the board sidewalk was extremely slippery this morning. Christina limped along slowly until she reached the path leading to the schoolhouse, which she knew would be slow going with the snow and her halting pace. She had left extra early to give her time to build a good warm fire in the potbellied stove and warm up the schoolroom before the students arrived.

She stepped from the boardwalk onto the path and stopped in surprise. She'd expected it to be clogged with snow, but the path had been cleared! Someone had tramped through the new snow ahead of her to clear her way, and she found she could walk along with no trouble. Even on this crisp, cold morning, the gesture made her feel warm all over.

Another surprise awaited her inside the school-room. On her desk sat a shiny tin can full of pink roses! What a miracle, roses in the wintertime!

By nine o'clock the little stove in the corner had heated the room to a toasty warmth and students began arriving. Christina greeted each one with a smile. Roxanna Jensen and Teddy MacAllister were late, but she knew they came on horseback through the snow so she smiled and let them slip into their seats without a reprimand.

To her surprise the morning lessons in arithmetic and spelling went smoothly, and by two o'clock that afternoon Kurt and Adam reported the stack of fire-wood outside was almost depleted. "Don'cha want to cancel school tomorrow, Miss Marnell?"

"Now, why would I want to do that?"

"'Cuz it'll be cold without a fire in the stove," Adam answered.

"And Mr. Panovsky don't want to cut firewood in a snowstorm," Kurt added.

"Mr. Panovsky *does not* want to cut firewood," Christina corrected.

"Well, he doesn't!" Kurt insisted.

"I thought that perhaps with your help, he—"

"Naw," Kurt interrupted. "He won't let me near his ax. Says it's sharper than Whitey Poletti's razor and I shouldn't touch it. So, if it snows again tonight can we skip comin' to school tomorrow?"

"No, you may not," Christina said firmly. But she did wonder how Ivan would manage to cut more fire-wood for tomorrow if it continued to snow.

* * *

The locomotive from the East puffed out a final blast of steam and rolled to a halt at the station platform. Ivan stopped pacing up and down and scanned the passengers visible through the train windows. Not a sign of Annamarie.

But it has been so long I might not recognize her!

He was more nervous than he could ever remember. The house he was building for them was not finished yet, so all week long he'd spent every spare minute setting up an extra cot in his tiny bachelor quarters and adding a chest of drawers with a mirror. He'd filled his meager pantry with cans of corn and beans and had even washed the single window that looked out onto the street. His little apartment over the feed store would scarcely be big enough for the two of them, but until he could finish the house he was building it was all he could manage.

Would she like it?

He groaned. A much more important question was whether Annamarie would like *him*.

Passengers began stepping onto the station platform and he jerked his attention back to the train. He watched women bundled up in wool coats and scarves, men in overalls and sheepskin jackets, townspeople, farmers…but he saw no young single woman. At least no one young enough to be—

"Ivan! Ivan!" He spun around to find himself clasped tight in a pair of eager arms.

"Anna!" He swung her off her feet. "Oh, darling girl, I didn't see you get off the train. Where did you come from?"

She laughed. "From New York, of course. You sent the ticket, remember? It arrived two weeks ago. I let you know I was coming and, oh, Ivan, I'm here! I'm really here!" She hugged him again, then looked up into his face. "Oh, my, you look just the same!" She smacked a hasty kiss against his cheek and burst into tears.

"Anna? Anna, what is wrong?"

"N-nothing, I'm j-just so happy! I never, never dreamed this would ever really happen, that I would leave that awful—that we would be together again." She drew back and gazed up at him, her blue eyes shining. "Oh, Ivan, you are so handsome!"

He couldn't help laughing at that. Handsome? Him? Only a sister who loved him could ever think of him as handsome. But she— God in heaven, little Annamarie was all grown up and so pretty with her creamy skin and long dark curls it made his throat ache.

He grabbed her frayed tapestry bag in one hand, draped his other arm about her slim shoulders and turned her toward town. "Come, my beautiful little sister, let me take you to your new home."

She danced at his side along the board sidewalk, and when they reached his small room over the feed store she was delighted with everything—the privacy curtain he had erected around her cot, the mirror over the bureau, even his collection of canned food. "Ooh, tomatoes! I *love* tomatoes!" She flung her arms around his waist. "Oh, Ivan, I am so happy to finally be here with you!"

He let out a long sigh of relief. He should not have worried.

Chapter Nine

Monday morning at nine o'clock Christina experienced two severe shocks. After her students tumbled into the schoolhouse and gathered around the potbellied stove, shivering and chattering as usual, Ivan Panovsky of all people walked through the doorway. Suddenly she could have heard a pin drop in her classroom.

Ivan led by the hand the most beautiful young girl Christina had ever laid eyes on, petite and slim, with a long tumble of dark curls about her shoulders and eyes the color of a summer sky. Kurt Jorgensen gaped at her and dropped into his seat with an audible thump.

Ivan and the girl approached her desk. "Miss Marnell, I like to introduce my sister, Annamarie, from New York."

The girl gave her a tentative smile.

"How do you do, Annamarie. Welcome to the Smoke River school."

"Anna," Ivan prompted, "tell Miss Marnell how old you are and what is your grade level in school."

"I am twelve years old, Miss Marnell. Well, almost twelve. My birthday is in December, so I won't really be twelve until almost Christmas, but…" Her lovely face lit up in a smile. "I promise I will *act* like I am twelve."

Ivan stepped forward. "Miss Marnell, I may speak in private?" He took her elbow and conducted her into the school yard outside. "I tell you some about Anna. I have not seen her for almost five years. When I came to Oregon after my father died, Anna was only six years old."

"Has she been attending school in New York?"

Such a look of pain crossed his face that she bit her lip.

"After I leave New York, Anna's mother, who is my stepmother, died and Anna... My poor sister went to live in orphanage. I work hard to bring her here to Smoke River and live with me. I am her only family."

"And it has taken you five years to do this?" Christina said. "You must have worked very hard."

"Yes. I build house for us to live in. That took a long time."

"Can Annamarie read and write?"

Ivan laughed. "Anna can read anything in print, and afterward she can write it all down from remembering."

Christina nodded. This girl would be a challenge for Sammy Greywolf. That should prove interesting, since Sammy's primary pesterer was Kurt Jorgensen, who had taken one look at Ivan's pretty, dark-haired sister and collapsed into his seat.

"There is something else," Ivan added. "Anna is very smart, and she loves books, but...she does not need much education."

Christina frowned. "Oh? And why is that?"

"She will grow up very beautiful and she will

marry. In old country, a wife does not need much education."

"What?" She almost screeched the word. "Ivan, that is outrageous! If your sister is gifted, as you say, she will want more for herself than just being a wife."

"No. Being a wife, it is enough."

Christina clenched her fists. "You are wrong, Ivan. Very, very wrong."

His dark eyes narrowed. "I am not wrong. That is how all girls are brought up in my father's family, and in my father's father's family."

"Where was this?"

"In Ukraine. And also in New York, when my father left Ukraine to come to America."

"What about your mother? Did she believe this?"

"My mother, yes. And Anna's mother, my stepmother, she obey my father's wishes."

Christina felt an explosion building inside. "Thank you for bringing your sister to school, Ivan. I will look out for her. But I must warn you that I will also fight your antiquated ideas about education for girls. I will oppose that with every ounce of strength I can muster."

His jaw tightened, but he said nothing. Then unexpectedly he grasped her hand. "Thank you, Christina. You will do what is right for my Anna."

She turned away. "I will look out for her, Ivan. Do not worry." She stomped back inside to find an unexpectedly quiet classroom. For once Kurt and Adam sat without sneaking punches at each other across the aisle or dipping one of Roxanna Jensen's long blond braids in the inkwell. Instead, both boys were staring in dumbfounded admiration at the new student, Annamarie Panovsky, who still stood uncertainly before Christina's desk.

"Please take a seat, Annamarie."

The girl turned and then stood scanning the available spaces. Most of the older girls had a desk to themselves; three or four of the younger girls shared seats. Christina watched with distress as the older girls—Sally Lynford and Edith Ness, spread their skirts wide to take up more space. Roxanna curled her legs under her to leave no room at all.

Annamarie stood still, assessing the situation, and then Manette Nicolet scrambled out of her seat. "Come and sit here with me. I have plenty of room."

Annamarie smiled at the little French girl and settled herself beside her.

"Thank you, Manette," Christina said quietly. Then she moved on to the day's geography lesson, pointing out where Russia and the Ukraine were. She assigned the advanced group a difficult set of long division problems. Annamarie and Manette worked together on one slate, and Christina quickly saw that Ivan's sister would become one of three girls in the advanced section, along with Noralee Ness and Roxanna Jensen. And she would make certain that Ivan knew of it.

By lunchtime it also became clear that Annamarie was reading at an advanced level. She would be the *only* girl in the advanced group; the others were Sammy Greywolf, Teddy MacAllister and Adam Lynford.

After their reading recitations, Christina released

them for lunch and sank onto her desk chair to eat her sandwich, idly watching out the window as the students milled about the school yard.

She did not like what she saw. The boys were engaged in a rough-and-tumble game of kickball; Manette and Roxanna were jumping rope, and all the other girls had formed a tight circle apart from them. Annamarie stood alone in the middle of the school yard, twisting her hands together and staring at the ground.

Christina's stomach tightened. How cruel young girls could be! What got into children that made them so mean to one another? Was it something they learned from their parents or from their brothers and sisters and the other students? She debated whether she should walk outside and reprimand them, and she was halfway out of her chair when something unexpected happened.

Little Manette dropped her jump rope, marched straight over to Annamarie and took her hand. *Oh, bless her sweet little heart.*

Annamarie smiled down at the girl, and after a moment the knot of older girls broke up and sashayed past the rope jumpers. When they entered the schoolhouse, Christina could scarcely stand to look at any of them. Her heart ached so much she couldn't have spoken if she had wanted to. She shook her head. She would never understand such behavior. Never.

Late that evening a soft knock sounded on her door, and when Christina opened it Iris Ming stood before her. "Charlie and I wish to invite you to supper tomorrow night," she announced with a broad smile. "And Ivan and his sister, Annamarie, will come, too. To make her feel welcome."

Christina hesitated. Whenever she was around Ivan she felt unsettled inside. She had no idea why, but the thought of sitting down to supper in the same room as Ivan Panovsky left butterflies careening around in her stomach. And after this morning's conversation about his sister's education she was so furious with him she didn't think she could be civil.

But she couldn't refuse Iris. She would simply conquer her butterflies and her anger and try to be a polite guest.

Christina tapped on the white-painted front door of the frame house opposite the back entrance to Uncle Charlie's bakery. The door swung open and a smiling Annamarie drew her inside. "Uncle Charlie is in the kitchen with Mrs. Charlie, so I am answering the door." The girl leaned toward her. "My brother is already sitting at the dinner table," she whispered.

Christina removed her blue wool shawl, squared her shoulders and followed the girl into the pleasant dining room. Instantly Ivan Panovsky jerked up out of his chair and stood beside the lace-covered dining table, smiling at her uncertainly.

"Good evening, Miss Marnell."

He looked so stiff and ill at ease in his dark trousers and crisp blue shirt that she wanted to smile. "Good evening, Ivan."

In the silence that fell Christina found her gaze

drawn to the man standing next to his sister. She was trying hard not to like him with his outdated ideas about education for girls and his plans for his sister, but when his gaze met and held hers, for a moment she forgot to breathe. His eyes were an odd shade of green, like forest ferns, and so clear and steady she felt a shiver crawl up her backbone. He looked...tired. Distressed in some way she couldn't explain. His expression was guarded and intent at the same time, and she found the combination oddly unnerving. Maybe he was afraid of her because she had made no secret of her opinions about education for girls.

And then his mouth curved into a smile and a fist slammed into her chest. Suddenly there wasn't enough air in the room. A soft, insistent thrumming rose in her ears, and she realized that she was hearing her own heartbeat.

What was the matter with her?

Annamarie chattered away as if nothing unusual was happening. But something *was* happening. Something extraordinary that she had never experienced before in all her twenty-three years. It was like being filled with sunshine.

"Miss Marnell? *Miss Marnell?*"

Christina jerked back to awareness. "Yes, Anna?"

The girl's voice was hesitant. "I wanted to ask you about school."

"What about school? I think you will do very well, Anna. You appear to be ahead of most of the students."

"It...it's not about that." She shot a glance at Ivan.

"It's about the other girls. Do you know why they don't like me?"

Christina drew in a long breath and flicked a look at Ivan. He had an odd, puzzled expression on his face. "Anna, I think people, young girls especially, are wary of things that stand out, things that are different from them. I don't know why this is so, but I know it is true because it happened to me."

Ivan reached for his sister's hand. "Go on," he said quietly.

She drew in a long breath. "Well, I was twelve when I was crippled on my way home from school one day. I was walking across a narrow bridge, and a horse and buggy ran me down. My ankle was crushed. From that day on, I walked with a limp."

"And the other students were unkind?" he asked.

Christina swallowed. "Yes, they were. Extremely unkind. But even before I hurt my ankle, my classmates, especially the girls, taunted me because I preferred books and spent so much time at my studies. After my accident, it was worse."

"The other girls won't talk to me," Annamarie said. "And…and…" Her voice choked off.

Charlie shot to his feet. "That not fair! Look same, talk same, no different." He crooked a finger at her. "You come to kitchen, help with birthing day cake?"

When Annamarie disappeared into the kitchen, Ivan leaned forward. "Can you help her to fit in?"

"I can certainly try, Ivan. But…there are two things I cannot change. One is that Anna is by far the prettiest girl in school. And the other is that she is smarter than most of the other students."

"Those are not good things?" Ivan questioned.

"Those are very good things, Ivan. And I have an idea that may help."

Chapter Ten

"Ivan?"

"Yes, Anna?" They had just left the bakery, carrying two loaves of day-old bread and a dozen chocolate cookies.

"You like her, don't you?"

He frowned at his sister. "Who? You mean Mrs. Ming, Uncle Charlie's wife?"

"No, I mean Miss Marnell, my teacher."

He drew in a careful breath. "What makes you think I like her?"

Annamarie gave a peal of delighted laughter. "Because every time you hear her name, you twitch."

"Twitch? I do not twitch! Anna, you read too many books."

"No, I don't. I am just very observant."

Ivan suppressed a groan. His little sister was more than observant. She was...she was intelligent far beyond her eleven years. Whatever he had revealed to Annamarie about his feelings, he prayed it was hidden from Christina. Annamarie had sensed something, but the thought of anyone *else* sensing it made him nervous.

The following day was Saturday, the air clear and crisp, and Christina persuaded Annamarie to accompany her to visit Verena Forester.

"You didn't tell me why we are visiting the dress-maker," the girl pointed out.

"No, I didn't, did I? You must wait and see."

When they entered the dressmaker's shop, Verena was arranging new pattern books on the counter. Her dark eyebrows rose when she spied Christina. "Well, now, Miss Marnell. Surely you haven't worn out your new shirtwaist already?"

"No, of course not. But now I am in need of a dress or two. Something in a soft blue, perhaps? And a nice calico print."

"I thought you preferred dark skirts and plain white shirtwaists," Verena snapped.

"I do. The dresses are for Miss Panovsky here."

"Oh?" The eyebrows climbed another notch.

"Oh!" Annamarie gasped. "Oh, no, Miss Marnell."

"Oh, yes, Anna." She leaned down and spoke in the girl's ear. "You should look more like the other girls."

"But Ivan—"

"I have made an arrangement with your brother, so it will do no good to argue. Now…" She turned to the dressmaker. "What would you advise, Verena? A lightweight wool challis?"

The three women pored over dress patterns and fingered bolts of fabric for over an hour until a decision was made—a gored skirt in blue wool, two pale blue shirtwaists with ruffles at the neck and cuffs and a pretty dress of rose challis. After all the measurements were made, Annamarie turned to Christina and her eyes filled with tears.

"Oh, thank you, Miss Marnell. I have never had such beautiful things to wear!"

When they left the shop, Annamarie impulsively took Christina's hand. "Ivan will be so proud of me!"

"Ivan," Christina said, suppressing a smile, "is a man. And because he is a man, he will most likely not notice."

"But he notices you," Annamarie said.

Christina stopped short in the middle of the sidewalk. *"What?"*

"He notices you all the time, Miss Marnell."

An inexplicable bolt of pure joy shot into her chest. "That is pure nonsense!" she protested. But she found she had to work to keep her voice steady.

"No, it isn't, Miss Marnell. I am very observant. Ivan does notice you, he really does. Just you watch him."

Watch him! She would do nothing of the kind. She needed to change the subject immediately.

"Anna, when are you moving into your new house?"

"Tomorrow, after church. Ivan is installing the windows today. We don't have very much furniture, but Ivan is building me a canopy bed. Just imagine! With a real curtain all around it, made out of printed flour sacks from Mr. Ness at the mercantile. And we have a big stove like Mrs. Charlie's, and next week he is building a table and some chairs."

"I am glad for you, Anna."

"Aren't you glad for Ivan, too? He has worked so hard! I think that's why he is so thin. He hasn't been eating enough. But now... Oh, Miss Marnell, now he can eat anything he wants, not just stale bread and cheese. Isn't that wonderful?"

Christina stared at her. Ivan Panovsky was a good man, even if he did have old-fashioned ideas. She admired his perseverance and what he had accomplished. He cared about Annamarie, and it showed.

They parted at the bakery, and Annamarie skipped across the street to Ivan's room above the feed store. Elated, Christina climbed the stairs to her small apartment to work on lesson plans for the coming week. She could hardly wait for Monday morning. Verena had promised that Annamarie's blue wool skirt and one shirtwaist would be ready.

Chapter Eleven

Ivan pounded another nail into the bottom bed slat, then muscled the structure into the room he'd planned for Annamarie. He had painted it her favorite color, a pale blue. All his hard work, the grueling shifts at the sawmill and the long hours at Stockett's Feed & Seed had taken its toll, but it had been worth it. Annamarie was here now. He would install the last window in the small front parlor, and then he and his sister would move into their new home.

He smiled as he drove in the last nail. He was bone tired and thin, his body well-muscled but under-nourished for so long his clothes hung off his body, but he didn't regret it. Annamarie still thought he was her handsome older brother, so what did loose trousers matter?

He wished that Christina would also think he was handsome. No matter how tired he was after work at the sawmill each day, he always looked forward to cutting firewood for the schoolhouse. He would bet a week's wages Christina didn't care if he was handsome. From what he had observed, she judged people by what they were like on the inside, not how they looked. At least he hoped that was true. Many things about the schoolteacher were puzzling; for one thing, he could not understand why she was so dead set on Annamarie's education. His sister was smart, yes. And beautiful. She would marry early, as her mother had.

Every male in town thought Christina was the prettiest girl in Smoke River, but it was puzzling that she showed no interest in any of them. One of her students, Kurt Jorgensen, the lad who occasionally helped him stack firewood, practically saluted when Christina spoke. She must be very strict to frighten a strapping boy like Kurt into behaving.

He could understand that. He himself was a little frightened of Christina Marnell. He did a lot of thinking about her, but he had to admit he did not know how to talk to her. Every time he looked at her his mind went fuzzy and his tongue seemed to freeze.

Christina shoved another chunk of firewood into the potbellied stove in the corner, brushed the loose bark off her hands and limped back to her desk. When nine o'clock came, students began trickling through the door in twos and threes. They seemed in high spirits for a frosty Monday morning; the two oldest boys, Kurt and Adam, shadow-boxed their way to their desks and sent sidelong glances at the girls who were finding their seats.

Roxanna Jensen scooted inside just two minutes after nine. "Teddy is still unsaddling his horse," she panted as she removed her knitted scarf. "And that new girl, Anna, is petting him."

"Petting Teddy? Or petting the horse?" Christina's question was met with a spatter of giggles.

"Petting his horse," the girl answered. "Not petting *my* horse—Jane-girl."

Christina blinked. "Your horse is named Jane-girl?"

Roxanna shrugged. "My pa named her," she admitted.

Kurt snickered. "Jane-girl, huh? That's a dumb name."

"Says who?" Roxanna shot.

"Says—" Kurt broke off when the schoolhouse door opened and Annamarie stepped inside. She was bundled up to her ears in a heavy knit shawl, but Christina saw at a glance she was wearing her new blue wool skirt and a striped blue shirtwaist. The girl's eyes sparkled and her cheeks were rosy.

Kurt's freckled face colored. He half rose out of his seat, his gaze fastened on her.

"Whew," Adam breathed, staring at her.

His sister, Sally Lynford, huffed out a breath. "Adam!" she said. "Close your mouth. You've seen girls before."

"Not like her," Adam murmured.

Oblivious, Annamarie unwound her shawl, tossed back her dark curls and approached Christina's desk. "I'm sorry I'm late, Miss Marnell. I stopped to help—"

"Teddy's been unsaddling his own horse since he was seven years old," Edith Ness muttered. "I'm sure he didn't need any help."

Kurt closed his mouth with a snap. Adam craned his neck to keep Annamarie in his field of vision, and Edith bit her lip and stared at the top of her desk.

Christina swallowed a smile and rapped the ruler on her desk to call the class to order. "Now," she said in her most teacherly voice, "this morning we will begin with reading aloud. Edith, would you start?" She handed a worn red volume to the girl.

Edith rose and read the title in a bored monotone. *"'The Adventures of Robin Hood.'"*

An excited cry erupted from Sally. "Oh, Robin Hood, really? *Really?* Ooh, let me read, Miss Marnell, please? I've always wanted to read about Robin Hood. Please?"

"Aw, siddown, Sally," Kurt muttered under his breath.

Christina sighed. All she wanted to do was teach her pupils how to read, to add and subtract with accuracy and to know something about the world beyond Smoke River. But she was finding that much of teaching had nothing to do with reading or arithmetic; it had to do with who her students were on the inside—what they liked or disliked or admired or envied, and how they expressed it. Some days she felt as if she were the student, not the teacher.

The morning dragged on through arithmetic problems and reading recitations, and when lunchtime came the class pounded out the door in high spirits. Christina nibbled on her apple and focused her gaze through the window at the school yard outside.

Three boys and a girl—Roxanna Jensen—hunched over a game of marbles. Sally and Edith Ness stood patiently turning a jump rope for Noralee, who seemed indefatigable as she skipped in time with their rhyme: "One for Monday, washday. Two for Tuesday

when we iron. Three for Wednesday when we…"
Adam was helping Kurt stack firewood, and Sammy
Greywolf, Teddy MacAllister and Billy Rowell were
gathered around Teddy's roan mare, discussing horses
or saddles or whatever boys discussed.

Annamarie was nowhere in sight.

Concerned, Christina ventured out the door and
walked all the way around the schoolhouse. No sign
of Annamarie. On her second slow circuit around
the building she glimpsed a spot of blue some yards
off the path, and there she was, leaning against the
trunk of a red maple tree, her new wool skirt pulled
down over her knees.

"Anna, whatever are you doing out here?"

"Oh, Miss Marnell. I am reading your book about
Robin Hood. The girls wouldn't let me jump rope
with them. They said I was too short. I'm not too
short, am I? I'm taller than both Noralee and Edith,
so…" She studied the hem of her dress. "I think they
just didn't want me. Maybe they're mad because…
because Kurt and Adam are nice to me."

Christina's chest tightened. The girl's words made
her hurt inside.

"Besides," Annamarie continued, her voice quiet,
"I love these stories about Robin Hood."

Good for her, Christina exulted. Nothing her
brother, Ivan, could say would squash Annamarie's
interest in learning; she would make certain of that.
She left the girl to her reading and slowly made her
way back inside. Did Annamarie talk with her brother
about school? Did she tell him how unkindly she was
still being treated or whether she was unhappy? She

wondered if Ivan would blame her for not protecting his sister.

Suddenly she realized she wanted his approval. That thought was so startling she sank onto her desk chair and stared absently at the open dictionary. *Ivan does not matter,* she reminded herself. *It is Annamarie who matters.*

Chapter Twelve

"Hey, Panovsky, ya goin' to the dance?"

Ivan lowered his peavey pole and stood to one side of the log feed chain, breathing hard. "What dance?"

Smitty, the heavyset sawyer, stood at the opposite end of a big sugar-pine log, waiting for him to prod it onto the chain that would feed it into the saw blade. "Saturday night, out at Jensen's barn."

A dance? In all the years he had lived in Smoke River he had never once attended a dance. Until he had laid eyes on Christina Marnell, there had never been a girl he was interested in dancing with.

But he knew Annamarie would like going to a dance. He remembered dancing with his sister when she was very young, her tiny feet balanced on his shoes. She had loved it! He had even taught her the steps to the dances Mama and Papa had danced back in the old country.

"Maybe I will come," he called.

"You dance American, don'cha, Ivan?" Smitty yelled. "We figured you never came to any of the dances 'cuz you were a Russkie and you didn't know how to dance American."

Ivan snorted. "I bet I can dance better than you any day."

"Big words, Panovsky. Prove it! And get that log up here! We're gettin' bored with nuthin' to cut up."

Ivan shoved the pine log forward and listened to the whine of the saw as it bit into the wood. Would Christina be at the dance? Just thinking about being close to her, maybe even dancing with her, made his heart race.

By Saturday Annamarie was so excited she could scarcely eat any supper. "I can wear my new dress!" she exclaimed. "It's so pretty, Ivan. It has beautiful red and yellow flowers all over it, and a flounce at the hem, and— Ivan, you're not listening! Aren't you interested?"

"What? Of course, Anna. You will be most pretty girl there."

"Oh, I want to dance and dance! Will it be like back home when I used to dance with you?"

Ivan laughed. "It will not. Your feet are too big now to balance on my shoes."

"Oh, it will be such fun! I can hardly wait."

Neither could he, but for a different reason. Maybe he would work up the courage to ask Christina to dance with him. He swallowed hard. Or maybe not. The thought of being close to her made his mouth go dry as a pile of sawdust.

Jensen's barn was overflowing with people— ranchers, storekeepers, gray-haired women who sat together on the sidelines gossiping while men in clean jeans and pressed shirts whirled about the floor with women in long ruffled skirts. In one corner a band of sorts—two guitars, a violin and a washtub bass—boomed a thumping rhythm into the over-heated space. Long tables were laden with potato salad and coleslaw, baked beans, corn bread, platters of ham and fried chicken and apple and cherry pies. A rotund, balding man stood behind a two-by-twelve plank propped on two sawhorses that served as a bar, dispensing shots of whiskey and glasses of lemonade. The air smelled of ladies' perfumes, hay bales, sweat and bay rum shaving lotion.

Annamarie clutched his arm. "Oh, Ivan, just look! Everyone looks so beautiful. So dressed up. And all that food! I could eat myself silly."

Ivan patted his sister's hand. "You eat. I am going to—"

"Hey, Panovsky!" A russet-bearded man punched his shoulder. "I see you made it. You bring your lady?"

"This is my sister, Annamarie, from New York. Anna, meet Simon Smalley. We work at sawmill together."

Simon snatched off his battered hat. "How do, Miss Panovsky. Thought we'd never get your brother to a dance, but you seem to have done the trick."

Smitty popped up at Simon's elbow. "So, Panovsky, where's all this fancy dancin' you been bragging on?"

Just then there was a lull in the music. Ivan gave the plump sawyer a long, level look, then turned to his sister and held out his hand. "Anna?"

Instantly she stepped to his side and reached her free hand to his shoulder. Ivan laid his fingers near her collarbone and began to whistle a folk tune, and together the two of them began a series of intricate side and back steps, ending in a stomp.

Simon stepped back as they danced past him, and suddenly Adam Lynford gave a yelp, shook his dark hair out of his eyes and reached out his arm to grasp Annamarie's other shoulder. The steps weren't complicated, and in the next minute Noralee Ness joined the line beside Adam.

Then an elderly woman gave a shrill hollo and rushed across the floor to join in, grinning as Thad and Leah MacAllister linked arms with her. A smiling Verena Forester reached her hand to Thad's beefy shoulder and began to step beside him. The violin player picked up the simple folk melody Ivan was whistling; a guitar joined in, and then the washtub bass player began thumping away in rhythm. Within five minutes the music was booming and the line of dancers snaked around the room and looped back on itself, with Ivan and Annamarie in the lead.

On the sidelines Christina heard the folk tune and turned toward the dance floor, a glass of lemonade in her hand. She gaped at the sight. Good heavens, was that Ivan Panovsky out there in the middle of the floor? It was! One arm clasped his sister's shoulder and the other was propped smartly at his waist. This was quiet Ivan, who chopped wood for the schoolhouse and scarcely spoke two words to her?

My goodness, still waters certainly run deep.

And what intriguing steps he and the line of dancers he led were executing! Annamarie obviously knew the steps, so she guessed it was a folk dance. She had to laugh at Adam Lynford's face; he looked positively transfixed at actually touching the smiling Annamarie. Years from now perhaps they would both look back on this evening and remember it with a smile.

At the head of the line, Ivan led the dancing townspeople around and around the hall, and when he glanced up, he caught her gaze. His eyes held hers as he executed a nimble turn in place with a double stamp at the end.

Yes, still waters...

He looked...commanding as he led the line of people that snaked behind him. His dark hair tumbled over his forehead like a little boy's, but his movements were smooth and assured and all male. He and Annamarie were smiling at each other as if sharing a wonderful secret. Annamarie's face glowed, and Ivan...

Christina caught her breath. Ivan looked so boyish and yet so handsome at the same time, so much in control at the head of the line of dancers, his tall form moving with such assurance, she couldn't take her eyes off him.

She set her lemonade glass on the bench beside her, stood up and joined in as the line looped and circled about the floor. Ivan led them around and around the hall, and when the line looped back on itself again he caught Christina's gaze and gave another double stamp.

Annamarie laughed and grinned up at her brother. Then a red-haired millworker grasped Christina's shoulder and shuffled through the steps at her side. She vaguely remembered him; he worked at the mill with Ivan.

Annamarie looked radiantly happy, but it was Ivan she watched. When his eyes met hers he looked both proud and a bit shy, and a little bubble of something fizzed in her chest. What an interesting man Annamarie's brother was! She had never known anyone who could chop wood and execute these complicated steps with such panache and still be so pigheaded when it came to his sister's schooling.

At last he brought the dancers to a halt with a final decisive stamp, turned to Annamarie and bowed. The musicians who had picked up the tune finished with a flourish, and a cheer went up.

Ivan conducted his sister to the bar, where she downed a glass of lemonade and he tossed back a shot of whiskey. And then another. The band started up again, this time playing "Oh! Susannah," and Annamarie drifted off on the arm of Adam Lynford.

Christina kept her attention on Ivan. Now he was talking with two millworkers who kept pounding him on the back and gesturing at the whiskey bottle behind the bar. Then a tall older man climbed up on an apple crate and called for a square dance, and the milling crowd quickly formed into sets of four couples each. In the next minute, the tall man began to call instructions.

"Ladies to the center, gents to the side, don't get lost, now swing 'em wide…"

The caller's words made no sense to her, but everyone else seemed to understand them, even Annamarie and Adam, who had joined one of the sets. Christina wondered if Ivan was as adept at this square sort of dancing as he was at his folk dance.

The caller raised his voice over the raucous shouts of the dancers. "Swing 'er out and back once more, then walk her home and 'round the floor."

To Christina the directions were confusing, but they seemed to make sense to the square dancers. How did they keep track of all those instructions?

"You would like to try?" a voice spoke at her elbow. Ivan stood near, still breathing heavily. He smelled faintly of whiskey and wood smoke.

"Oh! I could never follow all those directions."

He lifted the lemonade glass out of her hand and set it on the bench. "I will show you."

He grasped her hand. "Come, they start a new set." He pulled her out onto the floor, where they joined Leah and Thad MacAllister and two other couples to form a square.

"Ivan, I don't think I can do this," she whispered. "I—I have trouble walking."

"Ah, that I know. But you will have no trouble, because I *can* do this. Trust me." He handed her into the center of the square, where three other women were extending their palms until they touched and then walking around in a circle. She returned to execute something called a "swing" and suddenly found herself in Ivan's arms. He turned her around and around, and he kept his arm about her waist during the caller's next series of instructions. He was so close it was hard to keep her thoughts straight, and whenever he lifted his hand away from her, she missed it.

She quickly learned that a "grand right and left" meant that she clasped hands with everyone as they walked around in a circle, and when she reached

Ivan again he held her close and they spun round and round. Her entire body was flooded with warmth at being near him.

She also learned that in square dancing her limp didn't matter at all.

When the dance ended, she admitted she had liked it more than she had expected to. Much more even than she *wanted* to. She didn't want to think about why. She cast about for something to say.

"Anna looks very pretty tonight."

"Anna always look pretty. Kurt, the boy who helps me stack the wood, cannot stop talking about her."

Christina smiled. "I expect the rivalry between Kurt and Adam, the boy she is dancing with now, will be even more intense after tonight."

"That is way of it," he said quietly. "A pretty wom—girl can take her pick."

"I hope she chooses well."

"She will. I will guide her."

"Oh?" She couldn't help but laugh. "You think she will let you guide her, do you?"

His green eyes smiled down into hers and all at once she couldn't breathe.

"Yes. I will guide her. Why not?"

"Because," she said slowly, "a young woman often has a mind of her own."

He hesitated, then sucked in a breath. "So does a young man."

Ivan tramped twice around the outside of Jensen's barn, hoping the crisp night air would cool him down. It did not. And not for one minute did it take his mind off Christina Marnell. If holding her briefly in his arms during a "swing your lady" left him this shaken, what would happen if he held her close during a waltz?

God help him, he could not wait to find out.

The minute he walked back into the overheated barn, Annamarie grabbed his arm. "Did you see me, Ivan? Did you?" She seized both his hands in one of hers. "I love square dancing, don't you? Do you want some lemonade? Adam brought some for me, and it's not too sweet."

"Adam?" he queried. "Who is this Adam?"

"Adam Lynford. He's in my class at school. His sister, Sally, is one of the girls who…" Her voice trailed off.

"Who what, Anna?"

His sister's smile faded. "Who doesn't like me."

"And her brother does like you, is that it?"

"I think so. At least he doesn't make fun of me."

Ivan clamped his jaws together. He wanted Annamarie to be happy here in Smoke River, not be made fun of or shunned. "Anna…"

The music started up again, and Annamarie was whisked off by another young man. This time it was Kurt Jorgensen, the lad who sometimes stacked wood for him. An instant later he spotted dark-haired Adam Lynford cutting in, and a disgruntled-looking Kurt wandered over to stand beside him.

"There's no figurin' a girl out, is there, Mr. Panovsky?"

Ivan hid a grin. "No, there is not. But does not mean that a man gives up trying."

"Oh, yeah? Right!" Kurt turned back to the dance floor, his gaze scanning the circling couples.

Ivan found himself doing the same thing, only he wasn't looking for Annamarie; he was looking for Christina Marnell. He found her in the arms of Simon Smalley, and without a second's hesitation he headed across the floor toward her.

Christina was so tired of changing partners as man after man cut in and whirled her away she thought about leaving the dance altogether. But of course she couldn't do that; she had driven out in Uncle Charlie's buggy, along with Iris Ming and Verena Forester. She had no other way to get back to town. She pasted a patient expression on her face and tried to ignore the thick paw crushing her fingers.

"What 'bout you, Miss Marnell?" her partner wheezed. "You glad you come out West?"

She drew in a breath. "Yes, I—" Before she could finish her sentence her partner vanished and she found herself in Ivan's arms.

"My goodness, where did you come from?"

He chuckled. "From behind Simon's back."

Christina smiled. "Your shirt feels cool to the touch. Have you been outside?"

"I walk around the barn outside."

"Oh? Why?"

He didn't answer. Instead he expertly positioned her to block the group of men waiting to cut in, guiding her through a few steps and then moving her away from another hovering male.

"Thank you," she murmured.

"For what do you thank me?"

"For keeping those other men away."

Ivan blinked. "You do not mind? Most girls like when they are, how you say, in demand."

"I do not."

He drew back to see her face.

She looked him straight in the eye. "I do not want to be 'in demand,'" she repeated.

"You do not mind dancing with one man only?"

"That," she said quietly, "depends on the man."

"What about with—" he hesitated "—with me?"

"No," she said. "I do not mind dancing with you."

His heart soared up out of his body, and his hand trembled as it held hers. Suddenly he could think of nothing to say.

A long minute passed in silence. "Anna does look very pretty tonight," she said again.

"Yes. Her mother was very beautiful."

"Was she Russian?"

"From Ukraine. My father, too."

"Is that where you learned to dance in a line like that? From your family?"

He nodded. "Anna, too. But we learned in New York, after my father married Anna's mother."

"It must have been hard to leave your family when you came out West."

"No. I want to come. After my mother died, and Papa remarried to Anna's mother, Papa want to be sure Anna would have a good life. But not in New York. Papa grew up on little farm. He never liked big city."

"Anna seems to like it in Smoke River," she said slowly. "Especially her lessons at school."

"She is good student, is she not?"

"Oh, yes. Annais one of my smartest students. Her intelligence is not the problem, Ivan. The problem is how pretty she is."

"Ah, the boys. But that is good, is that not so?" He cut his eyes sideways to where Annamarie and Kurt were lining up with other couples for a Virginia reel.

"No, it's not the boys that are the problem. It's the girls."

"What? How do you mean?"

"I mean," she said firmly, "that the same thing happened to me when I was her age."

Ivan glanced at her tightened mouth. "What should my Anna do? What did *you* do?"

She gave him a wry smile. "I set my sights on what I wanted and I ignored everything else."

"Ah. And what was it that you wanted?"

"I wanted to excel at my studies. I wanted a good education so I could teach school. That is all I have ever wanted to do."

Ivan was quiet for some minutes. He was glad that Annamarie's teacher was so dedicated, that she understood things he had no idea about. He admired her for that. But an odd, heavy feeling settled behind his breastbone, and once again he could think of nothing to say. Not one thing.

He tightened the hand he pressed against her back and watched couples line up for the Virginia reel. He needed to think.

Chapter Thirteen

Christina sat on a wooden bench at the edge of the dance floor, resisting the impulse to pinch herself. Was she dreaming? Had she fallen asleep over her lesson book and would wake up tomorrow and find that this evening was nothing but a dream?

Oh, she did hope not. In the past three hours she had learned two new ways to dance, both of them exciting and a little bit wild—a real expression of the boisterous, free-spirited Western frontier. And she had exchanged thought-provoking words with Ivan Panovsky. Her memories of this night would stay with her for the rest of her life.

She sipped the glass of lemonade clutched in her hand and tried to calm her racing heart. Square dancing was certainly strenuous! She'd never dreamed her crippled ankle would allow her to execute such complicated steps. And it was exhilarating, floating across the floor in…in… Oh, mercy! In the arms of Ivan Panovsky.

Then another thought popped into her mind, one she desperately tried to wriggle away from. She would never forget the pleasure she felt being held close to Ivan Panovsky.

Across the floor Annamarie was now dancing a spirited two-step with Kurt—no, it was Adam. And now it was Kurt again. How competitive young men could be! The next moment the musicians struck up a waltz, and a shadow fell across her.

Ivan stood before her, holding out his hand. He looked as if he wanted to say something, but instead he tipped his head toward the dancers circling the floor, and his dark eyebrows rose in a question. When she hesitated, he bent, plucked the lemonade glass out of her hand and set it on the bench beside her.

She rose and took his hand. Without a word he led her onto the dance floor, turned her toward him and placed her hand on his shoulder. Then he pulled her so close the ruffles on her pink-flowered shirtwaist brushed against his chest. His gray-green eyes held hers, and she caught her breath.

The music was slow, a tune she didn't recognize, but apparently Ivan did because he began to hum the melody. In the next instant she became acutely aware of his hand at her back. Still he didn't speak, just held her close, and they moved together around the perimeter of the polished wood floor. Dancing with him was like floating.

Over his shoulder she watched the other dancers swirl and circle, and then she looked up into Ivan's face. He was almost smiling, but not quite. Instead, she saw an odd hesitation in his eyes.

"Ivan?"

He drew her closer, so close she could feel the warmth of his body. "Do not talk, Christina." His breathing hitched and then evened out. She liked that, knowing that he was feeling something unusual, because she was feeling something unusual, too. It was

a strange sensation, a kind of understanding between
the two of them that had nothing to do with the music
or the fact that they were moving together in the slow
steps of a waltz. Some kind of…recognition.

Ivan tried to swallow over the rock in his throat,
tried again and then gave up. He couldn't speak with
Christina moving so close to him. He wanted to drop
the soft hand he held and fold her into his arms. It
would embarrass her, here among all these people.
Perhaps it would even frighten her, and he didn't want
her to move away from him. He wanted to hold her
close and never let her go.

He sucked in a long breath and tried to ignore the
scent of her hair. Did all men feel this way being close
to a woman, like they were drowning? Every breath
she took, every movement of her warm body under
his hand sent his senses spinning. He felt like he did
when he was working at the sawmill, only now he
wasn't the man prodding a log toward the saw, *he was
the log*! Sharp iron teeth were ripping into his chest.
But not only did he want that, he wanted even more.

Am I losing my mind?

Maybe so. He did not care if he was going crazy.
All he wanted was to keep holding Christina in his
arms. He wanted it with every breath he took, and he
could not think beyond this moment.

She stumbled slightly, and he realized he had
turned her too quickly, trying to keep the other men
prowling at the edge of the dance floor from cutting
in and spiriting her away from him. He never wanted
to let her go. He would fight every man here to keep
Christina in his arms, even though he knew that a

fight at one of Peter Jensen's barn dances would mean he could never attend another one. Rancher Jensen was very strict about that.

Christina had not said a single word since he had asked her not to talk. He should never have said that. A man did not order a woman around in that way. She would think he was uneducated, which he was. Worse, she would think he was rude, which he was not. Or at least not up until tonight.

He wanted to explain. He wanted to say that he was content holding her close without talking. Now his chest felt hot and tight, and little birds in his belly swooped and darted about. And below his belly he felt himself grow hard.

What was she thinking? What was she feeling? *God.* He closed his eyes. *Speak to her, you idiot. Say something. Anything.*

He opened his lips. "Christina…"

She glanced up and looked into his face, her gaze calm and steady. "Ivan," she said with a slight smile, "do not talk."

Do not talk? Had she really said that? Did that mean she wanted to dance with him and *not* talk? He closed his eyes and breathed in the scent of her hair.

Perhaps it was a minute later, or an hour later—Christina didn't know and she didn't care. Riding back to town in Uncle Charlie's buggy, she touched her heated cheeks with fingers that trembled. She felt different.

She wasn't tired, not even after two Virginia reels and she didn't know how many waltzes with Ivan.

Not the least bit tired. In fact… She caught herself up short. *In fact, you feel wonderful, full of warm, sunshiny bubbles. Full of happiness.*

She would never forget this night. Through all the coming years of her life she would always remember this one evening.

But the following Monday morning, her glorious, floating-on-air feeling evaporated like so much soap-suds on a snowy day.

Chapter Fourteen

Monday morning was rain-soaked and miserable. Christina's stomach tightened anticipating the trial she faced in keeping her students inside at recess and at lunchtime. Already the day had turned out to be more of an ordeal than usual, which she attributed to Annamarie Panovsky. No matter what rainy-day diversion she undertook, Kurt and Adam focused all their attention on showing off for Annamarie, and the rest of the class either took sides and rooted for one boy or the other or started similar contests of skill or daring or just plain mischief.

Roxanna Jensen loudly challenged Teddy Mac-Allister to a horse race, which was a perfectly safe challenge since it was pouring rain outside. The other students teased and poked fun at Roxanna for her audacity, and even peaceable little Manette Nicolet couldn't resist laughing at the girl. This resulted in tears and a bloody nose for Teddy and a sullen Roxanna sitting alone in the corner, glowering at everybody.

Christina bit her lip. More psychology than teaching skill was required to bring education to the young people of Smoke River! Still, she wasn't going to give up. She had worked all her life preparing to teach these students, and she wasn't beaten yet. She rapped sharply on her desk.

"For the next hour we will not tease or fight or giggle—" she shot a meaningful look at Sally Lynford "—or make any noise at all unless it is to make a point for your team."

The word *team* snagged their attention. "We gonna choose teams?" Kurt asked, his brown eyes shining.

"We are. Roxanna, I am appointing you captain of Team One. Manette, you will be captain of Team Two. Now you may start choosing your team members."

"What are the teams gonna do?" Kurt demanded.

Roxanna ignored him, rose importantly and swaggered to the front of the room. "I choose…"

"Wait a minute," Kurt yelled. "We gotta know what the contest is gonna be."

"We *have to* know…" Christina corrected. She emphasized the correct grammar and raised an eyebrow at Kurt. "So I will tell you. This will be a Word War."

"Ooh, a war!" Sally Lynford crowed. "How exciting! Choose me, Roxanna! Choose me!"

Roxanna ignored her plea and chose Sammy Greywolf. "Sammy always gets a hundred on the spelling tests," she explained.

Manette scanned the expectant faces and pointed to Annamarie. "She gets hundreds, too."

Christina noted with amusement that Kurt and Adam ended up on opposite teams, as did Sally and Edith Ness. Nothing would ensure avid interest more than trying to best one's rival.

"Now," Christina began, "the first word is *monogamy*. You must spell it correctly and then you must use the word in a sentence." There were two lessons to be learned in this contest; first, the correct spelling and usage of a new word; and second, that being the oldest student or the strongest or the loudest wasn't enough to excel.

"Aw, that's easy," Kurt blurted out. He spelled it correctly, but his use-in-a-sentence effort made everyone laugh. "Uh…we drink monogamy at Christmas."

When the giggles faded, Christina announced the next word. "Epistle."

Not to be outdone by Kurt's performance, Adam Lynford puffed out his chest and easily spelled *e-p-i-s-t-l-e*. Then he wiped out the point for his team by announcing his definition, "An epistle is the wife of an apostle."

After the laughter died down, Christina supplied the next word. "Spouse."

"That's easy, Miss Marnell," Sally Lynford sang. She sent a superior look across the room to Annamarie, her rival for Kurt's affections. She spelled *"S-p-o-u-s-e."* Then she undid her achievement by announcing her definition, "After school we are all going home and spouse around."

The class roared. Defeat came hard to Sally; she sulked the rest of the morning.

Gradually each team came to rely not on the most popular or the prettiest member, but on the smartest. Thus Sammy Greywolf and Annamarie were left to break the tie, and that fact brought new respect and acceptance for both students. Sammy emerged the champion, though Christina suspected Annamarie had purposely let the boy win.

At the end of the hour Christina listened in disbelief as Adam Lynford blurted out, "Gosh, Miss Marnell, I hope it rains again tomorrow!"

She suppressed a groan and prayed fervently that tomorrow the sun would shine! By afternoon, she was as drained and limp as a wet dishrag. When school was over, she helped Manette into her galoshes, found Kurt's missing knit cap and gathered up her books and papers. Halfway to her apartment she was overtaken by Ivan Panovsky, who stopped her with a hand on her arm and pulled her around to face him.

"I, uh… I wondered if…um…"

"You want to discuss Anna, is that it?" She hadn't seen Ivan since the night of Jensen's dance. She hated to admit how glad she was he had stopped her.

"Yes…uh…yes, that's it. I want to discuss Anna. We could have coffee?" He gestured at the restaurant just ahead.

Inside, they sat across from each other in stiff silence until the waitress approached with her order pad. "Afternoon, Miss. Ivan. You folks come in for some fresh rhubarb pie?"

"No," Ivan said quickly. "Just coffee, Rita."

Christina's mouth watered. "Oh, yes, I would love some rhubarb pie."

"Say, aren't you the new schoolteacher? Can't say I liked the last teacher much, but you look about right."

"About right? Whatever does that mean?"

"Oh, you know. Real intelligent lookin' and not too pretty."

Christina gasped.

"I mean," Rita amended, "not so pretty that you're

gonna run off and get married all of a sudden like the last one did."

"Certainly not," Christina assured her.

Ivan's eyes looked troubled. When Rita disappeared into the kitchen he leaned across the table. "Christina, she does not mean insult to you."

"I was not insulted, Ivan. What she says is true. I am not used to the way people are so outspoken here in the West, but she is quite right. I am not going to 'run off and get married.' I don't ever intend to marry. I have known this since I was Anna's age."

A frown creased his forehead. "How can you be so sure?"

"Because—" She broke off when Rita returned with two cups of coffee and a slice of rhubarb pie. "Because all I ever wanted to do in life is teach school." She picked up her fork. "Anna could become a teacher, too."

Ivan shook his head. "No. Is not enough."

Christina laid her fork back on her plate. "Not enough for what?"

"Not enough for woman to be happy."

"But your sister is gifted, Ivan. She could—"

"No."

"I don't understand. How can you take it upon yourself to speak for her? Decide what *she* wants?"

"I am Anna's only family. I want her to be happy."

"But you don't want her to be like me, is that it?"

Ivan looked away, focusing his gaze out the window where an elderly woman picked her way across the muddy street. Then he looked back at Christina. Was he wrong to want the best for his Annamarie? He felt such responsibility for her, such love and concern for her future. Was he wrong to want her to be happy? How could he explain this to Christina?

"I know how much Anna admires you," he said at last. "But—"

"But you don't want me to encourage her in her studies, is that it? You want what *you* want for her."

"I want what is best for Anna." His hand shook when he picked up his coffee cup, so he set it back on the saucer with a click. "And there is more."

"Oh?" Christina's slice of rhubarb pie sat uneaten before her. "Yes, I thought there must be more. Tell me."

His throat closed. "I do not think teaching other women's children is enough." He took a deep breath. "Even for you." He could scarcely get the words out.

Her eyes widened and she stared at him across the table separating them. "Even for me?" she echoed. "What right have you—"

"No right," he said quickly. "I have no right at all."

She looked into his eyes. "Other women's children are enough for me, Ivan. I do not intend to marry." Then she stared down at her uneaten pie and signaled the waitress. "Could you bring another fork, please?"

She pushed the extra fork over to Ivan's side of the table, then pushed the plate into the center. "Please help me eat this. I am not as hungry as I thought."

He made short work of half the pie while Christina took only a few dainty bites. While they ate, she found herself telling him about the rivalry between Kurt Jorgensen and Adam Lynford for Annamarie's attention, and about her smart-as-a-whip student

Sammy Greywolf, the boy who withstood constant harassment but never missed a day of school. She confessed the difficulty she had in corralling her students' interest on rainy days, even her nagging fear that she wasn't teaching them enough to justify her annual salary of one hundred dollars.

He listened without speaking, but she could tell by the interested and sympathetic expression in his eyes that he understood every word. Finally she shoved the pie plate closer to him and laid her fork aside.

"The rest is for you, Ivan," she said with a smile. "You have earned it by listening to my troubles."

"I think is most fine, very brave of you to teach students. I think my Anna wants to be like you, but I also think—"

"You do not approve. What if an education is what she wants? What if she wants to teach, as I do? What if she chooses not to marry?"

He gave her a stricken look, his soft green eyes clouded with pain. "I love my Anna. I want her to be happy."

Christina rolled over on her narrow bed and closed her eyes for the tenth time in the last hour. She could not allow herself to think about Ivan.

Think about something else. Uncle Charlie's molasses cookies or the Christmas dolls and toy trains displayed in the mercantile window. Even Teddy MacAllister's horse.

But her thoughts kept circling back to Ivan.

Ivan.

Why could she not get the man out of her thoughts?

It was three o'clock in the morning and she should be planning tomorrow's arithmetic lesson or making a new list of spelling words for the advanced readers, Sammy Greywolf and Annamarie Panovsky.

Oh, botheration! Each morning she hurried her steps along the path hoping to catch a glimpse of Ivan Panovsky stacking logs on the woodpile or splitting kindling, his lean, muscular body arched into a clean line over the chopping block, his dark head bent in concentration.

She liked him. She had never known anyone quite like Ivan. But it went no further than that, really it didn't. She would not allow him to be...what? Part of her thoughts in the middle of the night?

And she most definitely would not allow him to be part of her life!

Chapter Fifteen

"Oh, Miss Marnell, please say you will come?" Annamarie grasped her hand, the one holding the now squashed molasses cookie Uncle Charlie had slipped her on her way out of the bakery. "Please, *please*?"

"Anna—"

"You don't know what this means, Miss Marnell. It's my birthday—my *twelfth* birthday, just imagine that! And it's almost Christmas. And…and also Ivan has been promoted to foreman at the sawmill. Just think, he is the foreman! Surely we should celebrate, should we not?"

The girl clung to her hand as she stepped out the back door of the bakery and started down the street toward the schoolhouse. "Life back in New York, at the orphanage, was so awful and lonely. I dreamed and dreamed of coming to be with Ivan, and he has worked so hard to make it happen… Oh, please come. Please!"

Christina studied the eager young face before her. It must be wonderful to be so excited about turning twelve. What she remembered about that age was fear. She had dreaded limping into her classes, hearing the snickers and cruel remarks of the other students. No one had befriended her, and at dances she'd sat alone on the sidelines, fighting to hold back tears.

But it would not be like that for Annamarie, so pretty and so full of life and happiness. And Ivan— how proud he must be! In his quiet, unassuming way he had managed to make a life for Annamarie and himself. She knew that being promoted to foreman at the sawmill would make the townspeople look up to him.

He deserved it. He also deserved her presence at Annamarie's birthday celebration supper.

"Ivan will come for you at five o'clock and walk you over to our house."

"Oh, he need not—"

But the girl was gone, skipping off down the boardwalk and disappearing into Ness's Mercantile. So, Christina acknowledged, she was to be a guest at supper tonight with Annamarie and Ivan. Under her starched white shirtwaist her heart thumped hard.

Promptly at five o'clock Ivan tapped at her door. As she stepped out, he took her arm and without a word guided her down the stairway and out onto the snow-dusted boardwalk. She tried to draw her arm free, but he tightened his grip. "Is slippery," he said. "Is starting to snow."

He didn't say another word until they reached the front porch of the house he had built. A huge wreath of pine boughs hung on the front door, decorated with white paper angels and tied with a wide red ribbon. Before he opened the door he stopped and turned her to face him.

"I thank you for coming, Christina. It means much to Anna." His green eyes held hers. "And me."

Her throat closed and she could only nod. It meant a lot to her, too, but she couldn't say exactly why. Of course, it was Annamarie's birthday and she had grown very fond of the girl. But underneath she suspected it was more than that. How much more she didn't dare think about.

The house smelled simply wonderful, of pine trees and an enticing, spicy aroma that made her stomach rumble in anticipation. Annamarie threw her arms around her, then took her blue wool shawl and draped it over the back of a chair near the fireplace.

Ivan hung his sheepskin jacket on a hook in the hallway and disappeared.

"My goodness, Anna, what smells so good?" Christina asked.

"Stuffed cabbage. And borscht."

"Anna, I didn't know you could cook!"

"Oh, I am not cooking. Ivan is making supper."

"Ivan!"

"Of course, Ivan," a male voice called. He emerged from the kitchen brandishing a wooden spoon in one hand, a shy grin spreading across his face. An oversize, food-splattered white apron hung from his neck.

Christina gaped at him. "Ivan, you are a man of unsuspected talents!"

"Is not true," he answered. "I chop wood. I dance a *berezka*. I build furniture. That is all."

All? Christina's gaze fell on the overcrowded bookcase next to the fireplace. He read books. Lots of books. She squinted at the titles. Shelley and Keats. Cervantes. Chaucer. Even books about architecture and…raising chickens?

Annamarie grasped her hand. "Miss Marnell, come and see the beautiful bed Ivan built for me. And my bedroom! Ivan painted it all blue, my favorite color, and I want you to see it!" She tugged on Christina's hand and drew her up the staircase.

The room was indeed lovely, the walls a pretty shade of pale blue with ruffled blue curtains on the windows. A handsome four-poster bed stood against one wall, the polished wood beautifully carved.

"Ivan built this?"

"Yes. Ivan built all our furniture. That chest of drawers—" she pointed to a many-drawered bureau on the opposite wall "—and my nightstand and the settee in the parlor. Oh, and our dining table. You must see it before I cover it up with the tablecloth."

Christina could understand the girl's enthusiasm for her brother's handiwork. Every piece of furniture was perfectly proportioned, and the details—the smooth corners, the drawer knobs, even the mirror stand on the bureau—showed great skill.

"Would you like to see the other bedroom? It's Ivan's, just down the hallway, next to mine."

Yes, I would. But she couldn't do that, no matter how great her curiosity. That would be most improper. "No, thank you, Anna. I think not."

"Anna?" Ivan called from the bottom of the stairs. "Come and set bowls on the table."

"I hope you like borscht," Annamarie whispered. "Ivan is very proud of his borscht—it's his grandmother's recipe."

Annamarie paused in spreading out the lacy white tablecloth so Christina could admire the beautiful walnut dining table. Then she helped lay out plates and bowls, and the three of them sat down, Ivan across from Annamarie and Christina. "To be close to the kitchen," he explained. He ladled a thick soup into each bowl from the big tureen in the center of the table and picked up his spoon. "Supper," he announced.

With her first mouthful of the rich beet soup Christina added another skill to Ivan's growing list of talents. He was a superb cook!

"You like it?" he asked, his voice hesitant.

"Yes, it's delicious. It tastes like…wine."

His grin lit up his entire face, and a faint blush stained his cheeks. He smoothed his palms over the apron covering his chest. "Good. I hoped you like. Is Anna's favorite."

"Ivan," Annamarie said, "tell Miss Marnell how you learned to make borscht."

He gave his sister a long look, then turned his gaze on Christina. "She is maybe not interested, I think."

"Oh, but I am interested!" Christina blurted out. "Tell me about your grandmother. Did she teach you how to make this?"

Ivan sent a quick glance to Annamarie. "My mother, Elena Kurasov, was born in Kiev. Her family very poor, only farmers. When she was little girl, tall enough to stand at stove, she learned to cook from her mother. When she marry my father and came to America, she brought all her mother's recipes with her. And—" again he looked at Annamarie "—when I was very young, not yet going to school, my mama teach me how to cook them. Is simple, really."

Christina stared at the man across the table from her. Somehow wearing an apron and cooking their supper did not lessen his appeal as a man. On the contrary, it made Ivan Panovsky the most unusual man she had ever known. She watched him gather up the now empty soup bowls and disappear into the kitchen as Annamarie laid blue-flowered china plates at each place setting, along with small crystal glasses.

"For wine," she explained. "Ivan said I could have some on my birthday. I can hardly wait to taste it!"

"You're growing up," Christina said.

"Ivan says I am growing up fast, and now I should learn to cook and sew and…" Her voice trailed off.

"And not read books about Robin Hood, is that it?" Christina said quietly.

Annamarie bent her head to study her wineglass. A familiar ache started at the back of Christina's neck, and in that instant she knew she was going to fight even harder for Annamarie's right to go as far as she wanted in school. It would make an enemy of Ivan, whom she genuinely liked, but so be it. Ivan was an interesting and handsome man, but he was wrong, so very wrong, about his sister's education.

Ivan held his breath and watched Christina taste his stuffed cabbage roll. Her lips closed over the morsel on her fork, her beautiful eyes widened and then she closed them. *She hates it.* All afternoon he had chopped and seasoned and rolled the spicy meat mixture into the blanched cabbage leaves. It would all be worthwhile if she liked the dish.

But she didn't. Well, then, he must learn to cook

American. A man liked to please a woman, but when he failed it cut deep.

Christina swallowed, opened her eyes and sent him a dazzling smile. "What do you call this?"

"Toltutt kaposzta," Annamarie blurted out. *"K-a-p-o-s-z-t-a."*

"This is absolutely delicious," Christina said, loading up her fork with another bite. "It tastes... like something a czar would relish."

Ivan bit his tongue. "The czar starved and persecuted my family until finally they escape to America."

Christina's face turned so pink he suddenly wanted to press his lips to her cheek. "Oh, I am so sorry," she murmured. "I didn't know."

He gripped his fork so hard his knuckles hurt. He wanted to kiss her. That thought was so unnerving his hand began to shake.

Annamarie laid her hand on his arm. "Ivan, what's the matter? You're white as a field of snow."

"Nothing, Anna. Nothing is matter. Eat your supper."

"But—"

"Anna." Instantly his sister grasped everything. It made her smile in that secret way she had, as if she knew...everything. And worse, that she understood.

"And what is this dish called?" Christina inquired, nibbling a slice of red radish.

"Rotkvica. Radish salad."

"And this?"

"Blitna!" Annamarie sang with enthusiasm. "It's my favorite."

"Green chard with potatoes," Ivan explained. "I teach Anna how to make."

Christina's lovely blue eyes rested on his sister for a moment, then rose to meet his. "Why? Why are you teaching her to make these dishes?"

"Because he wants me to marry a Russian!" Annamarie quipped. "But we are in America now, Ivan. *You* are the only Russian in town."

"I see," said Christina, her voice quiet.

Annamarie beamed. "Oh, thank you, Miss Marnell. You *do* see."

Ivan clenched his fist. Annamarie was against him. And now Christina was against him, too. God help him, he and the pretty schoolteacher disagreed on everything.

He barely tasted the supper he'd cooked, including the bottle of wine he'd brought home from the Golden Partridge. Annamarie wrinkled her nose at first, but after two swallows, she claimed she loved it. Christina proposed a toast to his sister and downed half of her glass; Ivan had three glasses, but it did not help his shaking hands.

He presented his sister with a lemon cake, topped with twelve tiny red candles. Annamarie made a wish, sucked in a deep breath and blew them all out.

"Ah, is good luck!" he said.

She gave him a sly smile. "Don't you want to know what I wished for?"

He shook his head and hugged her.

"It concerns you," she teased. "And—"

"Do not say out loud," he interrupted. "It will not come true."

Supper ended with an ecstatic Annamarie throwing her arms around him. "Thank you, Ivan. Thank you! I feel all grown up tonight!"

He kissed her cheek. "Almost," he whispered. "Wait a few years."

After supper he walked Christina back to her room over the bakery, moving as slowly as he could without making it too obvious. Snowflakes drifted down, frosting the boardwalk and dusting their shoulders. For the first block, they didn't talk, and then she broke the silence.

"Anna is a very fortunate girl, Ivan. That was a lovely birthday supper."

He did not know what to say. They walked a few steps in silence, and then as they crossed the street he took her hand. For the next five steps he held his breath, wondering what she would do. When she kept walking beside him as usual, her hand in his, he felt as if he could fly.

"What was your life in New York like?" she asked suddenly.

He hesitated. "New York is big city. We—my father and stepmother and Anna—lived in apartment building. Very small. Very crowded."

"Is that why you left to come out West?"

He hesitated. "Papa and I not agree on many things, so when he died, yes, is why I leave home. It has been hard."

"But now it is better?" she asked.

"Is better to have Anna here, yes. Her mother died and then Anna have to live in..." He swallowed. "Is better for Anna to be here with me."

"She is happy, I think," Christina said. "She is enthusiastic about everything at school."

"But not learning to cook," he said with a laugh.

Christina said nothing. She scarcely knew what to say to this man who was so quiet most of the time. She didn't know what to think about this proud Russian man, Ivan Panovsky. But, my goodness, she knew what she *felt* about him. She liked to be near him, liked the touch of his hand holding hers. It made her feel warm inside. She could not explain why; she just liked him.

Ivan was a good man. He was a simple man, not educated, as she was, but he was intelligent and knowledgeable in his own way, and he was certainly skilled at woodworking. It was plain that he loved his sister. Annamarie was lucky to have someone who cared for her and could guide her. All Christina had was Aunt Lettie, and Aunt Lettie had disliked her from the day she had been crippled. Having someone care about her, really care about her, would have made her life so much easier to bear.

"Christina, you are quiet. What are you thinking?"

"I am thinking about Anna, how fortunate she is to have you for a brother."

"You think I am good brother? Even if I want her to learn to cook instead of read books?"

"I think you are a good man, Ivan. And a good brother. Perhaps in time I can change your mind about Anna and books. She is only twelve years old. She has many years before she needs to decide what to do with her life."

"You are right and you are also wrong," he said.

"True, Anna is only twelve. But you cannot change my mind about what is best for her. But…but maybe reading books will be happy for her, too. When she is married."

Christina closed her lips. She did not want to argue with him, especially after such a lovely evening. As Annamarie grew up over the coming years, many things could change. Perhaps Ivan *would* change his mind. She would count on his sense of fairness and bide her time.

The bakery was dark except for the shaft of moonlight that fell across the back door. She dropped Ivan's warm, strong hand so she could open the door. "There is a candle here someplace, and some matches," she murmured. She felt around on the small table just inside the door, found the candle and struck a match. In the glow of light she could see his pensive face, his gray-green eyes looking troubled. She wondered what he was thinking.

He lifted the candle out of her hand. "Come. I take you up the stairs."

"So I won't stumble, is that it?" she said with a soft laugh.

"No," he said, his voice quiet. "So I can say goodnight at your door as proper man should." Holding the candle high enough to illuminate her path, he started up the steps, and she followed, touched at his gallant gesture. At the top step he reached down to again take her hand in his and pinched off the flame.

For a long minute they stood together in the dark, saying nothing. She could hear his breathing, feel the swirl of his breath against her temple. Her heart kicked against her rib cage. She did not want to move, did not want to break the spell that settled over them. In truth, she did not want the evening to be over.

Then he moved a step closer, and a funny floaty feeling started somewhere deep inside her. "Ivan…"

"Christina," he said in a low voice. "Do not talk."

In the next moment she felt his lips brush her cheek, and then—*oh, God*—his mouth found hers.

Chapter Sixteen

Ivan's senses filled and overflowed, and a kernel of happiness swelled up and burst inside him. He was tasting heaven, silky and sweet as honey. After a long dizzying moment he lifted his lips from hers. "I should ask permission, but was afraid you would say no."

She gave a gentle laugh. "I might have. But now…" She reached up and laid a finger against his mouth. "Now I think I would say yes."

He kissed her again, longer this time, and then deeper. He never wanted to stop. He wanted to hold her, keep her. She moved in his arms and he broke the kiss, but he was afraid to let her go. She touched his cheek briefly and after a moment he released her.

She disappeared into her apartment and he stood there for some minutes, then somehow made his way down the staircase and out the back door of the bakery. Instead of going back to his house on Maple Street, he began to walk. The air was bitter cold and smelled of snow. But inside, a warm glow spread over his entire body.

Tonight maybe it would snow again, and he had to smile. For days Annamarie had pleaded with him to take her sledding. His sister was still a little girl in some ways, wanting to play and laugh and enjoy being alive. He had fashioned a sled out of lumber scraps from the mill and waxed the underside until it was slick enough to slide over a farmer's field. Tomorrow was Sunday. He should take Annamarie to church, but… He quickened his pace. If it snowed, he would take her sledding.

The next morning Christina was so restless she decided to go for a walk. It had snowed during the night, leaving the town covered in sparkling white lace and the tree branches drooping with silvery icicles. Just as she turned onto the path to the schoolhouse a peal of girlish laughter broke the quiet, and in the next minute a sled whooshed down the gentle hill behind the schoolhouse and dumped two people into the snowbank. A tall man in a tan sheepskin jacket and a red knit cap floundered out of the powdery snow, followed by a boy—no, it was a girl!—dressed in jeans and a heavy red sweater.

"Miss Marnell! Miss Marnell!" The slim, red-sweatered figure ran toward her, and now she recognized Annamarie Panovsky. Ivan appeared behind his sister.

Christina found she was unable to stop smiling at him. A man who wanted to take his sister sledding… It made her heart sing. He smiled shyly, and his green eyes said something she just now realized. There was a bond between them. The feeling between them was there, and today it was even stronger than it was last night.

Chapter Seventeen

⁓⁓⁓⁓⁓

On Monday Christina finally ran out of things to engage her wriggly, snowbound students, so she turned to her new list of words from the dictionary and announced a new competition called Definitions. Two teams were formed.

"Team one, use *serendipity* in a sentence," she directed.

Kurt Jorgensen scrambled to his feet. "Serendipity is goin' swimming without any clothes on."

Christina suppressed a smile. Sally Lynford fared no better with *trespasses*. Sally rose and twitched her dress importantly. "Everybody knows that. It's part of the Lord's prayer. 'Forgive us our trash baskets as we forgive those who put trash in our baskets.'"

"Hey, Sally," Kurt yelled. "You don't go to church much, do ya?"

"Neither do you, smarty-pants!" Sally snapped.

Consternation proved to be the downfall of Teddy MacAllister, and his definition almost brought the competition to an end with guffaws from the students. "When you're, uh, in the outhouse but you can't go, that's consternation."

"No it's not!" Roxanna Jensen challenged when the laughter died down. "A consternation is what you see when you look up at the sky at night and see a bunch of stars."

Noralee Ness then stated that *miscellaneous* meant an unmarried girl called Miss Cellaneous instead of a married woman called *Missus* Cellaneous.

At that point Christina gave up and proposed an idea that had popped into her head in the middle of the night. "Now we are going to write a Christmas play, about Robin Hood."

"I want to play Maid Marian!" Sally Lynford announced.

"Very well, Sally. But you must earn your role by correctly answering a geography question. If you cannot give the correct answer, someone else can answer the question, and *that* person will play Maid Marian."

"What if it's a boy who gets the right answer?" Adam shot out.

"Well, what if it *is* a boy?" Christina answered. "Did you know that back in Shakespeare's time, boys played *all* the parts in the plays? Not just Romeo, but Juliet, too?"

Adam's face expressed disbelief. "Wow, honest?"

"Yes, honest," she replied. After that, a clamor rose to choose the next part, and by the time school was over for the day, all the parts were assigned. And, Christina thought with pride, a good deal of geography had been learned along the way. It had even been fun! More than ever she was convinced that teaching was her life's calling.

Tired but exhilarated by her success, she reached the bakery and ducked inside out of the wind. Iris Ming greeted her from behind the glass counter with a wave and a wide smile. "You are late today, Christina."

"I stayed after school to plan tomorrow's lessons."

"Ah. You like your students, is that right?"

"Mostly. But the unkindness and cruelty I see in some of the older girls makes me cringe."

"Teaching school must be very difficult," the Chinese woman said. "I could not do it. But you like it?"

"Nothing gives me greater satisfaction," Christina admitted.

Iris offered her a crinkle-topped chocolate cookie. "What about Ivan Panovsky?" she asked with a sly look.

"Ivan? What about him?"

"He likes you, Christina. It is plain to everyone."

Christina bit into her cookie. "I didn't know the whole town was watching," she said tightly.

Iris laughed. "Pretty girl, handsome man. Of course they watch!"

"I wish the townspeople would find something else to do." Absently she took another bite of the cookie.

"There is not much else to do in a small town like Smoke River." Iris watched her for a moment, then handed her another cookie. "Christina, I am your friend, so I will say something maybe you will not like."

"Oh? What is it?"

"It is just this. For an intelligent woman, sometimes you do not act very smart."

Christina stared at her. Quickly she decided to change the subject. "Iris, how is your garden coming along?" she said.

"What?"

"I asked about your garden. What are you planting now?"

"Do not distract me with questions, Christina." She wrapped up three more chocolate cookies and pushed them across the glass countertop. When she reached for them, Iris caught her hand. "Do you not want someone to love? To make a home with? Children?"

"Iris." Christina's voice hardened. "Stop."

The two women looked at each other for a long minute, then burst into laughter. "I am sorry," Iris said.

"No, you're not," Christina replied. "But we are still friends."

"Oh, good. Because I have many more questions… and *much* more advice."

Christina grinned at her, took her cookies and climbed the stairs up to her apartment. Once inside, she walked past the chest of drawers in her bedroom and caught sight of her reflection in the mirror. Her lips were smiling, but her eyes had an uncertain look.

She *did* want to teach school. More than anything. But Iris's questions popped back into her mind. *Don't you also want someone to love?*

No, she decided quickly. She did not. She wanted to teach her students to read and write and know about other countries in the world. When she was in the classroom she knew who she was and what she was meant to do in life. She was valued for her knowledge and her skill. She felt worthwhile.

And it made her happy. She could never give that up. Never.

* * *

The tree fell exactly where Ivan planned, and he lifted his ax to start lopping off the limbs. It was early, the school yard empty and quiet except for the sharp *thwack* of his blows. He worked steadily, and the pile of branches grew.

Christina's face floated at the back of his mind, her eyes shining in the glow of Annamarie's birthday candles, her eyelashes dusted with snow. He let the ax head slide onto the ground and leaned his weight against it. It was hard to keep his thoughts focused on cutting firewood when all he wanted to think about was Christina.

He had held her hand. Danced with her. He had even kissed her, and she had liked it. At least he thought she had. But he did not know how she really felt about him.

He picked up the ax and worked for another hour, splitting wood and thinking, until he was out of breath and out of ideas. *How do you know if a woman loves you?*

With a woman like Christina, maybe you never knew. Maybe she liked kissing you, but she also liked coming to the schoolhouse every morning and teaching arithmetic and reading to a room full of children. Maybe she liked that even more than kissing you.

He groaned aloud. *Is that all she wants from life?* It was not all *he* wanted from life, working at the sawmill and making a home for Annamarie. He knew what he wanted. He had known it ever since the moment he'd laid eyes on Christina, watching her limp with determination down the street in the pretty blue bonnet that matched her eyes.

What does she think of me? Does she feel anything special for me? The next time he had a chance to be alone with her, he would ask.

"Ivan, we're writing a play at school," Annamarie announced at breakfast the next morning. "About Robin Hood and Maid Marian. Miss Marnell says…"

Ivan spilled his coffee at the mention of Christina's name. "Yes? Miss Marnell says what?" He mopped at the puddle on the dining table with his napkin.

"She says I get to be Maid Marian!" She dipped her spoon into the pot of strawberry jam that sat between them. "I won the part by answering a geography question about Egypt when Sally Lynford couldn't. Now Sally is mad at me."

"And who will be Robin Hood?"

"That's the funny part. Remember Sammy Greywolf, that smart Indian boy I told you about? He answered more geography questions than any of the other boys, so he gets to play Robin Hood. Adam is going to play Little John."

"Adam?"

"Adam Lynford. Sally's brother.

Ivan remembered. "Ah, yes. The boy who can waltz."

"And who likes books as much as I do," Annamarie added slowly. She crunched into her jam-slathered piece of toast. "And Miss Marnell says…well, she says it doesn't matter that Sammy Greywolf is lots shorter than I am. She says that how tall someone is or how they look is not important."

Ivan carefully swallowed a mouthful of coffee. "What does Chris—Miss Marnell say *is* important?"

"She doesn't say." Annamarie buttered another slice of toast. "You like Miss Marnell, don't you, Ivan?"

He swallowed again. "Yes, I like her." And more, though he would not tell that to Annamarie.

"And she likes you, doesn't she?"

"I do not know. But I pray hard every night that it is so."

"I know it is so," Annamarie said dreamily.

Ivan's hand stilled on the butter dish. "What? How do you know?"

"I just do. There are all kinds of little signs."

"Signs? What signs?"

"Oh...the way she looks when she sees you, all soft and smiley. Are you going to marry her?"

He choked on his coffee. "I would if...if I knew how."

"Oh, that's easy," Annamarie said airily. "You just ask her."

He stared at his sister. "Just ask her? Don't you think I should first ask if she...if she cares about me?"

"You mean whether she loves you? First I think you should tell her how *you* feel."

"I—I cannot do that. She says she wants to be teacher, not wife."

His sister studied his face. "Are you sure?"

"Yes, I am sure. She has said so." He clenched his

jaw. He was sure of something else, too. He would go to his grave loving Christina Marnell and wanting her to be his wife.

Christina hurried along the path to the schoolhouse, noticing how deep the snow was this morning. She had come to school early, hoping to catch a glimpse of Ivan cutting wood in the school yard. She wanted to talk to him about Annamarie.

Oh, no, that is a lie. You just want to talk to him. About anything at all.

She liked Ivan. She felt oddly happy when she was with him. She loved seeing his smile and watching his eyes glow with laughter. His voice always grew quiet when they spoke. He didn't say much, but what he said was always thoughtful and honest. She liked talking to him. She liked being with him.

Maybe she more than liked him.

She gave her wandering thoughts a good shake. So what if she did like being with him? She knew what she wanted in life. She wanted to get up every single morning for the rest of her life and walk to her schoolroom.

She wanted to teach school.

Chapter Eighteen

"Miss Marnell!" a voice screamed. "Miss Marnell, come quick!"

Teddy MacAllister raced toward her over the expanse of frosty school yard where Ivan was splitting wood. "Roxanna fell off her horse and she's not moving!"

Ivan dropped his ax and caught the boy by the shoulder. "Where is she?" Teddy pointed back the way he had come, and Ivan began to run.

The schoolhouse door banged open and Teddy barreled into Christina. "It's Roxanna! She's hurt!"

"Run and get Doc Dougherty at the hospital," she ordered. "Hurry!"

Out of breath, Christina reached the riderless horse standing beside the path and saw the still form on the ground. Roxanna's face was white as paper and her eyes were closed. Ivan knelt over her.

"Get blanket, shawl, anything," he shouted, draping his sheepskin jacket over the still form.

Her stomach lurched. Christina stripped off her wool shawl and handed it to him.

She could see the girl wasn't breathing. She crouched beside the girl and picked up her small limp hand.

"Rub," Ivan ordered. "Rub hard."

Suddenly he tossed away her shawl and the jacket covering the motionless girl, bent over her and began pushing down on her chest.

"What are you doing?" Christina shouted.

He didn't look up. "I must try something."

Terrified, she watched his hands move rhythmically up and down on Roxanna's thin chest. A minute passed. Then another. It seemed like hours.

All at once the girl gasped and her body twitched. Ivan reared back in surprise, and then Roxanna opened her eyes. Quickly he piled his heavy jacket back on top of her and laid his hand on her forehead.

"I fell off Jane-girl," Roxanna murmured.

Ivan frowned up at Christina. "What is Jane-girl?"

"Jane-girl is her horse."

At that moment Doc Dougherty arrived on the run, a tearful Teddy a few paces behind. "I see that she's breathing," the physician panted. "Teddy said she was dead." He gripped the girl's wrist, then moved his forefinger back and forth in front of her eyes. "How many fingers?"

"Just one," Roxanna said, her voice faint. The doctor felt along her arms and legs, then lifted away Ivan's jacket and laid his ear against the girl's chest.

Ivan rose to his feet and stood watching. "Doctor, I tried pushing on her chest. You think I hurt ribs?"

Dr. Dougherty looked up. "You probably saved her life, Panovsky. Ribs are not important. Still…" He tentatively pressed his hand on Roxanna's breastbone. "Does that hurt?"

"No," the girl murmured.

"Good. No harm done." He gathered the girl up in

his arms. "I'll take her to the hospital and check her over. Good work, Teddy. And Ivan…" Awkwardly he stuck his hand out from under the girl's body and gave Ivan a hurried handshake. "She's lucky you were here, Panovsky. You did the right thing."

Teddy started after the doctor. "I'm gonna un-saddle my horse and then Jane-girl, Miss Marnell. I might be late to school."

Christina drew in a shaky breath. "Y-you're early, Teddy. T-take your time." She sucked in more air, but she couldn't seem to stop trembling.

"Christina." Ivan touched her shoulder. "Are you all right?"

"N-no." She stepped into his arms and burst into tears. He held her until she'd regained her composure, but he didn't release her. "Ivan," she said at last. "Ivan, I think you are the most wonderful man. How did you know what to do?"

"I did not know. Once when I was boy in Russia a troika turned over in our wheat field, and I watched driver do this." He hesitated. "Do you really think I am wonderful man?" he asked, his voice tentative. His breath ruffled her hair and his arms tightened around her.

She couldn't answer. The truth was she *did* think he was wonderful, and the last thing she wanted to do at this moment was move out of his arms. "Yes, Ivan, I think you are an extraordinary man."

"Because I accidentally help girl?"

She lifted her head and looked up at him. "No, not just because of Roxanna. Because of you."

"Christina…Christina, I have more wood to split, but first I want to kiss you."

She reached to touch his cheek. "The wood box is full, Ivan. You need not split anymore. But kiss me anyway." She stretched up on her toes and grazed her lips against his.

What heaven a kiss can be, she thought hazily. It went on and on and she never wanted him to stop. Inside she felt shaky, as if she had swallowed a mouthful of stars, and when he finally lifted his mouth from hers she couldn't remember where she was.

"We must stop," she whispered.

"Why?" He breathed the word near her ear, and for an instant she wanted to close her eyes and fly away somewhere with him.

"Because," she said, her voice unsteady, "Teddy and the rest of my students will be here any minute."

"I could kiss you until then," he said with a quiet laugh.

"If you did, I would forget all the lessons I planned for today. And…" She brushed her lips across his chin.

"And?"

She smiled up at him. "And I would have to send all the students home."

"That is very good idea."

She laughed softly and stepped out of his arms. "Anna," she said softly, "is very fortunate."

Ivan watched Christina's long blue skirt disappear into the schoolhouse, picked up his sheepskin jacket and strode over to the ax he'd dropped on the ground. He felt so good he could chop three more cords of firewood. Christina had said he was a wonderful man! Extraordinary. And she did like kissing him—he could tell. He could hardly wait to kiss her again. He wanted to kiss her all day! His heart began to hammer inside his chest. Maybe even all night.

The ax slipped out of his hand and plopped at his feet. You didn't kiss a woman like Christina all night unless…unless she belonged to you. Unless she married you. He was one step closer. Maybe. But now Christmas was coming, and Annamarie said Christina was very busy with the play about Robin Hood. And it was winter and snow was everywhere…

He stopped short, remembering something his father had once told him about courting his mother. "When the winter snow came, we went on picnics."

"Picnics! In the wintertime?"

"You will understand when you are older," his father had said.

Ah, Papa, you would have liked Christina. She is a girl who will like picnics in the snow.

Chapter Nineteen

"A picnic?" Annamarie exclaimed, her eyes shining. "Oh, Ivan, she will love going on a picnic!"

"In the snow," Ivan clarified.

"It is unusual, but then so is Miss Marnell. I think she will like it."

"A picnic with me," he added.

"Well, of course. Who else?

"Just me."

Annamarie stopped chopping walnuts to throw her arms around him. "Yes! Yes—yes—yes!"

Ivan bit his lip. He was not so sure. Maybe Christina would not like being alone with him. Maybe she had other things to do, lessons for school or books to read or… In frustration he ran his fingers through his hair. He was not sure taking her on a picnic was the right thing to do. Maybe it would be too cold. Or raining. Or even snowing.

This past week it had snowed almost constantly. The schoolchildren sledded down the hills, laughing and screaming with excitement, and then they all trooped into town and stood in front of the store windows along main street, gazing at the fancy dresses and leather baseball gloves. One by one Christmas trees appeared in front-parlor windows, swathed in red and green paper chains and strings of cranberries and popcorn.

He tried to think about Christmas, about presents for Anna and special cookies they would bake together, but mostly he thought about Christina. About inviting her to come with him on a snow picnic, like his papa had told him about.

He wanted to marry Christina. But if he wanted to marry her, he had to ask her first. And before that, he had to court her, invite her to go on a picnic with him. In the snow.

At the bakery he found Uncle Charlie working behind the shiny glass display case.

"Miss Marnell, she is at home?"

"Yes," the smiling Chinese man said. "Miss Marnell at home in apartment. Go upstairs and knock at door."

Ivan hesitated.

"What matter?" Charlie inquired. "Is not proper to knock on Sunday? I know she not go to church. Never go to church. Go to school only."

Ivan bit his lip. The day was perfect for a picnic. The sky was so blue it looked painted, and the snow shimmered in the sunlight like spun silver. Annamarie had helped him pack a picnic lunch into a big wicker basket, and he had rented a horse and buggy.

But maybe Christina was busy with her schoolwork? Or perhaps she did not like picnics?

Charlie reached into the display case, selected six chocolate cookies with crinkly tops and wrapped them up in a square of butcher paper. "You take these," he said with a twinkle in his black eyes. "Always better offer small gift." He waved away Ivan's offered coins. "Is also gift for you. Look like you need courage."

Ivan accepted the small packet, drew in a deep breath and started up the stairs to Christina's apartment.

She smiled when she opened her door, and the speech Ivan had thought about all night froze on his tongue. Instead, he thrust the package of cookies at her.

"Why, thank you, Ivan. I was just going out for a walk. Would you like to come with me?"

"No," he said. "I come to invite you on picnic. Anna and I pack lunch and—"

"A picnic? But it's the middle of December!"

"I know. But my papa say that is how he— I mean, I bring warm blanket and the sun is shining. It is beautiful day."

"Yes, it is a beautiful day," she said. "And I feel like doing something unusual. After all, it's almost Christmas!"

Ivan couldn't seem to stop smiling. "I am glad. I have buggy to drive us." He waited while she gathered up a shawl, then took her elbow and escorted her down the stairs past a grinning Uncle Charlie and out onto the board sidewalk.

She looked so beautiful his mouth was dry. She wore a long yellow wool dress that looked like it was made of sunshine and a yellow knitted wool shawl draped over her shoulders. He found he couldn't utter a word, so he handed her into the buggy.

She gazed at him in silence for a long moment, and finally he managed to choke out the first thing that came to mind. "Anna made fried chicken. And potato salad. You like potato salad? Is not Russian salad, but…" He flapped the reins on the chestnut mare and the buggy rolled forward.

"Yes, I like potato salad," she said as the wheels crunched over the snowy road. "And we have the cookies you brought."

Ivan could think of nothing more to say, so he concentrated on guiding the buggy out of town along the road that led to the river. The meadows looked like they were covered with whipped cream, and as they drew near the water, snow sparkled on the shrubs along the riverbank. The air smelled of fir trees.

He selected a quiet spot at the bend in the burbling river and drew the buggy to a halt. Christina wrapped her skirt around her knees and watched him unpack the wicker picnic basket.

"Are you teaching Anna to cook? Or is she learning from a recipe book?"

"Mrs Beeton's Book of Household Management," he said with a chuckle. "My mama would laugh."

"Your mother probably never looked at a recipe book in her life," Christina said with a smile.

"My mama was married when she was fifteen."

"Fifteen! But that's so young!"

"In old country, girls marry young. She learned to cook from *her* mama. Not from book."

"But Ivan, you can learn so many things from books!"

"Not most important things." He unpacked the chicken and potato salad and handed her a plate.

"All of human experience is contained in books.

Think of Shakespeare. What important things can you *not* learn from books?"

He touched her hand. "Those are stories *about* life, not life itself. Do you understand? Reading *about* happiness is not same as *feeling* happiness."

"Oh." She bit into a drumstick, but she kept looking at him, her blue eyes slightly narrowed and her expression thoughtful.

"I have learned something," he said. "Not from book, from you."

"Oh? What have you learned from me?"

"Is about Anna. I think is important for Anna to read books. To have education. I learn this from you, Christina. Not from book."

"Oh, Ivan, you are the most surprising man! I think you are a wonderful brother. You are a wonderful man!"

He sucked in a lungful of air and opened his mouth. "Christina, something more there is I want to tell you."

"Yes?" She lifted her head. "What is it, Ivan?"

"It is this." He took another breath and lifted the drumstick out of her hand. "I— Christina, I want to marry you."

A long silence fell. "Ivan," she breathed at last. "Oh, Ivan, there is no man I care for more than you. You know that, don't you?"

A bubble of joy floated into his chest and he could scarcely speak. "I did not know that."

She reached to touch his cheek. "But I told you once that I will never marry. Do you remember?"

"Yes, I remember. Only…only I do not believe,

not truly. That was before I kissed you. I thought you liked, because you let me kiss you again, and then I think…"

"I did like kissing you," she said softly. She took his hand. "I *do* like it. Every time you kiss me I am so happy it makes me cry."

He lifted the shawl away from her shoulders, pulled her forward and covered her mouth with his. When he broke away, he pressed her head into his neck and stroked her hair. "Do you love me, Christina?"

"Yes, Ivan," she said, her voice quiet. "You know I love you."

"But you do not want to live with me, is correct?"

She gave brief laugh and raised her head. "Oh, I would live with you in a minute! I just can't marry you. A married woman is not allowed to teach school in the state of Oregon."

"Ah, then I have lesson for teacher."

"A lesson? What lesson?"

"Christina, you must decide how you are going to live your life, what you in life value."

"Yes," she said softly. "And I know what that is, Ivan. It's being a teacher. I have spent my whole life preparing for it. I know who I am when I'm in the classroom. What I am worth."

He said nothing, just looked at her.

"Ivan, I would be no good as a wife. I can't even cook. And," she added with a soft laugh, "if I moved into your house, the sheriff would arrest me!"

"Because you are single woman?"

"Yes. That would be the most scandalous event in Smoke River!"

"This teaching, it means so much to you?"

"It does. Besides, love doesn't always last, does it?"

"Ah. I have another lesson for teacher. This I learn from my mama. When you love someone you do not love them all the time in same way. There are, how you say, downs and ups, just like in life."

She opened her mouth to reply, but he placed his forefinger against her lips. "Wait. If you become my wife, you cannot teach, and that is what you say you want. But if you keep your teaching, I will not have what *I* want, and that is to marry you."

She nodded, her eyes full of tears. "Oh, Ivan, I am sorry."

"Also me," he said, a catch in his voice. "I look forward to teach you how to cook."

She laughed, and then she cried, and he kissed her for a long time. Then he packed up the picnic basket and drove the buggy back to town. A heavy silence lay between them. When he left her at her apartment door, she clung to him and cried some more.

"Christina, I love you," he whispered against her lips. "I would make you happy."

"I know."

She kissed him again and disappeared inside.

The next week of school was the most miserable she could ever remember. Christina's students performed well, showing they had learned a great deal in the past few months. She was proud of them. Proud of herself.

But…but underneath her feeling of success over their accomplishments lay a hollow, dark, unhappy, empty sensation. Something was missing.

At lunchtime on Friday, Annamarie stayed inside at her desk, her head buried on her folded arms. Christina studied the girl with concern. "Anna, are you not feeling well?"

The girl raised her head. "I feel all right, Miss Marnell." But her voice was lifeless.

"Something is bothering you. Can you tell me about it?"

"Yes, I can," she whispered. "I shouldn't tell you, but I can."

Christina waited.

"It's Ivan."

Her heart thumped. "What about Ivan?"

Annamarie swiped tears off her cheeks. "He's so… unhappy, I guess you'd say. He doesn't say much. In fact, he doesn't say anything at all. It's like something has gone out of him. Every night he sits out on the front porch step in the cold, staring at nothing."

Christina bit her lip. She knew exactly what was wrong. It was the same thing that was eating away at her during all hours of the day and night. *Oh, God, how can loving someone be so painful?*

There was nothing she could say. She patted Annamarie's shoulder and turned away.

Chapter Twenty

"Please, mister?"

Ivan bent down to the little girl's level. It was Roxanna Jensen, the girl who'd been thrown from her horse a week ago. "Ah. Roxanna, what is it?"

"My daddy said to give this to you." She thrust a note into his hand and darted away onto the school yard.

Ivan straightened and unfolded the paper.

You saved my daughter's life. If there is anything I can do for you, please let me know.
Peter Jensen

By Saturday morning, after another week of sleepless nights and unhappy days, Christina finally admitted to herself what was wrong. Yes, she loved teaching school. But she also loved Ivan Panovsky. When she was with him her heart was so full of joy her chest ached, and when they were apart all she wanted was to be near him again. At night she tossed and turned, unable to sleep, and in the morning she had no appetite. Each day the first thing she wanted to do was be with Ivan.

Finally one afternoon she went to visit Iris Ming.

"Christina," the diminutive woman asked as she

poured out two cups of tea, "I can see you are not happy."

"Oh, Iris, I don't know what is wrong with me, I really don't."

"Ah. But your students are doing well in their studies. You like them, and they like you. You have everything you want, do you not?"

"Yes, I do have everything I want. Or I thought I wanted. Now I am not so sure."

Iris set her pink rosebud cup down on the saucer with a soft *click*. "For an intelligent woman, Christina, you learn very slowly."

Christina released a long sigh. "And I was always so convinced I knew everything about life," she said with a quiet laugh.

"Well," Iris said briskly, "it is never too late to learn. Old Chinese saying."

"Were you unsure when you married Charlie?"

"Unsure? No. Frightened, yes. Any intelligent woman would be frightened to marry a man she had never set eyes on."

Christina twisted her fingers together in her lap. "Iris, what can I do?"

"Listen to your heart, Christina." The Chinese woman reached over and squeezed her hand. "Listen hard."

Ivan propped his boots up on the front-porch railing and bent over with his elbows on his knees. Peter Jensen, the rancher whose young daughter he had saved, had just given him a heartfelt handshake and left with an encouraging grin. He dared not think what that meant.

Annamarie had left for church, and he was alone with his thoughts. He closed his eyes and breathed in the scent of Mrs. DuPont's fir tree next door.

Christina. Christina, I will make you a gift.

All at once he heard an uneven footstep across the street and his eyelids snapped open. Christina! And she was coming straight toward him. Slowly he straightened and stood up.

"Anna not here," he said. "She is at church."

Christina smiled at him. "Good for her," she said with a laugh. "But it is you I have come to see."

"Yes?"

"Yes." She moved a step closer, and his pulse picked up. "Ivan, I have something to tell you. Something important."

"I have something to tell you, too. Come, sit here beside me." He took her hand and pulled her down next to him on the top porch step.

She settled her blue skirt around her, carefully tucking her petticoat ruffle out of sight. "I have learned something," she announced. "Something wonderful."

He waited, scarcely daring to breathe.

"Ivan," she said with a sigh. She leaned toward him and he wrapped his arm about her shoulders.

"Yes?" he prompted, scarcely able to breathe. "What you have learned?"

"That I love you."

"You say that before, Christina. And you know how I feel. What I want."

"There is more," she said, her voice quiet.

He looked sharply at her. "What more, Christina? Say it."

"Ivan…" She hesitated. "Ivan, I love you. More than I love teaching. I have decided that I will give up teaching."

"What?" He could not believe what he was hearing. "Why you would do this?"

"Because…well, because I want to marry you. I want to marry you more than I want to teach school."

He stared at her, and then he began to laugh. "That is what I wanted to tell you, Christina. You can marry me and teach school, too."

Her blue eyes clouded. "But I can't, not in Oregon."

"But yes, you can! Peter Jensen came to see me this morning. You remember Peter Jensen? Is Roxanna's father. And also he is president of school board."

Christina stared at him. "Yes, I know, but—"

"Peter Jensen does me a service. He says it is all right if you marry me. You can marry me *and* you can teach school. He says you will be only married schoolteacher in all of Oregon!"

"But—"

He kissed her. And when she kissed him back, he kissed her again. "There are no buts, Christina. Just answer me yes."

Her beautiful eyes filled with tears and spilled down her cheeks. Ivan swiped them away with his thumb. "Do you want to marry me?"

"Yes," she said, weeping. "I do want to marry you. But…"

"I say no buts, remember? Just yes."

"Oh, Ivan, I scarcely know what to think!"

He cupped his hands around her shoulders and turned her toward him. "Not true, Christina. You *do* know what to think. Must think of now, and next year, and years to come."

She bit her lip and smiled, then wound her arms around his neck and laid her tear-sheened cheek against his face. "Ivan," she breathed. "Ivan, you are the smartest man I have ever known."

Annamarie returned from church an hour later. "Married?" she screamed. "*Married?* Really and truly married?"

"Yes, really and truly married," Ivan and Christina said together.

"Oh, Miss Marnell, let me be your maid of honor? Please? *Please, please, please?*"

Epilogue

Christina Marnell and Ivan Panovsky were married on Christmas Day in Iris and Uncle Charlie Ming's front parlor, decorated for the occasion with red ribbons and evergreen boughs. Christina wore a pale pink silk gown with a double ruffle at the hem and carried a bouquet of red poinsettias.

Annamarie, in her first long dress of soft blue wool challis, stood up with Christina, and Peter Jensen stood up with Ivan. Roxanna Jensen scattered a basket of dried rose petals in Christina's path.

After they exchanged vows, Iris and Uncle Charlie served a four-tier chocolate wedding cake topped with roses fashioned of white icing. The gathered townspeople drank toasts of champagne and hard apple cider, and Noralee Ness, the mercantile owner's daughter, caught Christina's tossed bouquet.

Following the reception, Christina and Ivan were serenaded by her students, who lined up on the wide front porch and sang "Comin' Through the Rye" in three-part harmony.

* * * * *

A KISS
FROM THE COWBOY

Carol Arens

Dedicated to the house at 22631 Kittridge Street
and the love that happened within your walls for 60 years.

Dear Reader

You might find it odd that I've dedicated this story to
a house. But 22631 was more than four walls. To five
generations it was sanctuary…a place to celebrate every
holiday.

It was the place my parents welcomed us home to.
Especially at Christmas. Coming in through its front
door, we were surrounded by the scent of roasting turkey,
green beans simmering in the pot, and the fragrance of
the Christmas tree. Once inside we were wrapped up in
loving arms. On Christmas Eve there were photos taken
of children in front of the tree, dressed in new pyjamas
and eager for Santa to come. Thirty-one stockings were
hung by the chimney with care. In the morning there was
the magic of a pile of gifts that filled the living room, four
feet high.

This will be the first year we will not celebrate Christmas
there. Our home has gone on to bless another family. But
we will take many things with us…toasts with eggnog,
Christmas music on the stereo, and love…lots and lots of
love.

So, my friends, three cheers for home—whether it has
sheltered you for six days or sixty years…I wish you the
blessings of it.

Very best wishes and Merry Christmas!

Carol

Chapter One

〜〜〜〜〜

December 1885, Sweet Bank, Texas

Cousin Edwina was coming to visit.

Livy York led Old Blue from the shelter of the barn and into the biting wind. Old Blue was no more blue in color than the sun shining down was warm. He might have been considered bluish in his youth, but when Livy had purchased him last week he was already gray with middle age.

Still, he was sturdy enough and she could afford him. Next week she hoped to purchase a cow or a goat.

Because Edwina was coming.

She crossed the yard, tethered the horse to a post in front of the modest ranch house then dashed up the front steps. Paint from the banister flaked off onto her gloves.

It was only a bit warmer inside since she had banked the fire an hour ago in anticipation of going to town.

"Let's go, Sam," she called to her four-year-old brother.

A lump under a blanket on the couch heaved. Sam's head popped out of the covers. His light brown hair stuck up at odd angles.

"What does four plus six make, Livy?"

"Ten—the number of seconds I have to put your hair in order. Hurry now, we don't want to miss the Christmas-tree raising in town."

"I want to miss it." Sam tossed off the blanket, already wearing his heavy coat.

He didn't really want to miss the ceremony, she knew. He'd been talking of little else since the tree had been delivered to the livery four days ago.

What he did miss was Ma and Pa. So did she. This would be the first year he had celebrated Christmas without them.

"You know, Sam, Ma and Pa want you to have fun."

"Can they see me from heaven?"

"Of course, and they love you just the same from heaven as they did when they lived here. I'm sure they will be at the tree raising right alongside of us. We'll just see them with our hearts instead our eyes."

"Reckon I wouldn't want'a make them sad by acting like a baby."

Sam raced for the door, his grin wide. It had been nearly a year since Ma and Pa passed of fever. It was good to see her brother smiling. She believed he was finally healing—in as much as that kind of healing could be done.

Livy still cried at odd moments; she suspected she always would. Sometimes for joy, when a scent or a sound would bring back the wonderful years they had shared as a complete family. Sometimes it was for just plain missing Ma and Pa.

But Christmas was almost here and she would

make sure her brother found all the happiness the season could give him.

If only Edwina was not coming to spend a week with them after the New Year.

Life would be a good deal less complicated if she stayed in her well-appointed home in her upper-crust neighborhood of Kendrick.

Her cousin had never felt the need to come and visit while Ma and Pa were alive. There was only one reason that Livy could think of why she would do it now. That one reason made her stomach turn.

Following Sam outside, she lifted him onto the saddle then climbed up behind him, pulling him close against the cold.

"You got the *St. Nicholas Magazine*, Livy?"

"Right here in my coat pocket."

After the raising of the tree, everyone was going to Ida's Sweet Shop for hot chocolate and cookies. As she had done every year since she was sixteen, Livy would read the children a Christmas story from the magazine. The tradition was a fine way to begin the holiday festivities.

She only wished she had been allowed to spend every Christmas at home in Sweet Bank. This small town was full of friendly people who had doted upon her all her life.

But Ma had wanted her to spend the holidays with her rich relatives in Kendrick. At twelve years old she had been put on a train and sent off to be her aunt and uncle's act of Christmas charity.

Oh, she had been indulged, given a new party dress and a gift or two—but even gussied to the gills,

Livy knew she had never measured up. Sometimes she would say something that smacked of small town and her aunt and uncle would look embarrassed. Livy would run from the room, her cheeks flaming with shame.

As hard as she'd tried not to seem the country bumpkin, all she'd ever accomplished was to become homesick.

When she turned sixteen, she refused to make the trip.

Ma hadn't been happy about it.

Her mother's wish had been for her daughter to have the financial and social advantages she had grown up with. As much as Ma loved Pa, she had turned her back on her family to marry a lowly rancher.

One time, Ma had told her in a whisper of the prominent politician she had been engaged to. It was clear that she loved Pa and was not unhappy with her life, but she had blinked away a tear that night. Livy was never sure if it had been because of the estrangement from her parents or from the politician.

In the end, and Livy was not sure why, Ma made up a lie about why her daughter could no longer come for Christmas. She wrote a letter to her sister explaining that Livy was spending time with a very prosperous, quite influential beau and was blissfully happy so she could not possibly come for a visit this year.

The truth was, the purchase of her train ticket would have come at a dear cost. Livy reckoned her parents would have gone hungry while she feasted. And the prosperous, influential beau? Well, she'd indulged in a kiss with Frank Gordon, the banker's son, one day behind the schoolhouse then run for home, too embarrassed to look him in the eye. But once the blush wore off, she'd let him kiss her again. The truth was, she'd grown starry-eyed over him.

On the day he ran off to join a traveling troupe of actors, she was waiting under a walnut tree with her lips puckered. Indeed, she had waited for him for three long hours.

The bruise to her heart, or maybe just her pride, had taken some time to heal.

"Look, Livy!" Her brother tried to climb to his knees in front of her as they rode into town. "They're bringing the tree out of the livery!"

"Ouch! Sam, get your knee out of my ribs and sit back down."

It was a lucky thing the ride from town took only half an hour. Her brother was like a wriggly worm, incapable of sitting still.

Also, the temperature was falling. She would be glad to get inside the bakery, where there was always a welcoming fire.

After delivering Old Blue to the care of Hank, the liveryman, Livy took Sam's hand and led him toward the town square and the gathering crowd.

"I want'a walk by myself!" Sam declared, wrenching free of her grip. "I'm big now."

Four and a half years old wasn't all that big, but he was fully capable of walking safely beside her. It was just that she liked the feel of his small hand in hers.

Sam had been born into the family after her parents had given up hope of having another child. What a blessing that squalling, lusty newborn had been to all of them. His birth had eased the grief of many miscarriages.

From the first time Livy held him, she'd felt as much his mother as his sister. She doubted that there had been a moment in his first nine months when he hadn't been held and coddled by Livy or Ma.

Passing the door of the train depot, she was nearly knocked flat by Mildred Banks rushing out the door. Mildred worked the depot counter as well as running a boardinghouse.

"Oh, Livy!" Mildred gripped her shoulders, steadying her. "I was in such a hurry to see the tree I didn't pay a bit of attention to what I was doing. I do so love the Christmas tree!"

Mildred hurried a few steps ahead then swung about. "Oh, and that man you hired isn't here yet. The train is running late." She rushed away but turned yet again. "I've set out some dirty laundry behind the boardinghouse for you. And there's some fancy-like curtains for you to borrow for your cousin's visit, if they are to your liking."

"Thank you!" Livy rushed after Sam, who had outpaced Mildred.

It would be a relief when the ranch hand she had hired got here. She needed his well-touted skills desperately. She had found him through an advertisement in the *Texas News and Review*. From the brief correspondence they had exchanged it seemed like he would suit her needs well.

She probably should not have led the man to believe that this was a lasting position, but she'd feared he would not come all this way for a two-week job. She only hoped that when he discovered the truth, he would not quit on the spot.

Of course, had it not been for pride, she would not need his services at all. Well, she would. The ranch had become run-down after Pa passed to his glory, but she just would not need him so urgently.

Several years ago, with all the maturity of a five-year-old, Livy had followed her mother's example and written regular letters to Edwina. Because she had begun them, and could not suddenly stop, she'd kept up the silly letters over the years, and they'd turned into stories about her grand life, how prosperous the ranch was and how she was the belle of Sweet Bank. How she had become engaged to the banker's son.

It was unlikely that her cousin actually believed those lies, although she had never hinted that she did not, but—

But Edwina was coming to visit soon and Livy would rather bathe in a public horse trough than let her cousin see the reality of her humble life. Edwina had fine manners and exquisite clothing. Women like Livy washed those expensive clothes.

Vanity was a part of the reason she had hired Mr. James—she could not deny the sad fact. But it was not the whole reason—not the most important one.

Her mother's family loved to appear charitable, especially when it came to their poorer relatives. What Livy feared the most was that Edwina would come, see Sam's humble life and want to take him with her—insist upon raising him with her own four-year-old son.

Livy's fear of being separated from her brother might be overblown, but wealth had a way of speaking very loudly.

In Livy's opinion, it did not matter how much money her Hall relatives lavished upon Sam, they could never love him like she did.

Everyone knew that love was the most important thing of all.

The train was still an hour outside of Sweet Bank when Kit James closed *The Common Man's Guide to Ranching*.

The sudden snap of the pages woke his small niece, Emmie, who snuggled against his ribs for warmth.

"Where's Papa?" she murmured, blinking and glancing around. All of a sudden her green eyes, an exact match to Kit's brother's, misted over. "In Kevin?"

"Heaven, honey. But I'm here."

It was a good thing she never asked about her mother because he didn't know how to answer that question. But she would ask one day and his heart would break.

Three years and six days ago, Emmie had been born to a prostitute. Three years and one day ago the woman had sent the baby across town to Kit's brother, insisting he was the father, which by looking at her, he clearly was. Three years ago the woman had left town, never to be heard from again.

Kit didn't even know her real name. He highly doubted it was actually Midnight Lillie.

His brother, Wilson, had done his best to care for

his infant girl, but he wasn't the most prudent of men. All Kit's life he had been cleaning up after his older brother's mistakes in judgment.

Although, one could hardly consider Emmie James a mistake. She was an adorable, curly-haired treasure and the best thing that had ever happened to Wilson—or to Kit.

She had come as a surprise, but one he would never regret.

And now she was whimpering into his shirt.

"Would you like for me to hold her again?" The matronly woman sitting on the other side of the aisle reached out her arms. "Sometimes a baby just needs to be held by a woman."

This seemed to be true with his niece. During the two months that he had been her guardian, he'd seen her calm to a woman's touch even if she didn't know the lady at all. For some reason, women were always eager to help him with her.

"Many thanks," he said, then placed Emmie into her comfortable-looking arms. "Again."

It was hard to say who was more comforted by the embrace, Emmie or the woman. Within moments they were both dozing, gray head bent to chestnut brown.

Maybe Kit and his brother had been held that way by their mother at one time, but he sure couldn't remember the occasion. Wilson claimed to remember it—on the night she abandoned them at an orphanage. What Kit remembered was that Mama was laughing and leaning on the arm of some strange man when she walked away.

Growing up in an orphanage had been hard on

Wilson. He was always pushing at the rules. One night when Kit was thirteen and Wilson fifteen, they ran away and joined up with a circus, which suited Wilson fine, but Kit didn't care for it. When Kit was seventeen, he joined an acting troupe, which was a little more respectable than the circus.

Over the years before he'd died, Wilson had kept in touch, often because he needed to be bailed out of some scrape or another.

Neither Kit nor Wilson ever saw their mother again. Word was that she had come looking for them, but they had been gone a year by then.

Shaking his head, he laid his mother's memory to rest—or rather, the lack of her memory.

Kit opened the book again, thumbed to the chapter titled "Herding Cattle."

As an actor, he'd played a cowboy many times, and indeed he'd often dreamed of being a real one. He knew the swagger and the drawl. "Howdy, ma'am" was nearly second nature to him. But getting a cow to do what he wanted it to? That was going to take some research—and practice.

The problem was, Miss Olivia York was expecting a man of experience.

He'd assured her that he could clean a barn, tame a wild horse and build a fence—all in a good day's work.

And he'd done all those things in *Cody Billings of Montana*. He'd known every line of that play; the character was a part of him—too bad he didn't know how to build a real fence.

He knew it was wrong as can be to lie to Miss

York. But he was certain he could learn all those things—he had a book and was a quick study.

Miss York needed a ramrod and Emmie needed a home. So Kit, known last week as Burton Kitson James, had quit acting and begun life as a cowboy.

Well, he hadn't really begun as yet, but he soon would and he'd make sure his boss lady was not disappointed.

With any luck she would not notice that he was book-learned. He'd do his best to put on a good show. If she discovered his lie she'd send him packing quick as the swish of a horse's tail.

She would notice Emmie, though. He hadn't mentioned he had a three-year-old during their correspondence.

The decision to keep her a secret was as rash as any his late brother had ever made, but Kit had worried that he might not get hired with a young child in tow. Emmie needed a home. He needed a job. A sweet little ranch would give his niece the security she deserved.

If he made himself indispensable to the ranch, pleased Miss York with his hard work, perhaps he would keep this job for many years.

"Building fences," he muttered, then flipped the well-worn pages to that chapter.

Chapter Two

"Old Blue's a finicky cuss."

Livy laughed because Sam made the pronouncement the same as Pa would have to the many horses they used to have on the ranch, just in a higher voice.

Unlike Pa, though, Sam thought it was funny that the animal refused to move.

It might have been funny if they weren't still a good distance from home and if the temperature hadn't dropped to well below freezing.

"Have your own way," she said to the animal, then dismounted. "Let's see if he'll walk with only you on his back, Sam."

With a tug on the reins and an encouraging click of her tongue she led the horse forward…two steps.

"Come on, Old Blue. Sam can't weigh much more than forty pounds." Clearly, that was forty pounds more than the critter wanted to carry. "I'll light the stove in the barn first thing when we get home."

Old Blue shook his head, jangled the reins.

"That means no," Sam clarified.

"There's no help for it. We'll have to walk." She lifted Sam from the saddle, ducking her head this way and that to avoid the poke of the pine needles on the severed Christmas-tree branch that her brother had insisted on dragging home.

The blamed critter followed along without hesitation now that no one was riding him.

Brrr! Cold seeped through her boots and up her legs. It wouldn't take long for Sam's small feet to be at risk of frostbite.

Heavy clouds threatened overhead. They had come as a surprise since the day had been clear. An icy wind blew them in quicker than anyone could have predicted.

"Let's hurry!"

Seeing a snowflake, Sam snaked out his tongue and caught it.

"Snow's coming, Livy!"

Clearly, to a four-year-old boy snow was fun. To his twenty-two-year-old sister, it was as dangerous as a striking rattler.

"I'll have to carry you," she said, winding the horse's reins around her wrist and reaching down to lift up her brother. "I don't want your feet getting wet."

"I'm too big!" he complained but allowed her to pick him up.

He wrapped his arms around her neck and clamped his legs about her waist. Every few steps she had to adjust his weight. He really was too big to be carried and continually slipped over the curve of her hip.

"You'll have to drop the branch."

"I want it."

"My back is hurting, Sam. Please just put it down."

"No! It's for Ma and Pa." His voice cracked. His small chest hitched.

Livy's back ached, her muscles screamed and even

her teeth began to clack. She could not imagine carrying her brother all the way home. But she could not put him down and have his feet get wet in the quickly mounding snow.

"How's your coat? Still dry?"

Sam shook his head. "I'm cold."

Apparently, they were going to die three miles from home because of a finicky horse and a branch that her brother refused to leave behind.

But—was that the jangle of tack she heard? The creak of wagon wood?

She spun about, spotted a man urging his team through shifting drifts of snow.

Bundled in heavy clothes, with a Stetson pulled low over his face, she did not recognize him.

Still, she had never been more relieved to see anyone—stranger or not.

When the wagon drew to a stop beside her she noticed that he carried a blanket in front of him. Yes, a wriggling blanket with a spray of brown curls bubbling out of the top.

"Howdy, ma'am." The stranger's voice sounded smooth, pleasing and friendly. She felt warmer already. "Your horse come up lame?"

"Came up stubborn, more like it."

The man thumbed his Stetson back on his forehead, revealing his eyes.

Oh...well...my goodness, they are arresting. She needed to say something quick so he didn't wonder why she stared at him as though she had just been struck by Cupid's arrow.

Wasn't that the most foolish thought to ever invade

her mind? It was Edwina who used to go on about love at first sight and all kinds of like nonsense. Of course, Edwina had never been left under a walnut tree waiting for a kiss.

But really, staring into those rich brown eyes made her feel like she'd just indulged in a pound of butter.

Well, she doubted she was the first woman to go dumb at the sight of them and she certainly would not be the last.

Besides, if a woman had to be rescued, wasn't it nice to have it done by an attractive fellow? Why, this was nearly like a fairy tale.

And while she stood here speechless, it occurred to her that kissing him would be even nicer than kissing Frank Gordon had been.

"I wonder if you might be Miss Olivia York? If you are, I'm your new hired man."

My word!

Kit paused with his hand on the barn door, glancing back at a large space. For all its size he didn't notice any drafts seeping through the timber walls. There must have been a lot of livestock boarded here once.

Now that he'd lit the stove on the north wall and the one on the south, the place was snug, cozy even.

His horse seemed content, munching hay beside his boss lady's stubborn old nag. The chickens, roosting in their coop, didn't seem to mind the sound of the wind whistling under the eaves.

During his time on the road with the traveling show, he'd stayed in far worse places than this.

The bedding in the loft was clean and fresh smelling. He couldn't complain about it. It was a nice space for a man on his own.

But there was Emmie to be considered. The drop from the loft to the barn floor had to be ten feet or more. Far enough that it would keep him restless all night long.

That was as far as his complaints went. He and Emmie had a warm place to bunk down and he was mighty grateful for it. He couldn't help but shiver, worrying about other folks who might be caught out on the road in the unexpected snowfall.

With a sigh of relief, but a concerned glance back at the loft, he opened the door, bent his head against the wind and pushed toward the ranch house.

White gusts blew sideways, twisted and swirled. All that was visible of the house was a vague outline of the roof.

Before he could lift his hand to rap on the door, it swung open. Miss York handed him a steaming mug while he kicked the snow from his not-yet-broken-in boots.

"I hope you like hot cocoa," she said, leaning against the door and closing it behind him.

He preferred coffee but—

Hell—Miss Olivia York was every bit as beautiful as he'd imagined she was under that big furry hat. She had a smile as warm and welcoming as the drink she had just placed in his hand.

Blamed if she was anything like he'd imagined on the train ride here. For some reason he'd pictured her as an older lady, probably a spinster no longer capable of keeping up her land—or her *spread*, as Cody Billings would have phrased it.

It wasn't a hardship that she was not a spinster—that her pretty brown eyes crinkled at the corners in welcome. Nope, he didn't mind that one bit.

"I likes cocoa, Uncle Kit." Emmie, sitting on the floor in front of the fireplace with a boy not a whole lot older than she was, grinned at him. A chocolate halo circled her mouth.

"I hope you don't mind her having it, but I think we all needed a good warming."

Sure were a lot of things he didn't mind just now. Being in a snug little house with a woman who looked sweeter than a Christmas sugarplum was one of them.

"Supper won't be ready for an hour, so make yourself comfortable." Miss York nodded toward the couch facing the fireplace.

When was the last time he'd stayed anywhere besides a hotel or a rented room? The house might be a humble place, but it was warm and happy.

Love lived here. He felt it coming from the timbered walls, smelled it wafting from the kitchen that his boss had just bustled into.

The couch sure did look inviting, but not more inviting than Olivia York's smile.

He followed the swish of her skirt and a slight fragrance of vanilla into the kitchen.

"I just want to say, ma'am…"

She was bent over, poking at something in the stove. Her hips moved and her skirt shimmied with the effort. His mouth went dry and he forgot what it was he wanted to say.

She straightened, turned to look up at him, her head tipped just so.

"I appreciate you hiring me on." Cody had said that once, and the next line had been—what—something? It was too provocative, as he recalled.

"Well, I just want to thank you." This was his own line, spoken with complete sincerity.

He only hoped she did not discover who he really was.

"I didn't know you had a child, Mr. James."

"Emmie is my niece, my late brother's girl." Here was where she would send him packing. Who could blame her? How was a hired man to get his work done with a little one underfoot? "I should have made you aware of her, I know."

"It does change things a bit, I'll admit."

He held his breath while she gazed out the window at the snow.

Hopefully, Miss York was as kind as her sweet expression indicated she was. He sent up a prayer that she would let them stay on until Christmas. It would break his heart if Emmie had to spend the holiday in a rented room. This was, for all intents and purposes, her first one. His brother had never understood the importance of celebrating the day.

Poor Emmie didn't even know who Santa was until last week.

"The barn isn't fit for a child." Miss York turned. She stared up at him, biting her bottom lip and frowning. "And I doubt if she will feel comfortable being separated from you."

She blinked, then looked suddenly away from him.

In a whisper of petticoats she walked to the kitchen door. Her gaze settled on the children, soft and indulgent.

"There's an extra room down the hall that will suit much better—for the both of you."

"Again, I'm mighty grateful."

"As am I." She leaned her shoulder against the doorjamb, tapping two slender fingers on her bosom while she watched the children laughing at the drip of chocolate dribbling down the boy's chin.

She glanced quickly at him then away. The ghost of an expression in her eyes made him feel unsettled. Must be his imagination, though. She'd just offered him a room in the house.

"Our parents passed away a little less than a year ago. It's good to see Sam being silly."

"I'm deeply sorry for your loss, Miss York."

"Yes, well, love does go on regardless of what sort of separation it is, don't you believe?"

"It's only been a couple of months since my brother died, but yes, I still feel him."

"I think that since we are going to be sharing a roof for a while, you ought to call me Livy. Everyone in town does."

For a while? He hoped she meant a long while. He'd have to do his best to make his services indispensable. Emmie needed a steady home, not a constant change of location. He'd seen firsthand, experienced it even, what happened to children raised on the road. That was not a future he wanted for his niece.

Besides that, he'd noticed that Livy's pretty hands

were chafed, redder and rougher than they ought to be. His job as her ramrod would be to take over much of the work she was apparently doing.

He would take pride in earning his money in that way.

"Lovely name, Livy. I'd be obliged if you called me Kit."

She smiled. He smiled back. Then something happened that he couldn't quite understand—a quiver in his chest that he'd never felt before—a sense that they would always be together.

She cocked her head at him. The shadow of a frown dipped her brows. Her sweet smile turned baffled looking. Could it be that she'd also felt a tug of destiny?

Could it be that the romantic aspect of his nature, the one that had led him into acting, was imagining the spark between them? Creating drama where there was none?

Perhaps the sensation was simple gratitude because he and Emmie had a roof over their heads, one that he wanted to keep for a good long while.

But then again, he'd felt gratitude for many things in his life—this was different.

He was pretty damn sure there had been a spark.

Chapter Three

It was late. The children were sleeping.

Time to get to work. Luckily, the storm had moved on as quickly as it had blown in.

Closing the front door behind her, Livy could see the barn bathed in moonlight—all pretty and snow spangled. She walked toward it, thinking that a fresh downfall made the world glitter—just like Christmas made one's soul glitter.

Just like having a handsome man in the house made a girl's heart glitter, or that was how it felt.

What a shame it was that after he made the ranch presentable enough for Edwina's visit, she would have to let him go.

After coming into the barn, she leaned against the door to close it, took a deep breath then sighed.

Something tender had happened earlier. It had happened when Kit said, "Livy." It seemed that he was suddenly no longer a stranger—like he had never been a stranger.

That was odd.

Even odder, she had the distinct feeling that her father had been standing behind Kit, grinning with his hand on Kit's shoulder.

This was confusing.

Luckily, washing laundry was not.

She lit a fire under her laundry kettles then went to get acquainted with Kit's horse while the water came to a simmer.

This barn used to be full of horses. Selling them was how Pa had kept his family clothed and fed. It hadn't been a grand business like some were, but they had gotten by.

"I'm glad you came along when you did." She stroked the animal's mane, ran her fingers along his muscled neck. "I sure do hope your master is good at what he does. I feel bad about leading him on about the length of the job, you know, but I'll be mighty humiliated if my cousin finds out I'm a fake. Worse— she will think Sam would be better off with her."

The horse shook his head, snorted. "You're right, he'd be miserable in their fancy home, just like I was. Let's pretend you are mine. You are ever so much more impressive than your stall neighbor."

In the end, pretending was as useful as a pebble in one's shoe so Livy crossed the barn to her laundry pots. She dumped lye soap in one, followed by the clothes that Mildred Banks had left beside her back door. She stirred them with a large wooden paddle.

The task was not as tedious as usual. For once she did not feel like she was going to fall asleep, tumble into the pot and drown, or boil.

Perhaps because there was a man living in her house. Someone to talk to. Someone to cook for. If something happened—an accident or if Sam fell ill, there was another adult to turn to.

Somehow she felt—

"Livy?"

Not so alone.

Funny how she hadn't noticed she'd even felt alone until Kit came—until he'd spoken her name and looked into her eyes.

"What are you doing out here so late?" she asked.

"That's what I was going to ask you."

"I wash clothes for the folks in town." She shrugged. "It's safer to do it when Sam's asleep."

He took the paddle from her hand then indicated that she should sit on a nearby stool.

"I didn't hire you to do laundry, Kit."

"Looking around, I wonder what you did hire me for." He arched his brows—and those eyes... *Oh, my.* "The only livestock I see are chickens and your horse."

"Yes, for what he's worth." She snatched the paddle from him and resumed stirring the clothes. "Thank you, Kit, but this is my job. And there is plenty of work for you to do, trust me."

"Well, ma'am, I didn't see any cattle to wrangle on the way in from town."

"No, you wouldn't. This has never been a cattle ranch. My father raised and sold horses, but when he passed I had to let what was left of the stock go."

"I reckon you hired me to get the ranch going again."

"I'd like to carry on my father's business someday, but I hired you for a different reason."

"Sure do hope I'm qualified to do whatever it is." His eyelids dipped ever so slightly. The playful expression he had worn coming into the barn dimmed.

"If anything you are more than qualified." She

lifted a paddle of dripping clothes from the soapy pot and placed them in the rinse pot. "In reading our correspondence, I was impressed with all you are handy at."

He stared at the water simmering in the pot, nodding his head without speaking.

"What I need you for—" Without warning an image of him touching her jaw, lifting her face and lowering his mouth to hers— Well. She shook her head to dispel the vision. "The work required of you will be to fix the place up. I'm sure you've noticed how it's fallen into disrepair."

"I noticed a fence in need of mending." He glanced up, his happy expression restored.

"There's that, and painting, lots of painting. What I need is for you to make my humble home look elegant."

She added more clothes to the rinse water.

"And I need it done by the New Year."

The doggone New Year!

He'd done a bit of artistic painting. It wasn't too hard to make a backdrop for a scene seem elegant. But a whole house? By the New Year?

He sure did hope his instruction book had something to say about that. It wasn't like he could go to the town library and find one that did. In a place this size, it would take all of an hour before he was found out as a fraud. Sure couldn't afford for that to happen.

"I wouldn't mind having a bit more time than that, Livy." Two weeks' time wasn't nearly enough to make a home for Emmie. "Even if I am good at what I do."

Or at least acting like he was good at it. But a whole house? There were broken shutters, the floor was splintered in spots and a stone was missing from the fireplace. All the fences needed work.

"Two weeks won't be long enough—and there's Christmas coming. I need to make it special for Emmie. My niece has never had a gift from Old Saint Nick, if you can believe it."

Livy dropped the paddle of clothes she was lifting from the pot back into the rinse water.

"That's just not right." She pressed her hips with curled fists, frowning at the black pot. "Children need Christmas. Well, we all do but—" She huffed out a sigh. "Between us, we'll make up for what she has lost. It's a promise from me to you."

"I do thank you." Even with her hands curled up, he could see how chafed they were. It was easy to see why. She was supporting herself and her brother by doing laundry. While other young women would be tucked into bed with sweet dreams of Prince Charming, Livy was scrubbing her youth away.

It troubled him to think she was going to pay his wages by working into the wee hours of the night.

Kit whisked the paddle from her hands again.

"Please, Kit. I can do this. You'll have enough to do getting this place in order."

"You help me with Christmas, I'll help you with washing."

Besides, he knew a bit about getting clothes clean. When the troupe washerwoman was near her time and after she gave birth to her twins, he'd helped with the chores. It was a relief to be able to do something that he didn't learn about in a book.

"Sit down while I wring them then hang these out to dry," he ordered.

With a nod, she settled onto a bale of hay. From the corner of his eye he saw her arch her back, heard her sigh of relief.

"I'll get this place in shape," he said. "But I'll need more time."

Time to figure out how to paint and such things. At least, those two weeks gave him time to figure out how to rebuild her ranch.

"Unfortunately, I don't have more time to give you. But I do aim to help out."

Finished with hanging the clothes on the rope that stretched from the north wall then twenty feet to a horse stall, he sat down beside her on the hay bale.

"I have a confession to make, Kit. I, well—I suppose you thought I hired you to ramrod my ranch. It's what I led you to believe, and I'm sorry for it. But you seemed to know so much about so many things. I reckon I made your duties seem more adventurous than they are." She gazed up at him, lamplight casting her face in an angelic glow. Water tapped an erratic rhythm onto the hay under the clothesline. "Please forgive me."

He'd like to meet the man who could not forgive a woman of such uncommon loveliness.

Especially when that man's deception was a far worse one.

"I don't see there's anything needing forgiveness. I'll fix up the house, then fix up the ranch."

"No, I'm sorry. That's not exactly what I meant." She breathed in hard. Let it out in a whoosh. "I can only hire you for the two weeks. I'm sorry I led you to believe otherwise. If you feel the need to decline my offer of employment, I understand."

He felt gut-punched, and it was an effort to breathe. He felt like he'd lost track of his lines midscene. If it wasn't for the fact that he was also deceiving her, he'd be blisteringly angry.

And even if he wanted to express his frustration, Livy was looking at him with eyes as brown and sweet as any he had ever seen.

Declining this position was not possible. Livy had been the only one to respond to his advertisement. He had no other place to go.

"I don't decline, Livy." But he would try to find a way to become so valuable to her that she would keep him on. Emmie needed a home and he would do whatever he had to make it happen. If it meant working hours on end for nothing, he would do it. "I accept. But I'll need more time for all this work."

"Like I said, I don't have more time. But between the two of us I think we can get it done."

He must have been frowning because she sighed.

"My cousin is coming to visit soon and I don't want her to see the place like it is."

"It needs some work, I'll admit. But your home is warm and welcoming."

"You feel welcome here?" For some reason her eyes misted over even though she smiled. "I'm glad. Ma and Pa always made folks feel welcome in our house—there wasn't a soul down on their luck that they didn't make welcome. Everyone in town knew they could count on Ma and Pa."

Her sweet yet vulnerable expression did something to him. His heart went soft, but down below he went uncomfortably stiff. It was all he could do to not cup that pretty face and kiss her mouth, especially when it trembled ever so slightly at one corner.

Cody Billings would have stolen a kiss.

The trouble was, Cody would forget the intimacy by scene four. Kit was sure he never would.

With some effort, he put Cody Billings back on the script page where he belonged.

"I'm sure your cousin will be comfortable in your home." Hell if she needed him here at all, really.

"Only if you help me." She reached across the hay bale and squeezed his hand.

Her small palm was more calloused than his was. This was not acceptable. A woman like her ought to be cherished, protected from tasks that would redden her hands. A man worthy of her would not have smooth skin and manicured fingernails like he had.

"I won't have you paying my wages by washing laundry in the middle of the night."

"If I don't pay you, I will pay someone else. I've got to have the ranch looking impressive—top hat, for my cousin's visit."

In two damn weeks?

"Won't she be satisfied with comfortable?"

"Not Edwina. She grew up with the very best of everything. Her goal in life is to impress folks. Even a simple country girl doesn't want to be found lacking."

"There's nothing simple about you, Livy. You're not lacking, either."

"Well…" She took a long slow breath that lifted her chest in an appealing way. She didn't notice him notice because she had looked away to stare at a blade of hay sticking out of the corner of the bale. She plucked it out and rolled it between her fingers. "But I won't be who Edwina is expecting. Over the years my mother and I led her to believe that I'm well-to-do in this town—someone of importance and engaged to a wealthy banker's son. Now Edwina is coming and I'm going to have to play the part."

Playing parts was something he knew about, but— "Wouldn't it be simpler to let her know who you really are? You've nothing to be ashamed of."

"It's not that I'm ashamed, Kit. My parents gave me a good life and I wouldn't trade it for all my cousin's fine manners and money. It's Sam I'm worried about. I know Edwina. She'll want to take him, raise him with her own boy. In her mind, she'll see it as her duty to give him advantages I cannot."

Livy flicked the tattered blade of straw away, covered her face with her hands and shook her head. After a moment she peeped at him between spread fingers.

"You probably think I'm being selfish to want to keep him with me."

"I don't. Everyone knows that love is the most important thing of all."

All of a sudden she dropped her hands away from her face, nodded her head vigorously.

"That's what I say!" She clutched his hand again,

this time with both of hers. "Exactly what I say! Thank you for staying on, helping me make my cousin believe what I've told her. She'll only be here for a few days."

"I'm your hired man, Livy—here for as long as you need me." Longer if he could find a way to make it happen. Hell—not if, when. She wanted the ranch restored and he wanted a home for his niece. There had to be a way of making that happen. "But I am going to help with the washing. I won't watch you wear yourself down when I'm here to lend a hand."

"I've been doing it by myself for a year, but if that's your condition, I accept, gratefully."

They ought to go back to the house. The laundry was drying fine and the children needed checking on. Still, neither of them made a move to get up from the hay bale.

For the life of him, all he wanted to do was to sit and gaze into her eyes. Even at this time of night, after caring for her young brother all day, after washing clothes into the wee hours of the night, they simmered, as warm and appealing as brown sugar melted in butter.

Since her hands were still gripping his, expressing what he guessed to be gratitude for him staying on, he lifted them, and kissed each reddened palm.

Something was definitely going on here—a yearning, a tenderness. Cody Billings never felt his damned heart tumble when he kissed a woman's hand.

Chapter Four

Unless Kit missed his guess, every resident of Sweet Bank was gathered in the bake shop to hear Livy read from *St. Nicholas Magazine*.

With so many children, parents and grandparents listening to Mary Dodge's story promoting country, home and Christmas, he found it necessary to stand outside and listen through the half-open doorway.

Heat from inside rushed out to warm his face. Too bad the chill of the icy evening made his backside feel frostbit.

Being able to watch what was going on inside was worth the price, he reckoned. A frozen bum for the pleasure of seeing Emmie sitting shoulder to shoulder with Sam, her eyes bright with the anticipation of Santa's visit? Yep, he'd pay it ten times over. He swore he felt the spirit of Christmas thrumming through his own veins.

It didn't matter that he was a man grown. There was something about picturing Santa placing gifts in stockings, piling them three deep around the tree, that made a fellow believe in magic.

All of a sudden Livy glanced up from the page she was reading, saw him in the doorway and smiled.

Now, that was a Christmas gift in itself. Why was it, he had to wonder, that the smile of a woman he

had only known for a few days made him sizzle—
not only his body, but his heart, too?

They had a common cause—a goal to protect Sam
and keep Livy from being embarrassed in front of her
cousin. Not that he thought she had a single thing to
be embarrassed about.

No, there was something else drawing him to her.
He felt it every time she gave him the smile she was
giving him right now. Blamed if he didn't hear Christmas music in his mind's ear.

Wait—he actually did hear something. It wasn't
music, though. From somewhere behind him, maybe
under the boardwalk, he heard whining. It was faint
but he swore—

"Mr. James!"

Kit turned away from the door to see a figure
crossing the street through the darkness. He carried
a box under one arm.

"Evening, Mr. Runne," he said to the liveryman.
"Looks like we're the only ones not inside listening
to the story."

"Oh, well, I wouldn't be. The missus is near her
time. Wouldn't do to be away for long."

"Congratulations. Will it be a Christmas child?"

"We're hoping so." Hank Runne's broad grin was
visible even under his bulky mustache. "Say, my wife
asked me to give this to Livy. It's the reason I came
out. Can you deliver it to her for me?" Hank shoved
the fair-sized box at him. "It's my Mary's fanciest
gown. She's loaning it to Livy to wear when her rich
cousin gets here. Oh, and under it is a small bit of
laundry that needs washing."

"That's kind of her." The whole town must know about Edwina's visit.

"We're all doing our part to protect Sam. Wouldn't want to lose him to the lure of the almighty dollar. If Livy had to fight for custody, Edwina's the one who could afford a fancy lawyer. Can't have our Livy looking like less than the prize she is, either."

Hank stared at him for a moment. That odd whine came again, seemingly from under the boardwalk directly below his boots.

"You do consider her a prize?" The liveryman's brows lowered. His gaze narrowed, searching for the answer on Kit's startled face. Of course he thought she was a prize! Any man would. "Living out there with her—well, we, and I'm speaking for the town, are expecting you to behave as a gentleman."

He was more a gentleman than Cody Billings was. The last thing he intended to do was soil Livy's good reputation.

"I admire Miss York greatly, Hank. You can trust her to my care. As for getting her place ready for her cousin's visit? I'm working night and day, but I've only got a week and a half left to get it finished."

And, he supposed, to be on his way. The last thing he wanted was for Cousin Edwina to take offence that he was living in the house and not the barn.

He doubted that Frank and the good folks of Sweet Bank knew about that, either.

"I'd best get back to the missus. If you get in a bind, let Mildred Banks know, and she'll rally the troops."

With a nod, Hank Runne jogged down the boardwalk then up the road to where his wife, no doubt, awaited his arrival.

He watched the fellow get swallowed up by darkness, thinking how lucky Hank was. It struck him that having a wife waiting in a cozy home of one's own was the greatest of blessings.

He couldn't remember having a home, other than the orphanage—which didn't actually count—that stayed in one place. The life of an actor was one of constant change.

Couldn't say he missed the traveling one little bit.

What he did miss was the small window of warmth spilling out of the bakery doorway. He turned back toward the gaiety coming from inside, but once again he heard a pitiful whine whispering up through the slats of the boardwalk.

With a shiver, he trotted down the steps to investigate.

Riding home from town in the wagon, Livy felt the warm glow of Christmas approaching. Not warmth as in a roaring fire in the hearth, or the heat that radiated from the oven while baking.

At the moment it was so blistering cold that it didn't even help to imagine that sort of heat. Why, the mass of stars overhead looked like chips of sparkling ice, so frigid and beautiful.

No, the warmth she felt came from her heart. The leftover melody of "Jingle Bells" tinkled through her veins. She hummed it out loud because she didn't want to let go of the glowing moments they had spent in town with everyone so full of good cheer and the anticipation of Christmas.

Glancing behind, she checked to make sure the children were still under the blankets heaped over them. Giggles and churning limbs made the covers heave.

All was well.

"Dashing through the snow," she sang under her breath, wondering if Kit would think her a fool.

"In a one-horse open sleigh…" In case his voice didn't sound rich and sultry enough, the wink he slid at her made her feel all fuzzy inside.

My word. Maybe she didn't want to go dashing through the snow after all. Gazing into Kit's eyes made her feel more like lounging on the couch beside him in front of a crackling fire, feeling his hands in her hair and his—

"Something wrong, Livy?" He waggled his brows. His eyes crinkled at the corners when he smiled. "Don't care for my singing?"

"Actually, it's very nice. Maybe you ought to take to the stage."

"Can you picture me there, entertaining the crowds? Making them laugh or cry."

"I'd rather not." Indeed she would not! Who would get her house ready if Kit suddenly ran off to become an actor? "Actors are not the most reliable of people."

He laughed, shook his head. "You believe that?"

"I have reason to. Frank Gordon, my friend—special friend, I thought—ran off with an acting troupe. He'd been gone a year when his pa found him and brought him home. But we all noticed he was never the same."

"Maybe the boy was capable of being unreliable even without joining an acting troupe."

Possibly. It was true that Frank had always been a bit reckless.

Something whined.

"What was that?" *How odd.* Funny that Kit didn't seem surprised at the sound.

"Mrs. Runne loaned you a gown and sent some laundry. It's in the box behind you."

"A gown?" She glanced behind in the wagon bed and spotted the wooden box nestled in with the paint tins with its lid slightly open. "One that whimpers?"

Kit's answer was to flash her a one-cornered grin.

Turning, she got to her knees, then reached over the buggy seat to lift the lid from the box.

There was something wrapped in oilcloth. She pulled the string to reveal what it contained.

Her breath caught at the sight of a dress as red as Christmas, as fluffy looking as whipped cream.

The fabric heaved. A small brown nose poked up from under the oilcloth. Tall tan ears twitched at her. Brown, doe-like eyes blinked up.

"You found a puppy!" Sam had been asking for one. It felt more like Christmas every second.

"Yes, ma'am. Keep on looking."

She stroked the small white blaze on the pup's head. What else could be in the box that was more pleasing than a pup? The sleeve of a smudged shirt shifted under the dress. No, not a sleeve, but a tail swishing madly.

Another pup burst into view. This one was as white and fluffy as a snowball except for its ears and the patches around its eyes, which were a mottle of gray, black and brown.

"That's all of them." He said in a reassuring tone.

"My word, that's a relief."

"I hope you don't mind. I couldn't leave them to freeze under the boardwalk. I'll care for them in the barn."

"I don't think that will do. These little—" She glanced at him, arching her brows in question.

"Girls."

"These sweet baby girls will find bucket loads of mischief to get into out there." She retied the oilcloth, then set the lid back on the box exactly as she'd found it to let in some air for the pups. She turned back around on the bench. Somehow she ended up a bit closer to Kit than she had been before. He didn't move to allow for a friendly distance…so neither did she. "We've got two children and two puppies. They will keep each other busy so we can work on the house."

"That's my job, Livy."

"And I'm sure you're capable, but it is my house, and imagine how much faster we can get it done together."

"A good bit faster, I imagine."

For some reason his tone sounded glum.

Kit sat at a desk beside his bedroom window staring out at the snow-crusted ground. The glow of the lamp spread golden fingers across the open page of his book.

He raked his hand roughly through his hair, feeling uneasy—no, more than that, downright worried. Livy was confident that he was going to get her house in order.

If he didn't dread waking the pup who had at long last fallen asleep on his lap, or the one dozing on his bed, he would laugh, or curse. Probably curse.

Livy had proclaimed him capable. Hell, he was capable of finding the single page that had to do with whitewashing a fence, but the truth remained that he was an unreliable actor. He could act the part of a handy fellow but that was not going to get any paint on the walls.

In ten days—no, rather nine now—Edwina would be here. It was up to him, in part, to make sure she did not take Sam when she left. Also, unless he set this place to rights, Livy would be humiliated in front of her cousin.

Humiliation was not something to take lightly. On stage, he'd experienced it a time or two. To be shamed in front of people who mattered? Damn, Livy did not deserve her cousin's scorn.

"Hell," he muttered, then ran his finger down the page.

"Stir paint well. Lather it generously on the fence with a paintbrush but avoid letting the paint drip. Once the paint has dried pick out any bugs that have adhered to it, then apply another coat."

That didn't sound so hard. It couldn't be much different painting a wall than a fence post.

The pup sat up with a start. Her long pointed ears erect and twitching.

"You hear a coyote out there?" He stroked her long forehead, smoothing away the anxiety.

Then he heard the noise that had caught the pup's attention.

"Sounds like something being dragged across the floor." The pup jumped off his lap. "We'd best see to it."

The fluffy white pup already had her nose to the crack under the door. Her pristine tail wagged back and forth over the floor.

"Oh, blame it!"

Kit rushed out of the room and down the stairs two at a time. The puppies scrambled past him.

By the time he burst into the parlor, the small beasts were leaping upon Livy, who sat on the floor cradling her foot in her hand, her eyelids squeezed tightly shut.

"You all right, Livy?"

She blinked her eyes open, giving him a nod. Clearly she was not all right; she just didn't want to admit to it.

"I smashed my toe," she gasped while pushing both puppies away from her face. "And I'm under attack."

"Let me help." Since the small canines were not about to give up lunging and licking, he scooped Livy up off the floor and carried her to the couch.

Slowly.

It wasn't every night that a man got to hold a woman in his arms—at least this man didn't.

Besides, this was not just any woman. She fit like she was meant to be this close to him. Soft and curved, the swell of her breast pressed against his chest, the line of her thigh nestled into the crook of his arm and—

And he ought to put her down.

Just didn't want to.

Maybe she'd give him half a minute more.

"Put me down. The couch is right there," she murmured softly a full forty-five seconds later.

"We don't know for sure if you can walk." That was a foolish thing to say. As far as he knew, a banged-up toe never kept anyone from taking two steps.

He did set her down, though. If he held her a second longer it would be considered improper, and he had told Hank Runne that he was a respectable man.

No doubt when he eased down beside her he should have sat a foot farther away, but she sure did smell good.

"Let me have a look," he said.

Blushing, she lifted her sleeping gown barely enough for the big toe of her right foot to peek out.

"How does it feel?" It looked red and was starting to swell.

The pups made a dozen leaps, trying to get on the couch but were still too small to manage that trick.

"It hurts some."

This was a lie. It had to feel like a dozen stinging bees.

"I'm going outside to get some snow for the swelling."

"It's too cold. Don't bother," he heard her say while he was closing the door behind him.

She wasn't wrong about it being too cold, especially since he'd rushed outside without putting on a coat or boots.

Luckily, there was snow just beyond the porch and he was back inside well before frostbite set in.

He found a cloth in the kitchen, wrapped it around the ice then hurried back to the couch.

This time he sat even closer than before. She'd probably think that it was out of necessity since he had to hold the cloth to her toe.

It wasn't the truth. She was capable of holding the cloth by herself.

His heart made a ruckus in his chest when he realized that the thought must have occurred to her, too. And yet, she made no move to snatch her foot from his ministrations.

So here he sat enjoying the scent of cinnamon and vanilla coming from her hair. And under that was the scent of—

Damn, why did he have to actually be the gentleman he assured Runne he was?

"How did you hurt it?" He lifted the cloth, peered at her purpling toe. "How does it feel? I imagine it hurts like blazes."

"It's much better." Not likely, in his opinion. "I'll be good as new by morning. I banged it when I was moving the couch."

"It's one in the morning. Why were you moving the couch?"

"Since I'm used to being up late, I hoped to get an early start on the painting by moving furniture away from the walls." She sighed, then flopped back against the cushion. "Not the best decision I ever made, as it turns out."

"That's a man's job—my job. Livy, I know what I'm doing."

"Of course you do!" Did she notice that he had set the snow aside and was still holding her bare foot in his hand? Stroking her heel with his thumb? "I have complete faith in you—I only thought I might help."

"You know, Livy, I'm grateful you hired me." He stared at how pretty her foot was. Not all feet were pretty. "But you don't need to go to all this trouble just to impress your cousin."

"You only say so because you don't know Edwina. The appearance of wealth is everything to her. She grew up believing that money and happiness are the same thing. Do you know that just because my mother married a common man, her family believed she lived in poverty and was therefore miserable? I would bet she was as happy as any of them—no, I'm certain she was happier."

He didn't know if rubbing her heel made her toe feel better or not. It sure did make him feel good, though. Good enough to trail his fingers up her ankle and rub the slender indentation near her heel.

Suddenly, she yanked her foot from his grip and placed it on the floor. The squeak she tried to stifle when it hit the wood made him feel like a cad.

"I'm sorry," he murmured.

"You only meant to help, I'm sure."

That wasn't what he was sure of.

What he was sure of is that he wanted to kiss her. And not as a way to ease the pain in her toe.

She placed her foot on his knee again, sighing deeply. "I hope you don't mind if I rest it here. It throbs like the dickens otherwise."

There was a nice soft pillow on the other side of her that she could have elevated her foot upon. Maybe she didn't notice that.

Then again, maybe she did. If she was willing to touch him this way, maybe she would be agreeable to touching him somewhere else—like on his lips. Could it be the kiss he wanted was closer than he first thought?

"I don't know why folks have to put on airs, try and be things they are not. Like happy. For all Edwina's imagined advantages, she was never as happy as I was. It's like she's an actress, playing a part."

"So you believe Edwina's unreliable, too? Like an actor?"

"Oh, not as bad as that. She does put on airs, though. Being upper crust is what gives her satisfaction, whereas I take satisfaction in making a grungy shirt white."

"Everyone appreciates a white shirt. Would you like to stay up for a while? I'll build up the fire."

"Oh, that is tempting. But there's so much to do tomorrow." She glanced at the cooling hearth, sighed. "And the children will be up early. In fact, I should check in on them."

"All right." He stood, then gathered her up into his arms. Again, he was struck, no, overwhelmed with the feeling that this was where she belonged.

"Put me down, Kit. I can walk."

"I reckon you can, but it will take you an hour just to make the stairs."

The puppies, who had fallen asleep, woke up leaping and whining while they followed Kit toward the downstairs bedroom where the children slept.

He opened the bedroom door.

"They look sweet as sugarplums all cuddled up together." Livy sighed.

She glanced up at him, a pink tint staining her cheeks. The children were not the only ones sweetly cuddled together.

To be honest, his thoughts were on her and not the children. The picture forming in his mind was a great deal less pure than sweet cuddles.

"I'm so grateful Emmie's here." Livy's voice brushed his ear, warm and a bit breathless. "She's filling up an empty space in Sam's heart."

"Mine, too."

Kit closed the door on the children, carried Livy through the parlor then began to climb the stairs.

Halfway up he stopped, caught by the glimmer of moonlight streaming through the stairway window. It shone on Livy's face, on her neck and on her bare feet, which peeked out from under the ruffle of her robe.

Did her skin taste like it smelled—like the tempting blend of vanilla and cinnamon?

"I think we should—" Damned if she wasn't looking at his mouth when she spoke.

"I do, too." He leaned forward, nuzzled his nose against her hair, brushing her cheek with his lips. This was a moment to savor—to cherish.

"Name the pups," she whispered softly. He felt the

sweet, moist warmth of her breath cross his face. "We should name the pups."

"White one's Penny. Brown one's Dixie."

"Oh, that was—"

"Not what this is about, Livy."

"No."

"It's not that I think you can't make it up the stairs on your own. It's that I want to hold you, and I reckon you want me to."

She nodded slowly, trapping him in her honey-warm gaze. In a light, ticklish stroke, her fingers trailed up the back of his neck then into his hair. She pressed his head down and tipped her face up for his kiss.

Chapter Five

Livy balanced a bowl of cookie dough on her hip. She didn't need to look at it to know what she was doing. After all, she had been stirring dough since she was small enough for Mama's apron strings to tickle her nose.

What she did need to do was look at Kit. All night long she had seen his face in her dreams, relived the scent of his breath on her face and the way his heart thumped hard and fast under her palm.

The kiss she shared with him had been nothing like the one Frank had stolen behind the schoolhouse that first time. The very last thing she wanted to do was run away and hide from Kit.

So, she stood in the doorway to the kitchen, leaning against the jamb and listening to the *click-clack* of the wooden spoon against the bowl.

She watched Kit paint the parlor wall. As she suspected, the flesh-and-bone man was even more compelling than the one in her dreams had been.

The dream version of Kit had caused intense feelings but he'd been shadowy. This Kit, dipping the brush in the paint and then smoothing it on the wall had arms whose muscles flexed, whose hair caught the glimmer of the afternoon sunlight leaking through the curtains.

Kit in the flesh cursed the drops of paint rolling down his arm and dripping off his elbow.

Evidently, even an expert painter had his struggles.

She laughed. He glanced away from his work and winked.

Turning back to the kitchen, she couldn't help but wonder what he would think if she boldly walked into the parlor and kissed him again.

She'd appear a regular Jezebel, but—

Shaking her head, she carried her bowl to the kitchen window and looked out.

Just beyond the back porch, Sam and Emmie played in the snow. They appeared to be having some trouble with the snowman they were building. Trouble in the form of Dixie, who dug away at the base, and Penny, who snatched the stick arm and ran merrily off with it.

In ten minutes she would have to call them all in from play. This late in the afternoon, the temperature could drop in a hurry. Also they needed a bit of rest before they went to town for the Christmas reading.

Livy set the bowl of dough on the counter then removed a tray of cookies from the oven. She was baking a large batch today, enough for all the children attending the reading. And a dozen for Mary Runne, who was confined to home until her baby came.

Also one for Jezebel, who could not get kissing Kit James off her mind.

Easing a cookie off the baking tray, she carried it behind her back into the parlor. A good night's sleep had done wonders for her toe, but she still limped a bit.

"I have to say, Kit, it looks like you're painting yourself as much as the walls."

He set the paintbrush aside then rose from a stoop to gaze down at her.

"Well, ma'am, I'm a mite better at rustling cattle and mending fences." His gaze settled on her lips before it lifted to her eyes. The smile he shot her lifted one corner of his mouth, crinkled the corners of his eyes. "I smell a bit of heaven coming from the kitchen."

"I was wondering if you might want another bite? I mean—" she whipped the cookie from behind her "—a first bite, since you haven't had one yet."

He lifted his fingers, which were coated in white paint, and wagged them at her. "Put the head of that gingerbread man in my mouth."

She lifted the cookie to his mouth, her fingertip somehow—accidentally—touching his bottom lip in the process.

"Yum," he mumbled, holding his dripping hands wide. "I reckon I'll take that second bite now, Livy."

She lifted the cookie, but he shook his head.

"Step closer, honey."

As if she had anything else in mind. As if she were anything more than a magnet being drawn to an attracting force.

His chest was warm, manly and solid against the front of her apron, against the imprudent yet eager thump of her heart.

He touched her face when he lowered his mouth to hers. Vaguely, she was aware of a cool smear of paint grazing her cheek.

Life did exist beyond the warm probe of his mouth,

beyond the masculine scent that wrapped her up, but for now she chose to ignore it.

There was life beyond this, beyond Kit, who would soon be leaving.

Still, for this one, exquisite moment she would pretend that this was all there was.

"It's beau-u-u-tiful, Uncle Kit!" Emmie declared while she squirmed in the crook of his arm. "I loves Christmas trees so much."

It was clear that each and every citizen of Sweet Bank was enamored of the huge tree. Tonight, a couple hundred candles mounted on fancy tin trays had been clipped to the branches. Bright pinpricks of flame made it look like the tree had drifted down from the star-studded sky.

"I've never seen anything so pretty, darlin'," he said but he was looking at Livy's face when he said it. She glowed prettier than the candles did.

"Can my papa see it from Kevin?"

Suddenly his attention was only for Emmie. "Why, darlin', I believe he's right here beside us and is enjoying the tree the same as we are. You know, your papa, he wants you to have a happy Christmas, he wants you eat cookies and candy and open lots of presents."

Sam looked away from the tree with a grin. "I'll eat lots of candy if it will make my ma and pa happy."

Livy yanked the brim of her brother's hat over his eyes. "A sensible amount of candy will make them happier."

"We gonna eats lots of cookies, then," Emmie declared with a great big grin at Sam.

Kit was about to laugh out loud and agree that they should all eat lots of candy and cookies when the minister stood on a box to lead everyone in singing "O Tannenbaum."

Since Livy had already taken note that his voice sounded polished he decided not to sing. Although, he wanted to. Caroling was one of his favorite things to do.

His acting troupe always entertained children in orphanages this time of year. He missed doing that.

While everyone sang, he watched their faces. After a moment he turned his attention to the tree and the pretty points of flame, reaching and twisting.

Sure did look nice, but lit candles and trees didn't go well together in his opinion. A lot of fires happened this way.

Even so, he couldn't deny that, like everyone else, he enjoyed looking at it. It was a rare sight with the tree all a-sparkle, and overhead the night sky a miracle of bright twinkling stars. It took the breath right out of him.

Chances were, this tree would be safe enough, since the candles would be put out after folks gathered in the bakery for hot drinks and Livy gave her reading. Also, Hank Runne and Dr. Baily were standing by with buckets of water and sand in case of an emergency.

When "O Tannenbaum" ended, the preacher led them in "O Come, O Come Emmanuel."

There was not a chance in a million that he would be able to keep quiet through this carol.

He began to hum. Livy glanced over at him with a smile. If she thought he ought to be on the stage, her expression didn't show it.

Closing his eyes, he hummed, wondering if there was some way to convince Livy to let him stay on after the house was finished.

Something was happening between them. Something tender and wonderful.

Damned if he wanted to leave before he knew if it might be something lasting.

The kissing had to stop! Kissing in the morning, at noon, all night long. It was distracting. How was Livy to get a thing done when Kit's lips never left hers?

Very well, there had only been the two kisses, but in her mind they were constant. It didn't matter that Kit was in the barn tending the horses and the cow they had borrowed last night, or that she was in the kitchen frying potatoes—his mouth was on hers.

Even if he was hanging fancy curtains on the windows, like he was doing now, it felt like he had his hands on places they should not be.

Something was burning. She stirred a pot of beans without really seeing it and drew her sleeve across her forehead. She certainly was warm. Thinking of Kit had her all fired up. Made her imagine that she was steaming.

No, not her. There really was smoke in here!

She grabbed a cloth, then opened the oven door and drew out a dozen charred biscuits.

From behind her she heard laughter.

"I don't know what's so funny," she huffed. Dinner without biscuits was not dinner at all. "It will take a week to get the stench out of the house. What will Edwina think?"

Kit set aside the curtain and placed it on the back of a chair. He crossed the room.

Gallantly, in her opinion, he plucked a biscuit from the baking sheet and took a bite, chewed and swallowed.

"Not bad. I could eat two."

Now it was her turn to laugh. He had no idea what had caused her to ruin the biscuits. How it had been her burning as much as the unfortunate dough.

"Even if you do, it won't get rid of the stench," she pointed out because smoke was miserable to get out of things. "Edwina will think I'm a bumbler."

He shrugged, touched her cheek then traced his thumb along the line of her jaw. "Does it really matter what she thinks?"

"It matters to me." But not as much as the fact that Kit was going to kiss her again. She should not let him. It was not prudent. Not a bit wise.

He closed his eyes, shook his head slightly.

"I know how to get the stench out." He dropped his hand and backed away. "Just give me a minute."

With that, he spun about and walked down the hallway and into his bedroom.

Clearly, he was running away from the attraction growing between them, just as she ought to be.

Just this one time she was not going to do what

she ought to do. She had years to be prudent but only another week to kiss Kit.

The children and the puppies were upstairs napping. There was nothing to keep her from following him down the hallway. No one would know if she quietly slipped inside his bedroom, stole a kiss and made a memory.

Of all the things she expected to see when she opened the door, it was not Kit sitting in a chair beside the window reading a book!

She had assumed he would be pacing, fighting the intimacy building between them, not absorbed in some story.

"Livy!" He slammed the book closed, shoved it behind his back then stood up.

"I didn't realize you were such a literary man, Kit." Well, clearly he must be to dash away like he had.

"There's nothing like a good tale."

"Um, there's also nothing like earning your wages."

"You're right. I'll get right back to it."

He would, but first she needed to know what was more interesting to him than their abandoned kiss.

"What are you reading?"

"Dime-novel trash."

"I adore dime-novel trash." She reached behind him intent on seeing what it was.

Blame it! All she managed was to knock it from his hand. It landed facedown on the floor. He reached for it but she was quicker.

Snatching it up she turned it over. *"The Common*

Man's Guide to Ranching?" She looked at him in bewildered astonishment.

He audibly swallowed. "I reckon there's something I need to confess."

Confessions were never what one wanted to hear.

Chapter Six

She closed her eyes, praying that he was not going to reveal something horrid.

He took the book from her fist and slapped it behind him on the table. "What's in these pages is all I know of ranching. That and what little bit Cody Billings knows."

"And who is Cody Billings?" This was an odd confession.

"Howdy, ma'am." He lifted her hand, kissed her knuckles. His voice suddenly sounded odd, smooth and seductive, given the conversation they were engaged in. "Mighty pleased to make your acquaintance."

"I don't understand." What exactly was the man confessing to? "Your name is really Cody Billings?"

All right. That alone was not unforgivable. Sometimes good-hearted folks needed a clean start.

"He's a character that I've played." He gazed at his boots for a moment, then looked into her eyes. "I'm— well, the truth is, I'm not a ranch hand. I'm an actor."

"I don't believe it!" She did not want to believe it. The man she'd hired was a well-qualified ramrod.

Extending his hands, he turned them this way and that. How hadn't she noticed they were not calloused?

The only marks on them were blisters; red and angry and painful looking.

"You kissed me," she hissed. "You cannot be an actor!"

"I'm sorry, Livy. I thought I could play this part like I've done every other part, live it and make it real."

"You kissed me and lied?" What was she to do now? It was far too late to hire someone else, to forget what her heart had discovered. And Edwina would be here in only a week. "Why would you do that?"

"For Emmie. I couldn't continue on as an actor and properly raise a child."

"It seems to me that you *have* continued acting," she pointed out waspishly.

"I have. I'm not proud of it, but it's the truth." His lips creased together in a firm, grim line. He narrowed his eyes at her. "You can't deny doing the same. Didn't you hire me for the very purpose of deceiving your cousin?"

"That's different—"

Then again, it wasn't all that different when she looked at it. Her intent *was* to blatantly deceive her cousin. She had even involved the whole town in the masquerade.

She'd involved Kit as well by misrepresenting what his duties would be. Led him to believe this job was of a lasting nature. Heaven only knew how much time he had spent learning to be a genuine cowboy.

Surely not as long as she had spent misrepresenting herself to Edwina!

"You'll have to leave," she stated, wondering if she sounded as much a hypocrite as she felt.

Unable to look in his eyes a second longer, she fled the room for the sanctuary of the parlor. But there was no sanctuary to be found. Kit followed her so closely that she could nearly smell him, feel the heat radiating from him.

All of a sudden the wind started to blow. It moaned under the eaves, sounding gloomy. That was appropriate background music for what was going on here.

A strand of brown hair dipped below his brow when he shook his head. He stepped several inches closer, not farther away.

"Here's the truth, Livy."

She backed toward the front door, ready to throw it open and firmly point the way to the barn.

"I deceived you, and you deceived me."

"I still want you gone." He followed—no, seductively stalked her was what he did, until her rump bumped the door.

"That's not what your eyes are telling me."

She closed them because she knew exactly what her eyes were saying, drat them.

Then she felt a touch, the barest pressure of his thumb tracing the shape of her pout.

"If I say there's nothing between us, that'll be one more lie." He was so close that she felt the rush of his breath on her cheek.

She opened her eyes to find him staring intently at her mouth. Once again, something was burning. She'd be a fool to think it was beans or biscuits.

"I won't lie again," he whispered. His hand slid up

her spine. His fingers tickled her neck then cupped the back of her head. "Will you?"

"No." It was one thing to deceive her cousin but quite another to deceive herself. There was something growing between her and Kit. She was not going to spend the rest of her life wondering what it might have been.

His lips came down upon hers, a gentle, affectionate kiss. With one arm circling her back, he lifted her. The sensuous upward glide pressed her breasts against his chest. She felt his heart slam against his ribs and wanted to feel so much more of him than that.

What she wanted was to ease this heat—to strip off her clothes and feel his skin against hers. It was wicked—given that he would be leaving soon and that the children were sleeping nearby—but she wanted this beyond what was reasonable. In this, her body and her emotions were speaking more loudly than good common sense.

All at once an icy blast of wind blew inside the parlor.

She hadn't opened the door. It must have been Kit; he was going to carry her away to the barn, lay her down in the hay and—

"Olivia Grace York!"

No! No! No! It could not be!

"Who is that man?"

Chapter Seven

"Edwina!"

Livy shoved out of Kit's embrace, making a sound halfway between a squeak and a gasp.

The woman standing in the doorway scowled at him while pressing her fingers over the eyes of a small boy huddled against her skirt.

Down in the yard, Hank Runne hopped down from a wagon piled sky-high with trunks. The glare the liveryman shot him was deserved.

The way he had been kissing Livy—the places his fingers had been inching toward… His behavior had been far from respectful.

"I ask you again, Olivia Grace." Edwina pinned Livy with an accusing stare. "Who is that man?"

Livy resembled a stone pillar, silent, her expression frozen.

"I'm Kitson James, Mrs. Spire." He indicated with a wave of his hand that she and her son should come in out of the cold. "Your cousin's husband."

Livy snapped her openmouthed stare to him. Two shocks in the space of thirty seconds; no wonder she couldn't speak.

"Welcome to our home," he said.

At least Edwina was no longer scowling. In fact, she looked downright pleased.

Too bad the same could not be said of Livy.

"You must be the banker's son!" Edwina stepped inside, steering her child before her with her hand clamped on his shoulder. "My goodness, Livy. This is a surprise."

"Yes." Livy cut him a razor-edged glance. It stung. "Yes, it is."

He smiled. "I'm the banker now. My father retired and I took his place at the helm. It's quite a pleasure to meet you, Cousin Edwina. I've been looking forward to it immensely."

Glancing past Edwina's shoulder, he spotted Hank standing in the snow, his face growing red and angry looking.

Feeling a tug on his pant leg, Kit glanced down. The boy gazed up at him through a pair of black-rimmed spectacles.

"Do you have fans?" the boy asked, then turned the question to Livy with a lift of his eyebrows.

Kit doubted she noticed the boy, given that her whole attention was focused upon her alleged husband. In spite of the moment they had shared only a moment ago, a life-changing moment in his opinion, she gazed at him as if he was a stranger.

Hell, in a way he was. Until a few moments ago she had believed him to be a hardworking cowboy.

"Bradley Spire!" Edwina bent over to whisper in her son's ear. Her voice carried anyway. "Remember what I told you. Only people of means have electric fans. Now, mind your manners."

"We have means—not nice?" The boy glanced again at Livy. "We have fans—and we are nice."

"We have puppies," Livy said. All of a sudden color flooded her cheeks.

Coming as quick as it did, he figured the blush had to do with temper. He could only believe she was hopping mad at him.

Still, when she turned to face Edwina, it was with a smile.

"Isn't this a treat!" Livy folded her cousin in a great hug. Kit thought he saw moisture in Edwina's eyes, but she squeezed them shut before he could be certain. "You're early!"

"Isn't it wonderful? There was so much happening back home, all the hustle and bustle, the social calls—well, it was making me dizzy. So many people coming and going, I was near to screaming. Unfortunately, your little hotel in town was booked, and naturally I wouldn't stay at a boardinghouse, so here I am!"

"My wife and I welcome you. There's always room for family. Isn't that right, honey?"

Livy agreed, even though he'd bet all the wages he'd earned so far that she didn't mean it.

"The children will be so happy to meet Bentley," Livy said.

"Children? I thought there was only Sam?"

"My—my—Kit. He has Emmie, his niece."

"Hank!" Kit hurried outside. He stood close to the liveryman and whispered, "I need a favor. When we come to town later for the reading, I'm going to marry Livy. Can you set it up for the preacher to meet us in private?"

"Good. I reckon I don't need to reach for my shotgun after all."

"You still might. I'm willing, but I'm not so sure about my bride-to-be."

"I hope you're a bit more than willing. Our Livy deserves more than willing."

"I care deeply for her. Reckon I'm no different than anyone else in this town. I didn't want her to be shamed in front of Edwina so I said what I did."

"You also said you were a banker."

"Livy's cousin assumed it and so I just embroidered a little."

Hands fisted at his hips, Hank nodded.

"I'll make sure the preacher is waiting for you at the chapel after the reading." All of a sudden, the man slapped his thigh, laughed out loud. "Help me unload all this baggage. I've been away from my missus for too long already."

"You claimed you were not going to lie again!" Livy whispered, keeping her anger discreet. Even though it was dark and secluded in the alleyway between the bank and the general store. Not a soul was nearby but she would perish if anyone witnessed her humiliation. "I am not going to marry you!"

She yanked her elbow out of Kit's fingers while the bullheaded man hauled her toward the chapel. For an actor, he was very strong.

"And I'm not going to share a room with you in sin," he answered, reclaiming her elbow.

She dug her boot heels into the dirt and tugged backward.

"When I do marry someone it will not be because I was tricked into it."

All of a sudden Kit stopped his forward momentum, and spun about to pin her with a level glare. "Look, Livy. The reason you hired me was to keep Edwina from taking Sam. Yes, I lied when I told her we were married, but at least I made sure that won't happen."

"I don't think your motives were so pure, Mr. Kitson James." She poked him in the chest with one finger. "I was about to send you packing—you made it impossible for me to do so. It was a purely conniving act on your part."

She yanked out of his hold then turned, about to walk away. True friends waited for her in the bakery.

Drat it! Why did she have to feel a thrill at the pressure of his big hand clamped around hers when he drew her powerfully back toward him?

"I can see how it might look that way."

"Yes, you can because it *is* that way."

"You are going to marry me because—"

"I'm *not*." She was not!

"Because of Sam."

For Sam—yes, she'd been through the arguments in her head for the past two hours without ceasing.

If she married the actor, Sam would remain safely with her. Edwina would not even suggest taking him away, not believing his guardian was a banker's son.

Kit was right about sharing a bedroom. She could hardly do that outside marriage. Since she could not send him to the barn without making Edwina wonder, for the time being, he would have to sleep in her room.

Drat her fickle insides for dancing a little jig at the thought of being alone with him in that virginal chamber.

"There must be another way—there has got to be."

"Might be, honey, if she hadn't caught you kissing me."

"It was you who was kissing me!"

She yanked away from him once again but found that she had taken a few steps toward the church instead of the bakery.

He caught up to her, walked beside her without touching her. "Damned if I'm going to ruin my reputation and yours by sleeping in your bedroom when we aren't legally wed."

She was good and caught. She could argue until the gust of wind that just dropped a snowflake on her nose turned into a blizzard. In the end it would make no difference.

It was clear that she had no choice about her future. She could have Sam and Kit, and Emmie. Her heart softened a bit at the thought of being able to raise that sweet little girl. Or she could have no one.

"Livy." He touched her cheek with his glove. She stopped, glaring up at him. "I know this is all happening too fast, and that I never gave you a say-so, but we could be happy together. You know we could."

Of all the fool things to do, Kitson James went down on one knee, right in the alleyway between the general store and the yard of the Chapel of Grace.

"Livy Grace York, will you be my bride?"

For some reason it touched her that he knew her middle name. He must have been paying attention to Edwina when she'd uttered it with such condemnation.

It sounded so much prettier coming from Kit's lips.

Many things would be nice coming from Kit's lips. Blasted wayward thoughts! From now on she would not think them.

From now on she was going to—

"All right. I will marry you."

He came slowly to his feet, reaching for her as though he was going to kiss her like any newly pledged man would do.

"But—" She held up her hand to keep him at a distance. "Only in the eyes of the law, for Sam's sake and for my reputation's."

"All right, honey. But maybe in time—"

"I'll seek a divorce."

How could he think she would welcome him into the rest of her life, into her bed, after he had manipulated her this way?

He needed a job and a home for his niece. He had seen an opportunity to have that and he'd pounced upon it.

Well, she would pounce upon her opportunity to be rid of him as soon as the time was right.

"You know," she said, when Kit knocked on the front door of the chapel, "everyone knows we weren't married this morning. Someone might point that out to my cousin."

"Not once Hank Runne lets them know what happened."

"Everything?" Of course everything. Hank would have witnessed the indiscretion that gave Kit the chance to declare them married. "Then I'm ruined anyway—married or not, I'm ruined."

"I care for you—deeply. I'll never do anything to make you feel ruined."

She huffed. The sound was not attractive. This was not the way she had always dreamed she'd feel at her wedding.

"What a shame you didn't think of that before you jumped on me at my own front door."

"That's not how I recall the event. Seems to me you were just as willing as I was."

And that was exactly the problem with this tawdry affair. She wondered if she would have been able to stop kissing Kit even had she known Edwina was on the far side of the door.

A few moments later she stood hand in hand with Kit, falsely pledging her troth to an actor. Staring into his sincere-looking face, she could only guess what character he was stepping into for this performance.

And what had come over Hank? All he needed to do was witness the event. Dashing a tear from his eye seemed a bit much.

Until she glanced up at Kit's handsome face and saw emotion glittering in his eyes, as well.

Without warning her heart went half-dizzy.

She was going to have to be very careful that she did not lay it at the feet of a man who could play a part more naturally than he could play himself.

Chapter Eight

Sitting at a table beside the bakery window, Kit watched a dozen snowflakes smash against the glass then drip to the sill. He'd need to get his family home soon, before a flat-out storm hit.

His family. He let the idea roll around in his brain, sink into his heart.

Funny how quickly a man could know a sense of bonding. He'd played the role of a family man many times. This was different. It was real and he liked the feel of it.

He and Emmie had been a family, but now there was Sam and Livy and, all of a sudden, life seemed complete. It was as though he had been missing something—needing this tie that had fallen to him like a Christmas blessing.

A lot of folks would feel trapped by the situation he had landed in. But he didn't. With the dust settling, looking at the future, all he felt was grateful.

His bride was the one who felt trapped. At the moment she didn't appear to be distressed, talking with Edwina and sipping hot tea. Under it all, though, he sensed her misery.

He and Livy did have something in common. They could both play a part. He wondered if the folks of Sweet Bank would be willing to do the same.

It was going to take some skillful playacting to perform this drama.

"Santa's going to bring me my own fan," Bentley said, sitting between Sam and Emmie while he licked cookie crumbs from his mouth. "With five blades."

"I wants a dolly in a pink dress," Emmie announced. She did? Where was he going to get one of those? He sure hoped the general store had one that he could afford.

Now that he was married, the money he had saved was no longer his own. It was for his family. He'd be a hog-tied mud licker if he was going to allow his wife to continue earning money by washing clothes in the middle of the night.

Livy had mentioned that she wanted to get the horse ranch running again. With the small sum he had put away, he could begin that.

As soon as Edwina went home, he'd retire from banking and become a rancher—a genuine range-riding, rope-throwing cowboy.

"I want a game of checkers!" Sam said. "I'll learn to win every time."

"I'm sure Santa is checking his list as we speak, young Sam," said Mary Newton, approaching the table in her flowered apron. The owner of the bakery carried a steaming teapot in her hand. With a nod of her head and a lift of gray brows, she asked if anyone wanted more.

Edwina set her cup on her saucer with a dainty click. "My goodness, this is such a quaint little place. It's not at all what I'm used to."

Livy stared at her cousin, flushed and embarrassed.

"I've got to say," Kit said because he felt the need to say something, "Livy and I just returned from our honeymoon in Paris."

He cast a quick glance at the children. Two of them would know this was not true. Luckily, they were distracted by Sam asking what ten plus fifteen made. They were counting fingers and trying to figure it out.

"We ate in many fine establishments, didn't we, honey?" He liked calling her honey. Didn't seem she liked hearing it, though.

"Very lovely places," she agreed with a tight smile.

"But the truth is—" he winked up at Mary "—for all the expense, all the glitter, even the most posh of them was not as warm and welcoming as Mrs. Newton's establishment. And the food? Not a single item compared to this delicious cookie."

Picking up one shaped like a Christmas tree slathered in green icing, he took a bite, making a show of savoring it then licking his lips clean of crumbs.

"Incomparable, Mary. Wouldn't you say so, Edwina? I know you've tasted the finest."

"I—I would say so, Mrs. Newton." A smile that looked genuine tipped her lips. "In fact, I'll have another."

Edwina picked one up, took a bite and made a show of licking her lips the same as Kit had. Her blush indicated that she might never have made a more unacceptable gesture in her life.

"Why, thank you, Mrs. Spire." Mary filled Kit's cup to the brim. She winked, smiled. "It's so nice to have you home, Mr. Kitson. We've missed you at the bank. My, but you and your bride have such a glow about you."

"It's good to be home."

Hank must have spread the word quickly. It was easy to see how much the people of this town loved Livy and Sam. It seemed that they were going to keep their secret.

Kit's life had taken him many places but none were as fine as humble Sweet Bank. This was where he wanted to make a home—a place to live the rest of his life with Livy and the children.

Some might say he was reckless to commit his heart so quickly. But he wasn't. Deep down he knew this was right. It was where he was always meant to be.

If only he could convince Livy of that.

Livy lay straight legged in her bed. She'd yanked the blankets to her chin, and still she shivered. Where was the nice cloud of warmth that normally built between her and the covers even on the coldest nights?

It had been stolen from her! Yes, stolen by one sneaky low-down man of many faces sitting in a chair only feet away. She stared at his silhouette, where it was dark against the snow falling past the window.

Even though he'd drawn a quilt about his shoulders, he trembled every now and then. Every time she thought he might have fallen asleep, his foot, which he had drawn up, hit the floor.

Blamed man. If he didn't fall asleep, how was she

to go to the barn and wash the laundry? She owed him his wages, and unless she delivered clean shirts to Horace and a few others, she would not be able to pay him.

If she did not pay him that would mean that their business relationship had been replaced by something else.

If it was replaced by something else, that meant there was no reason for him to be shivering in the chair and for her to be shivering in the bed.

It was precisely because she was watching him shiver that the warmth her blankets ought to offer her was not there.

The man was a thief—of many things. She wondered how many times he had played one in his less than respectable career. Probably so many times that it became second nature to take what was not his.

Like space in her bedroom, the warmth of her blankets—like her independence and the dream of a lovely romantic wedding to a man she held in high esteem.

She did not hold Kit James, clearly an actor to his bones, in high esteem! She certainly did not!

But…there was the one thing she did hold in high esteem. To be honest, there were two. Kisses and embraces.

"Are you awake?" She whispered this in case he was not and she could sneak out to the barn and wash the laundry.

"I'm as wide awake as you are, honey."

"I don't like it when you call me honey."

"I like it just fine." He sat up. Placed his big

stocking-clad feet on the floor. The quilt fell away from his shoulders.

No wonder he was cold! He'd removed his shirt. With the quilt bunched at his waist she didn't know what he did or did not have on other than socks.

She did not want to know! But then again, it was a slippery quilt. It wouldn't take much to—

"I just want to say thank you for that story about Paris." She sat up, dragging the blanket with her and tucking it tight about her. "I felt so awful about what Edwina said to Mary."

"I wonder what we would have done? You and me in Paris?"

"I reckon we'd have seen some fine sights." Why was she engaging in pleasant conversation? She needed him asleep so that she could finish the chores he had forbidden her to do. As if he had the right to forbid her to do anything.

"I reckon I'd buy you a fancy Parisian gown and take you for an elegant buggy ride along the Champs-Élysées."

"That's something Edwina would swoon over."

"Not you, though? I reckon you'd like something else."

"I would hate being an ocean away from Sweet Bank. I figure there's more beauty in our magical Christmas tree than all the lights of Paris."

"I like that about you, Livy." He stood up, crossed to her bed and sat down on it. "This is a good town. Folks are dedicated to one another. Just look at how they have rallied about you and Sam."

"You are not permitted to like something about

me." She shoved his hip with her foot but he didn't move. "I won't allow it."

"Some things are beyond your control, honey." He touched the blanket over her foot. She ought to kick his hand away. Cold from his fingers seeped through the blanket. Her toe was no longer so sore that she could not do it. Maybe she would, in a moment. "I like you and there's nothing you can do about it."

"Get off my bed! Go stand by the window and look out."

He shrugged but did as she ordered. She snatched her flannel robe from the foot of the bed and yanked it on, tugging the blue flowered tie about her waist.

"All right, you may turn around." She never should have married him. She should have told Edwina that no matter how much money, how many advantages she could offer Sam, this was home. Here he would stay.

But she hadn't said that. She'd gotten married instead. Not only married, but married to a man who had caught her by trickery. And she had to admit privately, a man who tempted her at every turn.

Why had she done that? Maybe she had been lured by the very smile he was giving her now. Why, you would think she was standing here in a sheer gown that revealed everything to his gaze instead of her all-concealing robe.

"This is my half of the room. Everything beyond that green line on the rug is your half. I demand that you keep to it."

"You going somewhere?"

"I have chores that you will not prevent me from doing. I'll return in an hour."

He took a long stride across the green line to stand toe-to-toe with her. She hated it that she had to look up to see his expression in the dim light.

"No more, Livy. I won't have my wife doing chores in the middle of the night."

"If she doesn't, how do you expect to be paid?"

"I don't. I won't accept your money." He stepped back onto his side of the line. "Go back to bed."

Of course he would accept it. He had to. This marriage was not real and that was how she intended it to stay. In her mind, holding money between them was the very thing that would keep them apart.

"We'll see about that." The snappish tone of her voice sounded good and firm.

But she did get back into bed. It was very cold and there was snow between here and the barn.

Kit resumed his place in the chair. He drew up his long legs then tucked the quilt around them.

"I checked on the children before I came up," he said. "They sure get along fine."

"Children tend to." She had noticed the same. Sam had taken quickly to Bentley—the bond growing between them would probably last a lifetime. And Emmie—well, there would be many tears shed when she moved on.

"They don't look a bit cold, the three of them all cuddled up together with the pups."

"I'm sure it's a sweet sight."

"Yep. There's nothing like another body for adding warmth."

"Go to sleep, Kit."

"Good night, honey."

Funny how she no longer felt that he was stealing her warmth, but rather smothering her with it.

Gathered about the Christmas tree, hands linked, the folks of Sweet Bank admired the candlelit wonder.

Sure was a magical sight with all those flames swaying this way and that in the whisper-like breeze. Kit was a newcomer to Sweet Bank, but already he loved the nightly tradition.

The singing hadn't yet begun so Kit closed his eyes to better listen to the quiet conversations going on about him.

"I'm gonna watch Livy and Kit play checkers," Sam was saying. "That way when Santa brings me the game I'll know how to play right off."

"I already knows how to play with dollies," Emmie said smugly. With Christmas in two days, he'd better hope that the general store had a doll dressed in pink and that he'd have the time to get to town and pick it up. "What do you want, Bentley, just a fan?"

"From who?" Even with Kit's eyes closed, he knew that Bentley would be looking at Emmie intently through those black-rimmed glasses of his.

"From me," Emmie answered.

"I want a hundred hugs."

"Here's the first one." Kit opened his eyes to see Emmie lean sideways and hug the boy.

"Here's two." On the other side of Bentley, Sam leaned in.

Right before his eyes was the spirit of Christmas. He was damn sure he was close to letting loose a tear.

He watched other people standing hand in hand.

Good tidings had put a smile on each and every face.

Except Edwina's. She gazed down at the children with a blank expression. It was as though she was somewhere else in her mind. Perhaps a fancier affair she regretted missing back in Kendrick.

The singing began. Since Livy already knew he'd been an actor and there was no point hiding it anymore, he let his rich voice ring out.

A sudden gust swayed the tree branches but amazingly the candles did not blow out. Hank Runne stooped to grip his pail of water but the wind quit and he began to sing again.

Life was wonderful. Or it would be as soon as he'd convinced Livy of it.

"Hank!" A voice cut the song, stilling the singers. A young woman ran down the middle of the road waving her arms madly. "Doc says the baby's coming and coming quick!"

Hank bolted, arms and legs pumping. Everyone else trailed after him, laughing and excited.

Chapter Nine

"Is this normal? Does everyone always gather for a birth?" Edwina asked.

Livy was sure that was not the case in every town. Especially in Kendrick.

"Mostly. Mrs. Long's baby came in ten minutes so we missed that one. But usually here we are, no matter the time of day or night or the weather, praying for a safe birth."

"The wind is picking up," Edwina pointed out. "And it's cold. I think we would be better off praying at home."

"Look around, cousin. You are the only one frowning. A baby's coming! What could be more wonderful?"

Edwina wrapped her arms about her middle. "I just thought the parents might like some privacy. I would not have wanted a crowd gathered outside my door when I labored with Bentley."

"Sweet Bank isn't like Kendrick. It's a small place. We're all family here. And new babies are—"

"I know about babies, Livy." Her cousin shot a harsh glance at her. "I've had one."

Hurtful silence stretched between her and her cousin. While Livy considered how to respond to that comment, a newborn's cry cut the night.

Cheers went up. Hats were tossed, each one a wish for a healthy, happy life for the infant. Edwina swiped her sleeve across her eyes.

The new father stepped outside, his grin as wide as the Cheshire Cat's.

"It's a healthy baby—" All at once Hank's proud grin faltered. His eyes bulged. "Fire!"

Everyone turned toward the direction he stabbed his finger.

"The Christmas tree!" Edwina shrieked, and was the first to pick up her skirts and run toward the disaster.

Twenty minutes later the folks of Sweet Bank gathered around the steaming ruins of the tree.

"It'll still be Christmas," Mildred pointed out.

"Santa's still coming," someone reassured a weeping child.

"The wonder of Christmas was never in the tree, anyway," added the preacher. "We are still bound in joy by the love the day represents."

"But it was a beautiful tree—and Livy hasn't read the last part of the story." The voice, coming from the back of the crowd was sniffling.

"I know how you all loved your tree," Edwina said. "And it was a lovely thing, but there is a new baby—a Christmas baby. You ought to take heart in that."

"I wonder if it's a girl or a boy," Livy said, puzzled by Edwina's sudden change in attitude.

"It doesn't matter." Edwina caught Bentley's hand, clearly ready to go home. "It's healthy and loved by both its parents."

* * *

No one had much to say on the way home from town. Gloom had them wrapped in its narrow-sighted arms. The Christmas tree was gone, and for now, so was the joy of the holiday.

Kit had tried to comfort them with a rousing rendition of "Jingle Bells" but it only made everyone sniffle, beginning with Edwina then on down to Livy and the children.

Upon entering the house, he hadn't bothered to light a fire in the hearth. All anyone wanted was the comfort of their beds.

The puppies, bounding with joy over their humans' homecoming, only accentuated the sadness.

"I don't know why Edwina even came," Livy declared, sitting on the middle of her mattress with her blue flowered robe tucked about her. "She does not seem a bit happy."

"No one does," he pointed out, whisking off his shirt then trying to get comfortable on an uncomfortable chair. "Seems to me there's plenty to be happy about, though. The baby got here safe and there was nothing but the tree burned."

Kit James had a good deal to be joyful about. It would take more than a ruined Christmas tradition to change that.

He was a happily married man, looking forward to convincing his wife that she was happy about it, too. Several images of the way to show her popped into his mind.

Too bad she was frowning so. He doubted she would welcome a proper courting at this moment.

"Only the tree! Why, it's what we love most about the celebrations."

"Christmas is about more than sparkling decorations." He stood up because his legs were cramping. Leaning against the window frame, he watched tree branches whip madly in the wind.

"Naturally, we all know that." She was silent for a moment, simply staring at him. "I suppose it will just take a bit for us to accept things."

"How long will it take for you to accept me, Livy?" A branch ripped off a nearby tree. It slammed against the side of the house, missing the bedroom window by inches.

"I won't accept you."

In three long strides, he crossed the damned green line in the carpet and sat down on her bed.

"I know you want to." He captured a strand of her hair before she could tuck it into the braid she was weaving. He rubbed it between his thumb and finger. It might be the single softest substance he had ever touched. "But I hurt your pride, honey, so you won't let yourself have what you really want."

"I don't want to be seduced by a smooth-tongued actor." She yanked her hair away from him, scooted closer to the wall. "Who are you even right now? Some character from a part you've played?"

"It's just me—Kit." He stretched across the bed. "You are a beautiful woman, Livy."

He touched her hand. Drew it away from the braid she was yanking tight. Like waves of brown silk, it came undone. The strands shifted between his fingers until it was a glimmering web in his palm.

Lifting the mass, he rubbed it against his cheek. It smelled like the cinnamon cookies she had baked earlier in the day.

She closed her eyes, sighed.

There wasn't much distance between them, only a few inches of rumpled bed. He leaned against her shoulder, kissed the top of her head, nuzzled down her temple then along her cheek with soft kisses.

"I'm the man you married, the man who loves you."

"What character recited that line?" she murmured, but she turned her face toward him when she did.

He inhaled the scent of her, leaned in for a kiss.

"How many actresses did you use it on?"

"This is only me, Livy, saying it only to you."

"That can't be true. I won't believe it."

So close, the heat of her lips scorched his heart. He would make her believe it—he had to.

Livy arched away from him, scrambling off the bed.

"I have something for you—just as soon as you get on your own side of the line." She pointed at the faded slice of color on the rug.

He was not giving up on his wooing, but it was going to take some time, possibly more time than he had.

"Here you are—this is your pay for last week's work." She reached across the line, waving money at him.

"I'm not taking money from my wife." He couldn't—it would be wrong.

"Very well, then." She set the short stack of bills on the carpet, directly on the line.

With a grunt, he backed into the chair and drew up his legs. Cold air seeped through the glass. Beyond it, the howling, whistling wind was bound to keep him awake all night.

Livy opened her eyes the next morning to find Kit gone and the money still on the carpet.

Blamed man.

She went to the window and looked out. A lamp glowed in the barn window. Smoke curled out of the stove flue. He must be in there doing her work, earning money that he would refuse to take from her.

While she dressed she recited his shortcomings, all the reasons she could not possibly accept their marriage.

Too bad he hadn't been a blacksmith, who would be reliably soot stained, or a baker who would always smell like yeast.

One never knew from moment to moment who an actor was.

She had learned that hard lesson from Frank Gordon. Until the day he ran off, she had believed him to be the best of men. One who put her first in his life.

Coming downstairs to prepare breakfast, her thoughts were consumed with how close she had come to kissing Kit in bed last night. Within an inch—a breath—she'd almost made a rash decision. One she would not be able to come back from.

Her only hope was that since Edwina had arrived

early, she would depart early and she could send Kit away sooner.

Life here in Sweet Bank must seem primitive to her cousin. No doubt she was counting the minutes until she could go home.

After rounding the hallway and coming into the kitchen, Livy stopped short.

"Edwina?" Her cousin had an apron tied around her middle. She gazed in confusion at the eggs and flour she had set on the counter. "What are you doing?"

"Making breakfast before I go to town with your husband."

"Why?" This was a side of her cousin she hadn't seen. Certainly in her own home the only reason Edwina ever went into the kitchen was to instruct the help on what to prepare for dinner.

"There aren't nearly enough gifts for the children." She pounded her fist on the counter, glaring at the eggs. "If there is one thing I know, it's shopping."

"Were you trying to make breakfast?"

"Why would I be doing that?"

"Eggs, flour?"

"Good morning, ladies." Kit came in from outside through the kitchen door, allowing a gust of frigid air to blow in with him.

He nodded at Edwina.

Before Livy had time to turn away, he crossed the room and kissed her.

It was a brief, husbandly greeting given for the sake of Edwina, but still—she wanted to slap him.

Or throw herself against him and make it the kiss she wanted in the darkest part of her being.

Since she could do neither of those things, she smiled and wished him a good morning.

"Since you are here to fix breakfast, Livy, I'll tend to the children." Edwina removed the apron and set it on the counter. "And the dogs."

As soon as her cousin's footsteps could no longer be heard clicking down the hallway, Livy grabbed a spatula, waving it furiously at Kit.

"Don't you kiss me again you—you—"

"Husband?"

He grinned at her and she stuffed down the urge to grin back. It seemed a very natural way to respond.

"It's a fine way to start the morning."

"It would be if we were really married."

"Preacher says we are."

Words! She wagged her fingers at him. "No ring! I had to tell my cousin I took it off because of the painting."

"If you weigh a circle of gold against the fact that we've shared a bedroom for two nights now, a ring doesn't mean so much."

"It does to me. I would never consider myself married without one."

"Got any coffee?"

Apparently, Kit James could change the conversation as easily as an actor could change personas.

"No." Blame it, she could change a conversation as well as anyone. "There was something odd about my cousin this morning."

"Last night, as well."

Kit sat down at the table, inviting himself into her space even without the excuse of coffee.

She sat across from him because she liked looking at him. She should be honest enough to admit that, even without wishing to remain married to him.

"She thinks we don't have enough gifts for the children."

"I do need a doll with pink clothes. But for Edwina, it probably makes her feel at home to buy things. I reckon she'll be welcome at the general store."

"Maybe, but I'll be relieved when she goes home."

"Too much acting the part of someone you aren't—having all the town involved in the deception, too?"

Clearly, he was trying to point out that they were both actors.

"Don't try and compare my little deception to yours."

"Because yours is bigger." He folded his fingers together on the table, arching his brows at her. "At least when I'm playing a part everyone knows it."

"I didn't know it."

"No, and I'm truly sorry for that. But, Livy, I'm not sorry for the way things turned out."

She stood up, pretty darn sure steam was whistling from her ears.

"I'll be relieved for her to go home so that I don't have to pretend to be your wife any longer."

Coming slowly to his feet, he rounded the table. She backed toward the wall and he stalked her.

Like a predator.

Her heart beat madly. Her palms grew sweaty. In the eyes of the law, the man was her husband. He could carry her upstairs and do whatever he wanted to her, and—and all it would do was make her insides melt in a delicious way.

She meant to push him away but somehow her arms looped around his neck instead. His hair slid through her fingers like a whisper.

"Who's acting now, Livy?"

He kissed her, and she wanted nothing more than to fall into his embrace, into his life. But how could she? He was no better than Frank.

Oh, drat it! To be fair, he was far better than Frank, but still, he had tricked her into a situation not of her choosing.

And just maybe, between the two of them she was the worse deceiver, accused an unwelcome voice in her mind.

"I love you, Livy. What do I have to do to convince you of it? We could be a happy family. I'm offering you my life, my future. Won't you take it?"

"When you came here you claimed you could do anything, fix anything. I believed that. I staked Sam's future on it." He did have the good grace to glance away and look ashamed. "Tomorrow is Christmas Eve, so if you can restore the town tree, maybe I will believe in you, in miracles, because that is what it will take."

She was being unfair. The logical side of her knew it—but the other side? It whispered for the miracle.

He shook his head looking discouraged, and something inside her wept.

* * *

Kit thought that Edwina seemed a different person while shopping in the general store. She purchased what seemed to be half of Geoff Goodwin's stock of toys. She smiled, laughed and put on an air of having a fine time, in spite of the fact that the goods would surely not be up to her higher standards.

Geoff had a big old grin on his face tallying up her bill. Which she paid without an apparent twinge of remorse.

"There's only one more thing I need," she mentioned before they went out the door. "Bentley should have a pup of his own. The other children have them and, well—he needs one, as well."

"I don't have any of those," Geoff remarked. "But I hear that Mildred's been feeding a stray behind the depot."

Kit found that he liked Edwina's smile, and if one more dog in the house helped make them appear more often, one more dog there would be.

It turned out to be true about the pup, and Mildred was happy to let it go.

Most of the way home, the shaggy peach-colored mop sat on Edwina's lap licking her face.

One time, Edwina even laughed. Christmas and puppies just went together as far as Kit was concerned.

But now that they were half a mile from home, his newly come cousin became silent, downcast.

"Are you worried your husband won't approve of that sweet, shaggy girl?"

"I hardly care what Mr. Spire thinks. Not any— Well, here we are, home just before dark."

Kit helped Edwina down from the wagon while she held tight to the pup.

He watched her go inside, heard childish shouts and puppies barking. When the ruckus seemed to settle down, he took the horses and the buggy full of toys to the barn.

Hours later, icy rain began to fall. It was warm and cozy inside the house, though.

Cheerful flames danced in the hearth. Homey sounds came from the kitchen. Livy sat on the parlor floor wrapping the mound of gifts that Edwina had purchased.

An hour ago he'd looked in on the children. Sweetly asleep in a row on the big bed—boy, pup, girl, pup, boy—they were a vision of contentment.

"Sleep now, sweet ones," he whispered. Come tomorrow night they wouldn't be sleeping so soundly, not with Santa on the way.

Too bad he was not so trouble-free.

His mind was in a knot trying to figure out how to make a dazzling Christmas tree out of ashes. It would need to be something spectacular so that his wife would have her miracle—and just maybe he would have his.

From time to time, Livy would attack him with a silent stare, unless Edwina happened to be looking, then she was smiling like a glowing newlywed.

At the moment, Edwina was in the kitchen trying to make cookies.

"What do you suppose has gotten into her?" Livy said, breaking her long silence.

"Maybe you ought to ask her?"

Footsteps tapped across the floor. Edwina emerged from the kitchen with flour on her face, her hands and her hair. Even her little dog, who hugged the edge of her skirt like she was tethered to it, was dusted in white.

"Sound does travel in this house." Edwina dusted her hands on the apron. "You, my dear cousin, make cookies nearly every day. I see no reason why I should not."

"You have hired help to do it for you," Livy pointed out, because no one believed that Edwina was taking pleasure in the creative task.

"No, not any longer." Edwina swiped her hand across her cheek, making a streak of dough and tears. The pup leaped on Edwina's apron, whining.

"No help? I reckon you'd better sit down and tell me exactly what's happened." Livy stood up, leading her cousin to the couch with a gentle tug on her elbow.

"I'll go on upstairs if you ladies would like some privacy."

"What I have to say concerns you, too, so you might as well stay." Edwina sat down. With the fire's glow reflecting off her face, it was easy to see that she had been weeping for some time.

With a hug, Livy sat beside her. Kit shoved a dozen gifts aside with his foot then drew a chair across from them and sat down.

"You might have noticed Bentley and I arrived early." Yep, and Kit was a married man because of it. "Well, we are not going home."

"You're not?" Livy cast Kit an appalled glance.

"Being here, I've come to see, to understand, that

family is sometimes all a woman has. And, well, I no longer have one of my own. Not a husband, at any rate."

"You don't?" Livy gasped.

"You won't mind if we stay here with you, just for a while, until—" all at once Edwina sobbed out loud "—just until I learn a skill to support me and my children, right here in your quaint little town."

His wife stared at her cousin, wide-eyed and gut punched.

"Won't it be grand?" Edwina asked with a hiccup.

With a quick, jerky nod, Livy hugged Edwina to her.

"Cousin." Kit rose from his chair and resettled on the couch on the other side of her. He lay his arm across her shoulders, because he had a feeling Edwina was going to need all the family care she could get. "When you said children, you didn't mean the puppy, did you?"

With one shake of her head, Edwina touched her belly then buried her face into Livy's shoulder.

"Why! This is wonderful news!" Livy declared, and held her cousin at arm's length to look into her eyes. "Is your husband unhappy about it? Is that what is wrong?"

"He doesn't know. I left him before I gave him the news."

"He ought to know." Kit squeezed her shoulder. "A man should be given the chance to rejoice at the happy event."

"Not this man!" She shook her head so hard the

puppy jumped off her lap. "He's a brute and cares very little for his family!"

"He hurt you?" Livy grew suddenly pale.

"Indeed he did. He demanded that we move to some primitive place in New Mexico. There is no polite society in the area—there is no society at all, in fact. The ranch he bought has only mad coyotes for neighbors. Everyone knows that's not a fit place to raise a child.

"He sold our house even though I refused to leave it. He's ripping the life I knew out from under me without any regard for my feelings. Well—I won't have it. Did you know there are scorpions in New Mexico? And it's so very hot and dry. He can go and be a rancher there without me."

"But, Edwina, he's your husband." Livy touched her cousin's hand where it trembled over her stomach. "You belong together."

"You would think that, Livy. I've seen the way your husband looks at you. I have not seen that kind of love in Grant's eyes for—oh, it's been years."

"Maybe you are mistaken—busy with other things on your mind," Livy suggested.

"I know love when I see it." Edwina glanced at Kit then back at Livy. "I see it when you look at your husband. It's all over your face."

It was?

"It is?" Livy looked astonished.

"Of course—I used to feel the same way about Grant. I do know what I'm talking about."

In Kit's opinion, Edwina's affections for her husband might not be as long gone as she seemed to believe. She was expecting a child after all.

"Well, I've decided that I quite like this sweet little town and I'm going to stay." She dabbed the floured apron across her eyes. "Won't it be outstanding, Livy, for our boys to grow up together? And dear Emmie with them?"

"But would you be happy here?"

"I've come to think so. I'll have my children and my dog—did you know Grant would never allow me to have a dog, even though I wanted one desperately?"

"I never knew you wanted a dog."

"Always! Mother and Father never allowed it, either. I always envied you. I used to imagine you with a dozen pups and no worries about fine furniture being ruined by them."

"You envied me?"

"I still do. Who would have imagined that people gather about a common Christmas tree, hold hands and sing? Why, it's a wondrous event. One that my children will take part in from now on."

"But life will be so different from what you are used to."

"You seem to have done well! My goodness, Livy, you married the town's banker."

"Well, I—" The only sound in the room was the patter of rain on the windows and the snap of the flames in the hearth.

Since honesty seemed to be paramount at the moment and Livy seemed unable to speak it—

"I'm not really a banker, Edwina. I'm an actor." Kit stood up because as soon as he spoke his piece, he was going upstairs to let the women sort things out between them. "A former one. When you assumed I was a banker I went along with that because I wanted to impress you. I'm sorry for the deception. You didn't deserve that."

"Oh, my." Edwina blinked and seemed at a loss for words.

So did Livy. It didn't mean that he didn't have one more thing to say, though.

"Your cousin and I never went on a honeymoon in Paris, either. We have yet to go on one. But this is the truth—I do love her."

What more could he say to either one of them? He'd acted the part of himself and that was all he could do.

Livy sat up talking to her cousin until a few hours before dawn. They came to know each other in a way they never had before.

To Livy's shame, she had misjudged Edwina, assuming she was part and parcel of her parents. And to be honest, of her own mother, too. On more than one occasion, Mama had felt the need to justify her lower position in society.

So, now here Livy was, climbing the stairs to her bedroom, and having misjudged her cousin, she wondered if she had misjudged Kit, as well.

Perhaps it was time to get off her high horse and speak to him with an open heart.

Edwina was convinced that they loved one another. Had warned sternly against false pride, which she claimed to know something of.

Livy quietly opened the bedroom door, looking forward to seeing Kit drawn up into the small chair, his legs and arms all akimbo.

The chair was empty!

Her heart fell apart within her. Looking down, she saw that she was standing nearly on top of the stack of bills she had deposited on carpet. Silent tears dampened her cheeks. Very distinctly, she heard one hit the money.

Did this weeping mean she wanted Kit here—in her bed and not the chair?

She didn't know that for sure. All she knew was that there was a big cold spot in her bedroom that didn't need to be there. All she had to do was trust him to be the person he claimed to be.

It shouldn't be so hard—after all, she did love that person.

Thankfully, Emmie was still here. He would not have gone far without her. Yes, chances were he was only in the barn.

That was exactly where he was. He would never leave his niece behind.

Chapter Ten

I̶t was nearly dawn on Christmas Eve when Kit's clothes finally dried out. The weather had warmed just enough for big, half-frozen drops of rain to soak him. The midnight ride to town had been cold and miserable.

Thankfully he was now in the shelter of the livery leaning against a pile of straw and reading *A Common Man's Guide to Ranching*. It was a good thing for him that folks in Sweet Bank did not lock up.

Just about the time his eyes blinked closed over the print, the door latch jangled.

"What are you doing here?"

Hank sure looked startled. He also looked dry. The rain must have quit while Kit was involved with studying.

"Figuring out how to build a Christmas tree from fence posts."

"Interesting thing to be doing." Hank greeted a gelding, stroking its face from nose to ears. "Why?"

"Livy's going to divorce me if I don't. Say, how's that beautiful daughter of yours?"

The smile of pure satisfaction on Hank's face told Kit all he needed to know.

"She spends plenty of time eating and not much sleeping."

"I reckon that's normal—healthy."

"More normal than finding you sitting here trying to build a tree from logs to keep from getting divorced."

"Are there any to be had, do you know?"

"Old Harvey just built a fence—had some lumber left over that he was going to sell to Geoff over at the general store." Hank moved on to greet the next horse. "If it ain't a private matter, why is she making you build a tree?"

On first thought, it was private, what went on between him and Livy. But on second thought, everyone already knew about their sudden marriage—and exactly why it had happened.

There was no reason not to bare his soul about how it was all falling apart—about how he was an actor pretending to be a cowboy. How it had hurt his wife.

No doubt folks would turn on him when they discovered how he had tricked their Livy.

He might as well tell him about Edwina, too, since her affairs would soon be common knowledge.

Hank listened intently until Kit finished talking. "In my opinion, it's good you are an actor. That Gordon boy hurt her, running off like that. Now you, another actor, will heal her." Hank shrugged, then peered over Kit's shoulder.

"This book is going to tell you how to rig a tree?"

"Only if you look at it sideways. See." He turned the book on its end so the fence suddenly appeared to be a ladder. "If I tweak things this way and that, it could be a tree. I'll attach candles, maybe some strips of tin cans painted silver, or whatever color the store has to sell."

"You won't finish it by tonight." Hank shook his head. "Not alone anyway."

"I won't ask for your help. You've got your hands full at home."

He grinned widely under his big mustache. "There's a whole town full of folks without sleepless newborns. Look for them to start showing up an hour after sunrise."

"This is quite a place, Hank."

"Wouldn't live anywhere else." He straightened, picked up his fork to finish feeding his stock. "You're one of us now. We'll watch out for you—Edwina, too, it looks like."

True to what Hank promised, folks started showing up shortly after dawn. Old Harvey came with fence posts, Geoff with paint and candles, Mildred with cut-up lace and a dozen or more people with open hearts and helpful hands.

Folks sang Christmas carols while they worked. Good cheer and hope of his Christmas miracle rang with every whack of the hammer.

"He's gone." Livy stared at the empty stall. "He left me without a word."

"You did demand that he build a Christmas tree out of ashes," Edwina pointed out unhelpfully.

"I did but—" Dawn light streamed through the open barn door, illuminating the area where Old Blue should have been standing, where his saddle should have been hanging on the low stall wall. "Why did I do that?"

Edwina snorted. Livy was certain this was the first time her cousin had ever made the common noise.

"At least he left us the good horse and the buggy so we can get to town tonight. I do so want to hear you read the last bit of the journal."

"He's gone, and he left Emmie behind." How could he have done that?

Edwina took three long steps into the barn, her fingers white where she gripped the hem of her dress, lifting it clear of straw and other barn debris.

"You are jumping to conclusions again, which, may I point out, is what got you into this mess in the first place."

"You may point that out, Edwina. I did misjudge you. And Kit does love Emmie."

"He also loves you."

"Maybe he did, Edwina. But I pushed him away with an impossible demand. Just like your husband did to you."

"That was entirely different. Grant wants to give away what I hold dear while Kit wants to give everything to you. I can scarcely believe he married you in order to protect your reputation. From what I've seen, that is not common behavior in a man. He could have left you to face your shame." Edwina tiptoed to the buggy, stepping lightly so she would not sully her boots. "Do you really know how to attach this thing to the horse?"

She nodded, so heartsick that she hardly had the will to carry on a conversation about a horse collar.

Edwina was right. Kit could have left her shamed. Instead, he'd given his future to her, handed it over to her keeping like—like he'd wanted to do it!

What had she done?

"I was so..." She sighed while she tried to come up with a word.

"Self-absorbed," Edwina supplied with a smile. "I do know a bit about that."

"Yes, I suppose it was self-absorbed of your husband to do what he did."

"Exceedingly, but I was speaking of myself—of the way I was when we were growing up." Edwina walked deeper into the barn and lifted the heavy collar from a hook on the wall. She grunted and groaned. "You're sure you know how to do this?"

"I grew up knowing how to do it—I just don't know that I have the heart to go to town and find Kit gone."

"Livy James!" Hearing her new name spoken out loud for the first time made her heart plunge, fall to a dark place where she feared it might never come back from. "He might have gone to town for any of a dozen reasons. To purchase a wedding ring, perhaps?"

"During a freezing rainstorm in the middle of the night?" No—it was because he could not face saying goodbye to Emmie. "Here, let me take that old thing."

Everything here was old—Kit had wanted to bring the ranch back to life and she'd told him to build a tree out of a smoking ruin.

All of a sudden leather snapped, and the collar slipped from her hands and hit the floor.

"That little thing at the top that looks like a belt broke." Edwina pointed out. "Is it important?"

"Critical. Looks like we won't make it to town after all."

This was going to be awful news to tell the children.

"Stop acting like a butterfly with a broken wing. We have all day to figure out a way to fix it."

Edwina, the one who ought to be broken, was lecturing her on being a survivor? And rightly so!

When had she become a weakling? Never was when. If she had to go on with her life without Kit, raise two children and their dogs on her own, that was what she would do.

Besides, she was not on her own.

Edwina was here.

Bathed, shaved and wearing a clean, borrowed suit, Kit stood in the middle of Main Street gazing south. From behind, the full moon cast his shadow on the road.

It also cast Hank's, Mildred's, Dr. Baily's, Geoff's and dozens of other folks' shadows on the earth.

"She should have come by now," Kit muttered, giving voice to what everyone would be thinking.

"Well, there's two women and three children to get ready," Mildred said. "Leaving on time is more of a challenge."

"Not one of them would miss a minute of the Christmas celebration," he replied.

"I'm sure everyone is healthy," added the doctor.

"I reckon they are just around the bend in the

road," added one of the men who had labored all day with him building the tree.

Or, Kit feared, Livy was at home with no intention of coming. She had never expected him to give the town a new tree. Clearly, she had tossed the demand out there believing it to be impossible. Something he could never do, and therefore she could dismiss him from her life like she would a bad day.

It would have been impossible for him to rebuild the tree on his own. Thankfully, the folks of Sweet Bank had rallied about him, contributing ideas and sweat.

It was a pure Christmas blessing that in doing so, they had accepted him, absolved him and treated him like one of their own.

If Livy did not come to town, see the tree and forgive him, he would be forced to gather up Emmie and leave the only place that had felt like home since— since ever.

As if to punch him in the gut, a shrill whistle announced the arrival of the evening train.

"Well, I doubt anyone is traveling tonight," Mildred announced. "Let's begin the singing."

He didn't want to. He wanted to wait for Livy. But the tree was not for him alone. It belonged to everyone here. They were anxious to celebrate.

"Let's do it." What was there to do but go along with it, even if he would not rejoice in the carols?

The one and only thing that would make Christmas come to life would be Livy reaching for him with love in her eyes.

He walked behind Mildred, hands shoved deep into the pockets of his borrowed trousers.

Looking north a block, he admired what he and the townsfolk had created.

It was a thing of glittering beauty, no doubt about it. The wooden tree stood fifteen feet tall, with a three-foot painted star on the top.

With three hundred or more candles reaching and twisting, it shimmered. When the breeze rolled gently through the wood branches, strips of painted tin cans tinkled against each other.

Behind it all, the great, bright moon shone down.

"It's so beautiful! More glorious than the first tree, I'll declare." Mary, the baker, slipped her arm through his and squeezed it. "Don't you worry. Your wife will see the glow all the way from home and come in a hurry."

"I hope so. I pray so."

"Everyone knows the good Lord listens to Christmas prayers with a loving ear."

"I'm gonna sit next to my window all night long," Sam declared.

"What?" Edwina turned on the front seat of the buggy, looking to where the children were bundled under a quilt. "How is Santa supposed to come if you are awake?"

"I is going to sleep," Emmie declared. "On Uncle Kit's lap!"

Livy cringed hearing the train whistle blow. How on earth could she tell a child her guardian had left her behind, and on Christmas?

Well, by the blazes, she wouldn't do it. Perhaps Kit was horrid enough to ruin the holiday, but she would have no part of it.

She would simply make something up, act like everything was fine for a few days.

Then again, acting was exactly what had landed her in this mess to begin with.

Mess or not, she could hardly let Emmie be heartbroken.

Livy only hoped she could be half the actor Kit was. A small, accusing voice in her heart reminded her that she was already a deceiver twice over, and that she was also judgmental.

What if Kit had gone to town to purchase a wedding ring? How would she react to that? Would she wear it with joy or tell him that he had failed to give her back the Christmas tree?

What good was a small voice in one's ear when it failed to give solid advice?

What she did know was that hearing the train whistle had broken something in her. All of a sudden the pride she held so dear when he'd maneuvered her into marriage suddenly didn't seem so important. If he was on that train, as he well might be, her house was no longer going to feel like home. Without him she had no home.

"I don't remember such a glow over the town," Edwina said, turning her face forward on the bench. "Only when the tree is—" *Lit!*

"It can't possibly be." The tree was a pile of ashes. The glow had to be the moon reflecting off rooftops.

"I hear singing." Edwina stood up but Livy yanked her back down.

"Be careful!"

"I do hear singing, and there's a huge star. Oh, my gracious word, I think he did it."

Livy also heard singing, but that did not mean— It could not possibly mean anything more than folks singing even without the tree.

If she truly believed that, why was her heart about to burst from her chest as she steered the team from Filmore Place onto Main Street?

After rounding the corner, it still took half a block for her eyes to accept what was before them.

Smack in the center of town square was the most spectacular, glittering, shimmering Christmas tree she had ever seen.

The singing faltered mid-carol. She hauled the buggy to a stop.

A lone figure stepped out from the crowd. He came forward in long, urgent strides.

Kit!

She shoved the reins into Edwina's hands.

"But I don't know how to—" she heard, before leaping down to the road.

Kit broke into a run, his long shadow reaching toward her.

She thought Edwina shouted something about running, but she already was. As if through a fog, she heard people cheering.

The one and only thing she knew was that Kit was reaching for her, the amazing new tree all a-sparkle behind him.

His arms went around her, and he lifted her up, spinning her about.

"Livy." His whisper warmed her neck. "You came."

"You aren't on the train." She held tight to him, feeling his neck grow damp because she was sobbing and laughing at the same time.

"I'll never be on the train, honey." He set her down and cupping her cheeks in his big hands, peered into her eyes. "I never will be—no matter what you make me build for you. I love you, Livy. From the very first, I have."

"I love you, too." For the longest time she couldn't think of anything to say. She only wanted to feel him, know he was here and had not quit loving her even though she had treated him like he didn't matter.

Slowly she found her voice. "Will you build me one more thing?"

"Please don't say a stairway to the stars." Moisture dampened the corners of his eyes, but it was not running down his cheeks like her tears were. "I don't reckon our neighbors will be up to that."

"Build us a horse ranch."

She accepted the long, joyful kiss he pressed on her mouth as a yes.

"I'm going to need a better book."

Someone turned her around and wrapped her in a great hug.

"Cherish that man," Edwina whispered in her ear.

"Edwina Spire!" a man's voice boomed over a dozen good wishes given all at once. "Where are you, Edwina?"

As one, the crowd looked toward the Christmas tree. Person by person, they shifted position, moving to block Edwina from the man in the expensive-looking coat.

"Father!" Bentley zipped past Geoff and around Mary.

The man caught up Bentley, joggled him in the air then drew him into a hug.

"Santa's going to bring me a fan and Emmie a doll and Sam a checkers game! What's he going to bring you, Pa?"

"Pa? We don't use that term, son."

"Everyone uses it here, Pa, and Mama says I can since this is where we are going to live now."

Grant Spire set Bentley on the ground, placed his folded fists upon his hips and shouted, "Edwina, I've come to take you home."

Livy was pretty sure she heard her cousin curse before she pushed her way through the crowd and marched up the street toward her husband.

"If you recall, you sold my home." She matched his stance, but had to look up because her husband was every bit of six and a half feet tall.

"I bought it back again."

"Too late. I like it here with Livy. Her husband might not be the banker but no one even cares. He could muck stalls for a living and the good folks in this town would like him just fine."

"What?" He shook his head as though a fly had just buzzed in his ear. "I love you, Winna. I'm sorry for what I did. I miss you and I want you back. I'll live wherever you want to." He glanced about frowning. "Are you sure it's here?"

"Exceedingly sure. And I have a dog."

"A dog? I don't—I suppose that won't hurt anything. I'll have someone build it a nice kennel."

"She lives in the house with me, or you can get right back on that train, Grant Spires."

"A dog in the house?"

"She's a good pup, Pa."

"Father."

"You'll get used to Pa. Oh, and there's one more thing." Edwina went up on her toes, circled her arms about her husband's neck and drew his head down. She whispered in his ear.

He gasped out loud, then held Edwina at arm's length to look her in the eyes. "We did it?"

Livy had never seen such a sweet smile on Edwina's face.

With any luck, she hoped to whisper that same secret to Kit one day.

Kit hugged her tight, and winked down at her with a look that said he felt the same.

Perhaps she and Edwina would have the joy of raising their children together.

"All right then, Edwina. I'll build you the biggest house in Sweet Bend."

"Sweet Bank—and, yes, you will. One large enough for all our new neighbors to come and visit. Warm up your voice, Grant, it's time for singing. After that, Livy is going to read us a story."

Livy tried to count how many minutes that was going to take. The one and only thing she could think about just now was rushing home, tucking the little ones into bed, then closing her bedroom door to everyone but Kit—her husband.

Her husband! She tried the title out in her mind one more time because it was such a wonder.

She hoped the children would not really be awake all night, because she had a very special gift to open, and his smile was the most beautiful wrapping she had ever seen.

Kit had learned a lot about patience tonight. It seemed to take forever for the singing to end, the reading to be finished and Christmas wishes given to one and all.

At one point he had despaired of the children falling asleep, but they had, one by one with the pups snuggled between them.

Edwina had finally convinced her husband that her small bedroom was a perfectly acceptable place to spend Christmas Eve, and with a dog at their feet.

Now, after much joy and anticipation, the house was quiet.

Climbing the stairs, he noticed snow falling prettily past the window. The storm had come on quickly, but it didn't matter. Everyone was home where they ought to be.

Especially Livy, who waited for him behind the closed bedroom door.

He opened it slowly, closed it quietly and leaned against it.

Livy was dressed in a pale blue nightgown, sitting in his chair with her hair unbound. She glanced quickly up at him, her eyes shining softly while twirling a lock of amber-hued hair around her finger.

The only thing separating him from his answered prayer was a filmy layer of fabric.

But before he touched her, there was something that needed doing.

He reached into the pocket of his rumpled shirt, rubbing his thumb around the wedding band that Geoff had sold him at seven o'clock this morning.

Clearing his throat, he went down on one knee, and opened his palm to show her the pretty circle of gold.

"I do love you, Kit," she murmured.

"Will you marry me?"

"I already have—but now I do again, because I want to. I want you."

Sliding the ring on her finger, he kissed her hand, then drew her up. The bed was mere steps away but it felt like he had to walk a hundred miles to get to it.

He led her toward it then felt a crunch under his sock.

Glancing down, he spotted the short stack of bills still on the rug. Livy saw them, too.

She bent down and scooped it up, waggling the money back and forth in front of his nose. He shook his head.

"Give me your sock," she demanded, but with a tender grin.

"Here, you can have both." One by one, he yanked them off then placed them in her palm. "You want my long johns, too?"

"I do, but for now just one sock."

With a quiet laugh she shoved the money down it.

"This is the start of our horse ranch." She kissed him and while she did, she placed the sock in his hand.

He took it and returned her kiss, adding a dash of heat. She responded, bringing the simmer to a boil.

Downstairs, Santa had already filled the stockings and set out the gifts. The children were dreaming of what they would find when they awoke.

But Kit had no plans for sleeping this night.

While snow fell past the window and the wind moaned softly under the eaves, he touched Livy's shoulder, trailed his fingers down her arm.

He didn't need a script or a book to know how to love this woman. It had been in his heart from the first time he'd seen her shivering on the road.

His wife was the gift of a lifetime, a present he intended to open slowly and with loving care.

* * * * *

*If you enjoyed this story, you won't want to miss
these other Western collections:*

DREAMING OF A WESTERN CHRISTMAS
by Lynna Banning, Kelly Boyce and Carol Arens

WESTERN CHRISTMAS PROPOSALS
by Carla Kelly, Kelly Boyce and Carol Arens

MAIL-ORDER BRIDES OF OAK GROVE
by Lauri Robinson and Kathryn Albright

All available now!

MILLS & BOON®

& HISTORICAL

AWAKEN THE ROMANCE OF THE PAST

A sneak peek at next month's titles...

In stores from 2nd November 2017:

1017/04